hide &SEEK

SCARLETT FINN

I0743981

Copyright © 2023 Scarlett Finn
Published by Moriona Press 2023

All rights reserved.

The moral right of the author has been asserted.

First published in 2023

No part of this book may be reproduced in any form on by an electronic or mechanical means, including information storage and retrieval systems, without permission in writing from the publisher, except by a reviewer who may quote brief passages in a review.

All characters in this publication are fictitious and any resemblance to real persons, living or dead, is purely coincidental.

ISBN: 9781914517914

www.scarlettfinn.com

Also by Scarlett Finn

GO NOVELS
GO WITH IT
GO IT ALONE
GO ALL OUT
GO ALL IN
GO FULL CIRCLE

EXILE
HIDE & SEEK
KISS CHASE

WRECK & RUIN
RUIN ME
RUIN HIM

**THE BRANDED
SERIES**
BRANDED
SCARRED
MARKED

**FORBIDDEN
PREQUEL DUET**
ALL. ONLY.
ONLY YOURS

TO DIE FOR...
TO DIE FOR TRUTH
TO DIE FOR HONOR
TO DIE FOR VIRTUE
TO DIE FOR DUTY
TO DIE FOR LOVE

**LOVE AGAINST THE ODDS
STANDALONE COLLECTION**
SWEET SEAS
HEIR'S AFFAIR
RESCUED
MAESTRO'S MUSE
GETTING TRICKY
THIRTEEN
REMEMBER WHEN...
RELUCTANT SUSPICION
XY FACTOR

NOTHING TO...
NOTHING TO HIDE
NOTHING TO LOSE
NOTHING TO DECLARE
NOTHING TO US
NOTHING TO SAY
NOTHING TO GAIN
NOTHING TO YOU
NOTHING TO THIS

THE FORBIDDEN NOVELS
FORBIDDEN DESIRE
FORBIDDEN WANT
FORBIDDEN WISH
FORBIDDEN NEED

KINDRED SERIES
RAVEN
SWALLOW
CUCKOO
SWIFT
FALCON
FINCH

THE EXPLICIT SERIES
EXPLICIT INSTRUCTION
EXPLICIT DETAIL
EXPLICIT MEMORY

MISTAKE DUET
MISTAKE ME NOT
SLEIGHT MISTAKE

**RISQUÉ & HARROW
INTERTWINED**
TAKE A RISK
FIGHTING FATE
RISK IT ALL
FIGHTING BACK
GAME OF RISK

LOST & FOUND
LOST
FOUND

ONE

AURORA MAGUIRE WAS LOOKING for her last hope, so it made sense that the bar she'd been told to find him in was called Last Resort.

Even while riding in the back of a cab to get there, she kept her heavy coat pulled around her body and her hood over her head in a feeble attempt to protect herself. Last Resort was located in the center of the worst part of town making her fearful of what she might find when she got there.

The first four cabs she'd gotten into had refused to bring her to this district. The driver of the one she was in now had agreed to take her only after she gave him a hundred-dollar advance tip and she proved to him that she was armed. Pepper spray was feeble, but it was all she had to protect herself.

Her last hope. All she knew was his alias. One of them at least.

Venturing down this path was beyond dangerous, crazy most people would say. But she wasn't crazy. Not crazy. Just determined… and desperate.

The cab stopped in the middle of an unlit block. Rain battered the window and the usually comforting sound of raindrops on the roof made her edgy.

Though she couldn't see anyone or anything other than the narrow space between two dilapidated buildings leading to an alley even darker than the street, she knew that she was in the right place. The only man capable of helping her save Benjamin was right down there.

He could say no. He could tell her he wouldn't help and if he did, she had nowhere left to turn.

The cab driver twisted to rest an arm over the chair beside him to look through the scratched screen between them. "Want me to take you back uptown, miss?"

"No," she said quickly, but swallowed just as fast. "No, I… I'm fine. Thank you."

Giving him the fare on the meter, Rora, as she was known to her friends, licked her lips and steeled herself. She'd known this wasn't going to be easy, but she hadn't fought this hard for this long, just to give up at the first bump.

Not that this was the first. It seemed that since she'd started this mission, all she'd hit were bumps. If anything, she hoped this fear was going to be one of the last. Best case scenario, she went down there, found this guy without any trouble, and he agreed to help. If he was as good as his legend told, she could be back out of there in minutes, on the street, clutching an address and embracing a glimmer of light at the end of this arduous tunnel.

"Word to the wise," the cab driver said, sorrowful when their eyes met. "At the first sign of trouble, turn, run, and don't look back. Even the cops don't venture into these parts."

Good to know. That knowledge didn't ease her anxiety, it reinforced her determination. "I passed the first sign of trouble a long time ago, sir," she said, and didn't let herself take the time to appreciate his sympathetic smile.

Rora opened the cab door and got out. Taking a few steps forward, she waited for the cab to speed off, but it didn't.

So, holding her hood over her face, she kept going, crossing the sidewalk to venture into the narrow alley. The further down she got, the greater the darkness became. It closed around her, consuming and polluting her with its intensity and hunger. But she didn't stop.

Her skin began to vibrate and the vague sound of heavy rock music met her ears. There was something down here. Something she couldn't see. The rain got harder. It was a wonder it managed to penetrate this enclosed alley at all, but she felt it on the back of her hands that clasped the edges of her hood.

When she heard the spin of tires, she paused to glance over her shoulder; the end of the alley was little more than a slit, giving a sparse view of the dark street beyond. The cab driver must have been making sure she wasn't going to change her mind and flee. Either that or he'd seen something, or someone, approaching that made him nervous. Whatever the reason, he was gone.

But she was here now. This was it. There was no backing out.

Venturing forward again, Rora zeroed in on the grimy brick wall up ahead. In it were two doors, painted black, neither more appealing than the other. Having no idea which to choose, she wondered if it made a difference, one could be locked, or maybe they led to the same place.

Her eyes were darting back and forth between them, trying to make a decision, when the one on the left opened. The flare of music and the escape of smoke gave her the only clue she needed.

Hurrying on, Rora meant to catch the door before it closed. She did manage to catch it and was grateful that she had because the smooth surface didn't appear to have any handle. What she hadn't counted on facing were the two mammoth-sized bikers who came out, almost knocking her onto her ass.

The first, chewing some kind of stick, glared at her, but stepped aside, more confused by her presence than intrigued by it. The second seemed to be the same; he clucked at her and followed his buddy to the right, without saying anything to her, but mumbling something to his friend.

Few people knew this place existed; she never had.

Holding the door, she had no choice except to round it and go inside. The bass of the music hit her. It wasn't too loud that she couldn't hear the susurration of conversation—

some pleasant, some questionable—but it was turned up so high that it knocked her heart from its rhythm.

There was so much to take in that her senses almost overloaded. It was dark, so dark that her eyes couldn't adjust for a clear minute. When they did, she could that she was at the top of three stairs, with the room laid out beneath her.

Lewd graffiti graced the walls along with posters of naked women, heavy rigs, and choppers. The vague lighting came from random neon signs dotted on the walls around the room. One stated, "Girls! Girls! Girls!" But she didn't see any girls.

It was man after man, at least sixty of them, packed into this space probably meant for less than half that number. But the fire code wouldn't be the main concern of this establishment. She didn't know if this kind of place had any concerns.

The Last Resort wasn't on any map or in any phone book.

The room smelled of beer and weed. Smoke hung in the air, and just about every patron held something in their hand that shouldn't be there. Guns, spliffs, chains, everyone was prepared for fun or violence, and she'd guess these guys would consider both a good time. The smoking ban had been in place for years in this state, but she supposed that wasn't a consideration either. Like the cab driver said, cops didn't venture near here, and God help anyone who tried to hand out a fine in here.

Fearful of drawing attention to herself, Rora knew she should move from her slightly elevated position. Though at only five foot five inches tall, she wasn't towering above any of these guys, most of whom seemed to be six foot tall and then some, and all appeared to be over two hundred pounds.

With her heart pounding in her chest, she took a step forward, still scanning the room. The darkest corner, that's where she'd been told to find her last hope. The bar was in one back corner, the restrooms in another. The third corner was probably the best lit in the place and the fourth, over her right shoulder… there was no light, but there was a booth… she was almost sure there was… something…

Squinting to see if there was a person seated there, she saw a brief flash of red light. It didn't come from a person, it came from a… laptop. Yes, on the table was a laptop, as black as the night she'd left behind the door, that's where the red light had come from.

Figuring he had to be there, she hurried down the stairs thanking her lucky stars. He was right there, twenty feet from the door, she didn't have to go deep into the place to reach her last hope, she could—

A hulking form stepped in front of her making her gasp and come to an abrupt halt so she didn't run right into him.

Tipping her head up slowly, Rora inhaled again when she registered his narrow eyes boring into her. This guy had to be seven feet tall. Twice the width of her, with room to spare, he was the epitome of what she imagined mean would look like if it morphed into a person. His massive, bare arms were adorned with chain link bracelets at the wrists and a length of actual chain hung around his shoulder, swinging over his tattooed bicep.

Though it wasn't just his bicep that had ink, it appeared to be all over him, down to the backs of his hands that rose when he folded his arms across that impressive chest. Color of some sort adorned his neck, creeping right up to the beard on his chin.

This was no accident, he hadn't just happened to cross her path, he was blocking her way, and she had no idea how to deal with him. Rora couldn't fight. She could run, but that meant giving up, and she had no intention of doing that. Not that running was any guarantee of escape, she'd passed a few tables already, if this hulk called out and told his buddies to stop her, she'd be trapped in an instant.

"You're in the wrong place, tiny," he said, his voice so deep it was almost inaudible.

Snatching her shoulder, he spun her around and began to haul her back toward the door. "No," she said, but fighting was useless. Her resistance was insignificant and though she tried to turn back, and to pull away, he just kept on going. "Please, no! I need to—please!"

He hauled her up the stairs, grabbed the door and tossed her out. "Don't be coming back, crazy kook!"

Oh, that was one button no one was allowed to push. "Hey!" she said, grabbing his wrist in both hands before he could go back inside. "Don't call me crazy! I am not crazy!"

Bending, he scowled into her. "Any woman who walks through that door is crazy. We got a no-woman-allowed policy."

"That's sexist bullshit," she called out, determined to hold on even when he tried to shake her off. "I am coming in there! I am going to keep on coming back until I do what I came to do!"

"And I'll keep throwing you out," he said. "Don't matter if it's once or a hundred times, I'm here every night, knock yourself out, keep me entertained. And we don't bar women by choice; we do it for their safety."

Again, he tried to turn and walk away. Rora bent her knees, pulling him back harder, using all her weight to make her point. "Please," she said. "I just need to talk to someone. Let me talk to him, after that, I'll leave, I won't cause any trouble. I won't come back. I promise." Considering her, he was probably trying to figure out why she'd put herself at risk like this, but that should prove how serious she was. "Please, would I be here if I had any other choice? I'm desperate… please."

"Who you looking for? I'll go bring him out."

"Yes," she said. "Yes, that would be amazing. Thank you!"

"He didn't knock you up, did he?" he asked, holding up two hands, each twice the size of her face. " 'Cause I ain't getting my hands dirty in any bastard's personal shit like that."

"No," she said, shaking her head. "No, nothing like that. I need to talk to Exile, that's it. Just him."

His slightly parted lips closed causing his teeth to clack together. His expression didn't change and for half a beat, she wondered if maybe he didn't know the guy she was looking for. That would be just her luck. But before she could recount what she'd been told about where to find Exile, the guy dropped the door, letting it close hard behind him.

His burst of laughter hit her hard. Rora was still stunned by its force when he slapped his belly, laughing so hard that she thought there might be moisture in the corners of his eyes. Well so much for him being mean. Displaying this kind of hilarity made him lose his edge.

"Did I say something funny?"

He breathed in, arching his back and tossing his chin toward the wet sky. "Oh, I was right, you are loopy-loo," he said, sighing out a high-pitched sound of humor.

"Excuse me? I don't appreciate you calling me names. All I want to do is talk to the guy, what's so funny about that?"

"Yeah," he said, trying to recover from his laughter. Once he'd managed to straighten his face, he took another breath. "There's no one here by that name."

He tried to turn away, but she grabbed his wrist again. "No one has a reaction like that to someone they've never heard of. You know him. It's obvious that you do."

"Tiny, you're insane," he said, tugging his hand away from her with enough force that she stumbled forward. "Exile doesn't come out and talk to strays. He doesn't talk to no one."

"I'm not a stray… and I can pay."

His brows rose. "You say that to any other guy in there and he'd bite your hand off. Ex doesn't give a damn about money."

"What does he give a damn about?"

He folded his arms, returning to his intimidating pose. "Best I can tell? Not a damn thing," he said. "But he's not a big talker."

"But, I—"

"Look, lady, I don't know what you think you read on some website or what your nutso friends told you, you don't play with Exile. No one plays with him. And the guy's got no sense of humor, about anything. What do you think you know about him?"

"He has skills," she said and he bobbed his head in agreement. "Skills that I need him to use to help me."

Instead of the pity the cab driver laid on her, this guy was incredulous, but not in a sympathetic way. He seemed to be getting more annoyed by the second. "You don't have a fucking clue what you're inviting into your life if you talk to him. You know they say his only goal in life is to break every law there is. Do you know why they call him Exile?" She shook her head. He came closer. "Because they say he has no nationality, no country. He doesn't come from anywhere. He has no parents. No family. And he sure as hell has no friends. They say he was spawned by the devil, some say he isn't even human."

"A fairytale," she said, recognizing exaggeration when she heard it.

"Maybe," he said. "But I can tell you he's wanted in every state, by every major agency across the world, and Interpol couldn't track him. He's impossible to hold. Evidence disappears. Information vanishes… People die… He doesn't exist."

"Yet he's sitting in that bar right now," she said, nodding past him.

He shrugged. "Maybe. We've been out here talking for a few minutes; he could be out of the country already."

"I'm not law enforcement. I don't care about what he's done or where he's wanted. All I want is help."

"He won't help you. He's not for hire."

"I heard he likes a challenge," she said. "And that he has an interest in the Black Jewel."

This time when he scowled at her, Rora read ignorance; he didn't know what she was talking about. She didn't expect him to, she hadn't heard of the Black Jewel before she started this journey. Rora still didn't even know what it was.

The door opened, hitting her associate in the back. Anger made him tense as he spun, but when a guy in jeans and a leather jacket came out of the bar, her new acquaintance relaxed.

"Strike, you out?" he asked.

"Sure am, Buddy," Strike said, glancing at her. Buddy lifted a fist, Strike bumped it with his. "Little vanilla for you, isn't she?"

"You want her?" Buddy asked.

Her mouth fell open.

"You paid for the privilege?" Strike asked.

Rora inhaled her shock, but they carried on discussing her like she was deaf.

"Not yet, but I might be able to make a deal. I know what she wants."

Strike's chest expanded. "They all want the same thing. The last fucking shred of our dignity." He turned up the collar of his jacket, scanned her figure one more time and then went the same way the other guys had gone, down the perpendicular alley. But he wasn't done. Without slowing or turning, Strike called out to them. "Let her in, Bud."

She smiled, feeling triumphant, figuring that guy was the owner or manager or someone who had authority at Last Resort.

Buddy twisted and stepped back, hooking a finger into a hole at the top of the door she hadn't seen. It was a good thing he was here to open it for her because she'd never have reached that notch herself. No wonder they had a no woman policy and every guy in there was so tall, the only way in was to reach that tiny groove, all the way up there.

This time because she knew what to expect, she didn't let the place shock her. Rora also didn't spend any time loitering on the stairs. Hurrying down them, she ignored the music and the smell and the patrons and went straight to the table in the corner.

The bubble of her optimism that had been infused with adrenaline and hope, burst in one devastating moment. There was no one at the table, it was empty. No one sat on either of the two seats fixed against the corner wall. There was no computer. No drink. No sign anyone had ever been there. Had she imagined the computer? The red light? The shadow seated in the corner?

A small rectangle, paler than the rest of the tabletop, drew her closer. What was that? Peering at it, she tilted her head and leaned down to inspect it. Except... Rora gasped when she recognized her own face on her driver's license!

In a panic, she dug her hand into her pocket to tug out her wallet. She'd known better than to carry a purse tonight, thinking she'd hold onto her possessions if she kept them on her person. Apparently, even that hadn't been a guarantee because when she opened her wallet, sure enough, there was an empty slot where her driver's license usually fitted.

How had he done that?

Grabbing it off the table, she scrutinized it, but saw no notes or clues he may have wanted to pass to her. It was the same as it always had been with a nick in one corner and a glue smudge in the other.

It was her driver's license.

How the hell did he get it? And why would he want it?

"That you?"

Slapping the card to her chest, Rora peeked up to see Buddy looming over her shoulder. "He stole from me."

Buddy stuck out his bottom lip and nodded again. "I heard he does that."

And if he took that, what else did he steal? Searching her wallet, nothing else appeared to be stolen. She had her phone in her other pocket and inside the case was...

Rora gasped. "Oh no."

TWO

HER HOTEL ROOM was ransacked.

Rora had done her best to keep her cool when she went to the front desk to ask for a new keycard. Turned out that a lot of people lost them, so it wasn't a big deal for them to create a new one.

She'd been chewing her lip as the elevator ascended to her floor and walked at twice her usual pace to get to her room. But as soon as she opened the door, she knew he'd been there.

Damn it.

The closet and bathroom doors were open, her clothes had been dumped on the floor, her cosmetics upended, even her shampoo bottle was in the tub. Rora discovered all that before she even went into the body of the room where she found even more mess.

The bed had been trashed, pillows were slashed, the sheets were torn… she'd have to pay for all that. Her drawers had been emptied, everything she'd brought was scattered across the floor and bed like confetti thrown at a wedding, landing any which way in any random place. It felt frivolous. Even if he was looking for something specific, he didn't need to make this much mess.

Sinking onto the end of the bed, her hands fell between her knees. What was she going to do now? She couldn't go to the cops and report this because if she ever wanted this Exile guy to help her, she couldn't incriminate him. Except if he'd heard she was looking for him, he might not go back to the Last Resort.

She'd lost her last hope.

Benjamin had been missing for six months. Every second was one more that he was imprisoned, possibly being tortured. Rora had promised to find him, and that's what she'd planned to do. But there was only one man with the skills to track down her friend and superior, and she'd just lost her only lead on him.

The first thing she'd have to do was tidy up.

Forcing herself off the bed, she began to pick up clothes. With her underwear bunched between her inner elbow and her torso, she went to open the drawer of the dresser that the TV was on. Before she even touched the handle, the TV flicked on, making her gasp and drop her bundle of panties to the floor.

The white noise faded up and a picture came onto the screen, one she recognized as her personal desktop. The wallpaper, the folders and icons, all of it was identical. How did…

The cursor moved and she turned around, trying to figure out how this was happening. Rora was stunned to see her laptop there on the corner table, exactly where she'd left it earlier, apparently untouched.

"Miss. Maguire," a deep digitized voice echoed through the TV speakers, making her gasp again. "You made a mistake tonight."

The cursor on the screen moved and started to open folders, data was being deleted, one bit at a time. All her research information on Exile was the first to go. Everything she'd gathered about Benjamin disappeared too.

"No," she whispered, her fingers curling over her mouth.

"Your friend Benjamin is dead. You can't help him," the digitized voice said. "You're right, I might have been able to do something about it. If I'd wanted to help him, I'd have done it. I didn't. You're going to forget everything you heard about me. Forget about Benjamin Gallagher. And you're going to keep your pretty little vanilla snout out of matters that don't concern you."

Vanilla? Why would… No! She'd heard that word once tonight already, but it couldn't be! It couldn't be that the man who'd left Last Resort while she was talking to Buddy was…

He was going through her pictures now, maybe deleting them, maybe just viewing them; he lingered longer over some than others. "Is this live?" she murmured to herself, looking around for a camera, and finding nothing.

Darting over to the computer, she opened it and tried to turn it on, but it stuck on the welcome screen and wouldn't load.

"A woman with your history should know better. Watching your family slaughtered by your own brother, that's got to mess a person up. How do you get over something like that? By screwing your revered and talented boss I guess."

Whether or not she'd slept with Benjamin was her business, not his. But how did he know about her family and why would he bring that up? Fury clenched her teeth. This guy thought he knew everything.

Stealing her driver's license must have given him what he needed to track her down. A guy with his computing skills would be able to check government records kept on her, and the media coverage about her family. He'd know everything about her in a flash.

"Now we've dealt with the past, let's move to the future…"

The future? Leaving her laptop stuck on its welcome screen, Rora turned, creeping back toward the television that showed him accessing her bank accounts.

"What the hell…" she hissed.

"Looks like we have something in common," the digitized voice said while the cursor moved over the figure on the screen stating her bank balance.

She'd inherited her family's money, their life insurance policies, and a hefty settlement figure for wrongful death after her brother was convicted. In short, she had never had to worry about paying bills.

But she didn't understand, what did they have in common? Was he saying she was rich and he was too? Except, without moving the cursor, he did something that caused her balance to change. One digit at a time, the amount began to decrease, slowly at first, then faster and faster, until…

"Oh my god," she said when it flashed at zero.

"That's your trust," the digitized voice said. "Let's see your checking…"

"No," she breathed.

But her other account came up on the screen and the same thing happened, the balance dropped all the way to zero.

"No," he said. "I'm not a monster…" The figure rose until it stopped at a thousand dollars. "Treat yourself."

"Bastard," Rora said.

The digitized voice came back, this time much heavier and more sinister than before. "Crossing my radar was the stupidest thing you've ever done," he growled. "Every cent you make from now on, you'll make for me. I own you, Miss. Maguire. All of it. All of you. It's mine." Snarling at the screen, she really wished she had something to hit… like his face. "Unless…"

"Unless?" she said. "I'm not your puppet!"

"If you can answer one simple question, I'll return every cent… might even erase those parking tickets of yours too."

"A question?"

She didn't get it and didn't think he could hear her. None of this made sense. She'd wanted him to help her and now he was asking her questions?

"What's the point?" he asked.

The television went off, at the same second the laptop sang out its tune to tell her it was on, causing her to spin around.

The TV came back on, and began racing through channels, hanging on one for a few seconds before moving onto the next. The AC turned on full and the fixed hotel hairdryer began to blow out air too. Every one of the lights flashed on and off in a haphazard rhythm, and music blasted from her laptop at the same time the ceiling fan started.

Something light hit her on the chest, but she ignored it to cover her ears against the noise of every electrical thing in the room taking on a life of its own. Rora dropped to a crouch with her hands over her ears, prepared to ride it out.

Just as she was overwhelmed enough that she might scream, the din stopped as suddenly as it had begun.

Breathing into the silence, her own heartbeat couldn't keep up with the demand of her panting. Gradually, hoping it was over for good, she let her eyes open, still poised, expecting something else to happen. When it didn't, she relaxed and noticed a rectangle on the floor.

Grabbing it up, she saw it was a driver's license, but it wasn't hers. It was…

***

"WHERE DID YOU GET this?" Rora asked, slapping Benjamin's driver's license down on the same Last Resort table she'd found hers on the previous day.

The man seated in the corner blinked, his eyes going from the laptop in front of him up to hers. He didn't lift his chin, only glared up at her. His unimpressed anger infuriated her.

"Miss. Maguire," he said, his voice somehow sounding distorted even now.

Maybe it was the music, or the smoke in this depraved place, it didn't matter, all she wanted were answers. "This isn't funny, Strike, Exile, whatever the hell your name is. Answer my question!"

"Are you here to answer mine?"

"The point? I don't know what the goddamn point is, ok?"

His sinister glare returned to his computer, his fingers moving fast over the keys. "Then we're done," he said.

"No, you can't just dismiss me. You can't give me this," she said, slamming a finger onto Benjamin's license. "And then just dismiss me." But his fingers didn't slow, and he didn't look at her again. "If I knew the answer, I would tell you the answer. Not because of the money, I don't give a damn about the money, keep it. I planned to offer it to you anyway. I'd give every cent willingly if you'd just help me find Benjamin. Where is he?"

"Dead," he said in a flat syllable, his typing never slowing.

"No," she said. "No, I don't accept that. He's not dead!"

"How do you know?" he grumbled.

"Because he told me!"

His fingers stopped, poised on the keys, and slowly his attention ascended to hers. He waited a breath before he spoke. "Well, fuck," he said. "He's in communication with you."

"No, he's not," she said, cursing her mouth for talking before she'd considered her words.

"How the fuck did he do that?" he asked himself rather than her. "He's better than I gave him credit for."

"Benjamin's the best," she said, proud in her resolution.

"Oh," he said, easing away from his laptop to look up at her.

A sense of doubt and amusement had flavored his tone; he was good at conveying a lot in just a single syllable.

"What he is doesn't matter. What matters is where he is."

"The Black Jewel has him," he said. "Just like you told Buddy."

Confused, Rora chewed her lip. "I thought he had the Black Jewel."

"No one has the Black Jewel," he said, going back to his keyboard. "Trust me. I know."

Still chewing on her lip, Rora was looking at nothing but the space above his head, desperately searching for clarity. "What is it? What is the Black Jewel? A drug? A location? A riddle?"

"How are you not dead yet?" he asked, snapping her focus back to him. "Seriously, you've been on his trail for six months?" She nodded. "How are you not dead yet?"

"I have money, had money… and a kind of unthreatening thing going for me."

"I'll say," he said, working on his laptop. "Do yourself a favor, forget Gallagher."

Slapping a hand onto the top of the laptop, she closed it, almost trapping his fingers in the process. "No," she said, incensed that he could be so casual about telling her to give up.

Clenching his teeth, he bared them, still focused on where the screen had been. "I've snapped men's necks for less."

"Good thing I'm not a man," she said, keeping her hand flat on his computer. "Listen, Mr. Exile, I have travelled across the country and back again looking for the only man who ever gave a damn about me. He was taken, against his will, and I am going to find him, whether you help me or not."

"Not," he said, grabbing the laptop and sliding it out from under her hand.

He stood up and rounded the table to start for the door. Rora hurried to keep up, but it was difficult; he was over six feet with long legs, and people moved for him, like they could sense him coming. But his dark aura was enough to push people from his path. She on the other hand was invisible; no one gave a damn if they got in her way.

One man didn't get out of the way fast enough, or he stumbled, either way, he interrupted Strike's flow and it was enough to make Strike grab his wrist. Still with the laptop in his other hand, he twisted the guy's hand causing him to turn away and call out in excruciating pain.

With little effort, Strike lifted the guy's twisted arm, forced him forward to thump his face into the wall, and bent the arm to such an ungodly angle that the crack of bones snapping echoed even over the sound of the music.

The guy dropped onto his knees when Strike let him go. Strike didn't even blink, just stepped over the cowering guy who was cradling his arm and continued on his path to the door.

No one else got in his way. No one questioned what he'd done. That guy had been standing with five other guys, all built bigger than Strike, but not one of them pursued him.

It wasn't until he'd ascended the stairs and opened the door that she got with the program and started to run across the room. Swerving around the carnage Strike had caused, Rora got up the stairs and caught the door just before it closed.

Dashing into the alley, she looked straight ahead, right, left, and it was only then she saw him striding down the perpendicular alley.

Going after him, she had to almost run to catch up. "You just broke that guy's arm!"

"His hand too."

It was unbelievable. She couldn't keep her mouth closed around this guy; he was shameless. "Why? Why would you do that?"

"Because you pissed me off," he said and took a right that she hadn't known was there.

"You hurt him because of me?" she asked, nausea making her swallow. "Why not just hurt me?"

"He knew better than to get in my way. Now you know it too," he said, entering a large space filled with motorcycles.

The concrete ground worked as a makeshift parking lot while the exposed brick walls of the surrounding buildings gave them security and cover.

"So next time you'll break my arm?"

"There won't be a next time," he said and slid his laptop into a custom pouch on a black motorcycle. "Until you can answer my question, you're useless to me."

Dashing forward, Rora managed to get to the motorcycle, putting herself between him and it just a fraction of a second before he could throw his leg over it. "You're not useless to me."

Her fingers trembled and her heart pounded. She'd never been so scared in her life; this guy could kill her with his bare hands. He'd said he knew how to snap necks and he'd proved he could break bones.

But she ignored her terror and swallowed hard, balling her fists. She was Benjamin's only hope and she didn't ever again want to feel the despair that had touched her last night when she thought she'd let him down.

"What is it you want from me, Miss. Maguire?" he asked, the bass of his voice reverberating through her.

Keeping her lips sealed, she breathed through her nose, trying to steady her breaths to slow her heart. At least that was what she told herself it was for. A tingling between her thighs rose to her gut that grew heavy as heat began to permeate through her.

Was she… turned on? Were fear and desire so closely linked?

What the hell kind of woman got turned on by a brute like this? He'd just broken a guy's arm for getting in his way, and he hadn't given much consideration to self-preservation.

"Weren't you scared?" she asked. "You hurt that guy, but… what if his friends had got hold of you?"

"Then I'd have hurt them too," he said.

"I've never… I've never known a man like you."

"That's because there isn't another one," he said. "And you don't know me, Miss. Maguire. No one does."

He moved for the bike, but she moved with him, staying in his way. "I always hated myself," she said. "I hated the fear. If there had been no fear, maybe I would've got in his way… Maybe I would've stopped him."

"Your brother," he said and she nodded. "You worry too much about the past, when you should be thinking about the future."

"I don't understand what—"

Bending a fraction, he put his lips just above her ear to murmur. "His blood runs in your veins, Rora." His voice had dropped to a sinister whisper that made her shiver. "What might you be capable of?" Something thick and heavy touched her palm and she dropped her eyes to see what it was… a switchblade. "Defend yourself or die."

With the tip of his index finger, he pushed up her chin as if telling her to hold her head high, but he said nothing else. Pushing her aside, he got onto the bike, bringing it to life and roaring away, leaving her standing there alone in the parking lot with the knife in her hand.

Violence was something she'd witnessed but avoided. Yet, it seemed that no matter what she did, she wasn't going to be able to turn her back on the thought Strike had put in her mind. Her brother had it in him to take the lives of those closest to him.

So just what was she capable of?

THREE

WITH BENJAMIN'S LICENSE in both hands, she gazed down at his picture. It was a wonder to her to have him here so close to her and yet, nowhere near. Stroking the image, she wondered what had been in his head when the flash went off. Was he thinking of his work? Was he thinking of her? Maybe he was thinking of what he was going to have for lunch.

One thing was for sure, he wasn't thinking that his life would turn out this way.

"You're in my seat, Miss. Maguire."

Yes, she was, and that was exactly the point. Looking up to find Strike standing on the other side of the table she occupied in Last Resort, she smiled. "I don't see a reserved sign."

"You're new," he said. "You'll learn in time that it's implied."

Her being there didn't stop him from coming around the table and sitting. Physically shunting her down the bench out of his way, he nestled himself in the vee where both sides of the wooden seat met.

A day had passed since he'd given her the knife in the parking lot, but Rora was prepared to show up here every day until Strike agreed to help her.

"You know what I realized when I came in here tonight?" she asked. Strike put his laptop on the table to open it up. It didn't start up like any computer she knew, not that it looked like one either. It didn't matter that he didn't ask her what she'd realized, she was going to tell him anyway. "Every guy moved out of my way... Do you think that's because we left together last night?"

"We didn't leave together," he said, and pulled his laptop closer to him, preventing her from seeing the screen when he began to type.

"I've never seen you with a drink. Why would you come to a bar and work on that thing all night and then just leave without ever drinking or interacting with anyone?" she asked, tucking the license into the pocket of her coat to lean over. "What are you working on anyway?"

Grabbing the side of the laptop, he pulled it down enough to block her view, then glared at her, his mouth set in a grim line. "There's something wrong with you," he said. "You saw me break that guy's arm last night, yet here you are again."

"Yes, I am. That's how much I want to find my friend," she said, sliding her hand into her pocket to take strength from the license she'd just put in there. Beneath it, cool against her knuckles, was the knife Strike had put in her hand the previous night, and much as she might not like it, she did feel safer having an actual weapon to help her protect herself.

"Go look somewhere else. You haven't figured out he's not here yet?"

"No, he's not. But you are."

"Yeah," he said, his fingers working so fast, it was a wonder he could keep up with their conversation. "You found me. Now you're it. Go hide and I'll seek this time."

"And Buddy said you didn't have a sense of humor," she said, swaying sideways to push him with her weight.

He stopped typing to eye her up and down like she'd just suggested foreplay or grown an extra head. "Don't make contact with me like that," he said, putting a hand on her thigh to push her further down the bench.

But as soon as his hand moved, she slid back up the bench, getting even closer this time. "No, see that isn't my plan, Mr. Exile," she said, figuring if he could call her Miss. Maguire when he was pretending to be polite that she could play the same game.

"A plan," he said, typing again, pretending like he hadn't noticed her proximity. "Finally got one of those, huh?"

"These guys around here," she said, pushing herself up off the seat to lean in closer to his ear. "They're curious about the girl you went home with last night."

"Home with?" Turning, his scowl wasn't as intense as it had been before, probably because he didn't expect to find her mouth just an inch from his. "You've got a season ticket on the crazy train, don't you, Ro?"

"Don't call me crazy," she murmured, shaking her head a little. "Don't ever call me crazy. I spent my whole life being called crazy by everyone who ever met me. Except after what you said last night, I'm thinking… maybe I am. Maybe it's unavoidable for me."

"But I shouldn't say it?" he asked and she shook her head again.

Like there were drugs in her system, she moved slowly. Her tongue slid across her lips, and when he noticed it, she needed to work harder to pull oxygen into her lungs. That shiver of need she'd felt by his bike last night was back, disrupting her system.

Rora wasn't here for sex, and certainly not for a relationship with this guy, but there was something about the smell of leather and the finesse of his fingers that entranced her. His gaze snared hers. She couldn't look away, couldn't blink, she could barely hold her own head up.

Tipping his head an inch, he touched his lips onto hers. It wasn't a first kiss like any she'd experienced before. It was so short, it was like a test. Had he expected her to pull away?

Being defiant was in her blood, that was something she knew for sure, because she'd always been headstrong, and if he wanted to test her resolve, she'd let him.

Rora might not like it, but she needed him. With what little she knew of him and what little he'd shared with her, she'd established that Strike was aware of Benjamin and likely knew exactly where he was. This was the right place for her, the only place, and Strike was her last hope at saving Benjamin.

"So, you tell these guys we fucked and then what?" he asked. "I'll help you just so you won't tell them I'm shit in the sack? You think I'd give a crap?"

"I don't want to sleep with you, Strike," she said. "And I don't want to tell these guys anything. I was afraid when I first came here, but now these guys think I'm yours, I'm not afraid."

"You aren't mine," he said, returning to his keyboard. "Just your money."

Because he was taller than her, she had to stay in this half crouch, with her ass off the seat, so she could lean closer into him. "They don't know that, Strike… So, anything I tell them about you, they'll believe. And I won't start with your lack of sexual prowess, I'll start with something much more believable… like maybe the names of some crime bosses you've ripped off. Pillow talk makes you so boastful, my naughty new flame."

This made him stop to look at her again. Rora kept her gaze sultry and her pout wide. They might be in shadow, but she didn't know what the others could see, meaning that details mattered. Unbuttoning a couple of buttons on her shirt slowly, she shifted onto her knees to give herself better lift and angled her head to kiss the side of his neck.

"What the fuck are you doing?" he hissed, his fingers curling over his keyboard.

"Giving them something to believe," she whispered and tongued his earlobe into her mouth.

She didn't expect him to move, but he scooped a hand around to the back of her neck to grip her tight. A breathy yelp leaped from her throat and as he squeezed, she winced.

His force was absolute and the glare in his eyes wasn't one of desire. "Threatening me will be your last mistake," he growled.

She tried to get away from his grip but couldn't. Her body got heavy, she went limp and then darkness closed in around her.

***

RORA WOKE UP with a start.

Her body clenched, and the quick motion sent pain bursting through her skull. The music wasn't making her headache any better. It was as she drew up her leg that she remembered she was in Last Resort.

Sitting upright, she looked around and ran a hand down her body to check she hadn't been violated. Strike was gone, he'd left her lying here on the bench where she'd been sitting with him before he assaulted her. Anyone could've…

"I tried to tell you."

She turned to the sound of the voice too fast, sending another spike of pain through her forehead. Cupping the front, where the pain was, she tried to peek under her fingers to see over her shoulder. Buddy was leaning against the wall at the end of the bench, swinging a beer between his fingertips.

"What did he do to me?"

"He didn't kill you," he said, holding the beer toward her. "That's something to be happy 'bout."

Funny that she wasn't overwhelmed with gratitude. That bastard had done something to her to make her pass out in this room full of drunk criminal bikers. Anything could've happened, unless he'd deliberately left Buddy to keep watch over her.

Even so, the bastard had assaulted her.

"Where did he go?" she asked. The laptop was gone, so he wasn't just in the restroom.

"When he leaves here? I always guess he goes back to hell."

"He's not Satan," she said, rubbing the back of her neck, though she wasn't a hundred percent sure.

"Take the beer, it's cold. He said you should put it on the back of your neck."

Grabbing the edges of her coat together, she thrust to her feet. "And when he shows up again, you tell him to shove it up his ass," she said, storming for the exit.

Every time she thought she had a chance of getting him to give in and help her, he trumped her. It wasn't that it wasn't fair, even though it wasn't. His attitude infuriated her. Any other human being would be satisfied with a payoff, but he'd drained her bank accounts and done nothing for her. He hadn't even told her what he did want. Maybe he was right about his question, what the hell was the point?

***

HER HEADACHE ONLY subsided after almost an hour in the shower. Rora didn't just use the time to preen, she used it to fume and to strategize. Over these last few days, she'd held out hope that Strike was just playing hardball. Tonight had proved he wasn't interested in game playing. And Buddy had been right; Exile had no sense of humor.

Well, he wasn't the only computer genius out there. Benjamin might be the man she considered the best, but there were other names. Going after Exile had seemed like the best plan, she hadn't banked on him being so unmovable.

On her way home from Last Resort, she'd put a call out on a message board that Benjamin had shown her. It might take a few days, but someone, somewhere would get back to her.

Frustration kept her under the shower steam. Months had been lost in her pursuit of a man who she'd believed would be her savior. There was no accounting for people's selfish attitudes. If it took her another six months to find another capable hacker, and he ended up being like Exile...

The water was beginning to run cold, and she was getting tired. It had been a fruitless night, a wasted week. It was disheartening to be rebooting this late in the process.

She moisturized, brushed her hair and teeth, going through the motions to get ready for bed, and then left the bathroom. Rora traversed the short hallway, combing her fingers through her hair. When her phone began to ring a second later, she froze.

It was late for someone to be calling and she didn't know of anyone who would want to reach out. Spinning around, Rora dashed over to grab her phone from her coat pocket, but it didn't display a name.

Putting it to her ear, she listened for a second before she spoke. "Hello?"

A computerized voice spoke, "What's the point?"

Outraged, she opened her mouth in a silent squawk. "What the hell? Do you think I'm going to forget what you did to me tonight, Exile? Use all the games and tricks that you want, there's no way in hell I'm helping you after you left me lying there like that! Who knew kissing a guy could get a girl concussion? You are unbelievable. Don't call me again!"

She hung up and thrust the phone back into her coat pocket.

Great! She'd just managed to calm down and he'd gotten her riled up again. Stomping over to the bed, she took off her robe and tossed it to the floor before she got beneath the covers. She needed to sleep because she needed to be fresh to help Benjamin, but the question wouldn't go away.

What was the point?

FOUR

TWO NIGHTS LATER, she was standing in an alley next to a bar.

Not Last Resort, no, she hadn't been back there since Strike knocked her out.

This was the place her latest contact had asked to meet. Rora would have preferred to meet inside the bar, but only because it was warmer in there. After finding the gumption to walk into Last Resort, working up the courage to stand in this slimy, shady alleyway was nothing. It was even in a halfway decent part of town that she didn't have to bribe cab drivers to take her to.

But he was late.

Looking at her watch, she began to shift her weight from her left foot to her right. Her oversized wool coat might be good for concealing her identity, but it wasn't so good at standing up to all this rain, even with its hood.

She thought she heard a click but wasn't sure until her hood was pulled down from behind. Her hair was caught in the grip of whoever had hold of her hood, and she called out in pain when whoever it was wrenched her back into a partial dip before she was let go.

Despite expecting this to be a mugging, she still panicked when the weight of a gun barrel touched her head behind her ear. It dragged around past her ear to her temple and then when her eyes stretched to see her assailant, she opened her mouth to squeal again, except he clamped a hand over her mouth and pushed her face-first into the wall.

"Who the fuck are you, Rora, huh?" Strike asked, digging the gun into the back of her skull, bumping her head off the concrete wall he'd just forced her against while he dipped his hands in her pockets.

"If you wanted to mug me, you should've done it after you knocked me out," she hissed, but when she tried to turn her head, he grabbed her hair and shoved her face into the wall again.

"I thought I had you. I thought I was a step ahead, how did you do it?" he snarled and grabbed the back of her coat to haul her around. He slammed her against the wall, keeping the gun barrel between her eyes. "How did you do it?"

"I don't know what you're talking about," she said, noticing the cut above his vicious eyes and the bruising on his jaw. The thin shallow cut running across his throat made her wince, she didn't want to feel sorry for this bastard, but that looked nasty. "What happened to you?"

"Your mistress," he hissed, leaning in close, pushing the gun deeper into her. "I should put a bullet between your eyes and send you back to her in pieces just for sport. Bitch."

Rora didn't know if he was calling her a bitch or this mistress. "I don't have a mistress," she said, her neck hurting almost as much as her head where it was being squashed between the wall and gun barrel. "I don't know what you're talking about, Strike."

He growled. "You tell her the games are over, and if she wants me, she should show herself. I get no pleasure from killing her minions. Her on the other hand…"

"Killing… oh my god, Strike, who did you kill?"

Baring his teeth, he almost spat venom when he spoke. "I don't give a damn about Gallagher. I told her. Sending this little innocent babygirl to dangle him in front of me won't change a fucking thing. I'm better. I'm stronger. I will get there first."

Rora had never been so lost, she wanted to say something, her mouth opened, but she didn't know where to begin. Strike did know Benjamin, that much was clear, but his role in whatever else was going on was a mystery to her.

"Get where first?" she asked.

"Are you ten?" he asked, shoving back to put a couple of feet between them, but he kept the gun aimed at her.

"Like, years old? No," she said, descending deeper into confusion.

"Ten, the gang, like the roman numeral, X. Do you belong to them?"

Pushing her head to the side, he pulled back her ear, making her wince, but whatever he was looking for back there, he wouldn't find it.

"I don't even know what that means," she said when he yanked her back to stab the gun into her forehead again. "I'm not ten. I'm not in any gang. I don't have a mistress, and I still don't know what the point is… And your call the other night was bullshit by the way, don't do that again."

"My… phone call?"

"Yes," she said, pulling the lapels of her coat, trying to regain some dignity. "I already told you I don't know the answer to your stupid question. Did you think violating me and leaving me to the dogs in Last Resort was going to jog my memory? Even if it had, I wouldn't have told you after you were such a dick."

Biting the inside corner of his lip, he seemed to be struggling to hold back his own frustration. The gun dipped once, then rose, before he let it fall to his side, hanging in his loose hand.

"You got a call the night I left you in Last Resort?"

It didn't even occur to her that the call might not have been from him. Looking left then right, she was even more confused. "Yes."

"Saying what?"

"Just one thing," she said. He waited, giving her nothing but time to tell him. "What's the point?"

"They asked you that?" he said and when she nodded, he cursed. "What did you say?"

"I… I don't remember… I probably swore and told them some variation on go to hell. I thought it was you."

"You used my name, didn't you?" Did she? She couldn't remember. It was foolish of her to think he'd call after what had happened that night, and in the previous days. Rora shrugged and he threw up his hands, backing off further. "How are you not dead yet?" he called out, his head falling back.

"Strike," she said, pushing away from the wall, but he held his hands up.

"You're still doing it, would you shut the fuck up?"

Curling her lip into her mouth, Rora bit it hard. He turned away from her, a hand on his hip, the butt of the gun resting against his hairline. Whatever assumptions he'd made, he was obviously changing them now.

Taking solace in the fact that she no longer had a gun pointed at her head, Rora slipped her hands into her pockets to find her wallet, her phone, and the knife he'd given her all still there. If he hadn't been taking her possessions, why was he searching her pockets? She couldn't begin to figure what he'd thought he might find.

Shocking her with an abrupt move, he spun toward her and held out a hand. "Give me your phone."

"What? Why?"

"Because if Bella calls again I'm going to end this."

"Bella?" she asked, taking her phone from her pocket. Strike snatched it from her before she could decide if she was going to hand it over or not. "Who's Bella?"

"My ex-girlfriend," he said, putting the gun into his waistband to begin doing something with the phone.

"Oh," she said, watching him work almost as fast on the phone as he did on his laptop. Whatever he was doing had to be important, his brow was creased in a frown. In fairness to her, she had no idea that anyone else was interested in her situation. How many people should she have expected to ask her the exact same question so soon after each other? "It didn't sound like a woman, it was a male voice."

"She has tech," he muttered. "My fucking tech."

Maybe she wasn't as ex as he'd said. "I don't get it. If she's your ex, why can't you just call her and tell her what's happening? Don't you have her number?"

He glanced up at her just for a split second, then went back to work. "She's off the grid at the moment."

"Must have been a bad breakup," she said to which she got a grunt. "Are you still in love with her?" No response. "Is she still in love with you?"

"Bella despises men. All men. All the time," he said. "She thinks they're a subspecies. Scum who should be despised."

"Very bad break up," she murmured, casting her attention to the street. "You must have really hurt her."

"She was like that long before I met her," he said. "It was one of the things I loved most about her."

"That she despised your gender?"

"That she hated me," he said. "Because she loved me and that made her hate herself. Watching that bitterness fester really was something."

"You wanted to make the woman you loved hate herself?" she asked, wondering if there was anything about this guy that made sense.

With one foot planted, he bowed toward her and dropped the phone back into her pocket. "Your life is in danger. Leave the city. The state. I'd tell you to leave the country, but your passport's expired. Get a fake one if you can and split."

"Split? No," she said. "I… I have to find Benjamin."

Like he was talking to a child, he took a slow breath and blinked. "Then what? You find him, and then what? You're going to save him?" She shrugged. "You make a target of yourself, Ro. Do you know how many times I could've killed you?"

"Then why didn't you?"

"Nothing in it for me," he said. " 'Til now. Use my name again, to anyone, and you won't get another chance."

So because she'd used his name on a phone call, his ex-girlfriend had sent people to cut and beat him? "I don't understand," she said, biting her lip instead of using his name. "Why did she send people to hurt you? And what is the point?"

"You're not the only one asking that question," he said.

"No, I mean, I don't get it. I don't understand the question. What is…" Slowing the question changed it and clarity made her pause before finishing. "The point… Oh my God."

"What?" he asked, but she was lost, coming to terms with this new understanding. Grabbing her arms, he shook her hard, forcing her out of her stupor. "Rora, what is it? Did you remember? Did you figure it out?"

"I… I… No, I… never mind. Sorry, I have to—"

"You're a terrible liar," he said, hauling her back when she tried to walk past him.

"I have to go."

"Tell me, what's the point?"

But there was no way she was going to share what she'd remembered with him, not here, and definitely not now. "Help me find Benjamin and I'll tell you."

"What? No."

"No, you're right," she said. "Not just find him. Help me save him, and I'll tell you."

"Save him? This isn't a movie. If I get killed helping you and your—"

"Fine, I'll wait until Bella calls again," she said, and tried to leave again, but he slammed her to the wall so hard the air was forced out of her lungs. "Get your hands off me!"

"Bella will give you what you want. In her own twisted way. She'll slit your beautiful Benjamin's throat and deliver him to you in time for you to watch him take his last breath. She's evil incarnate."

"So says you," she said. "But I've heard similar rumors about you."

"Difference between me and her is, I'll tell you the truth. I am evil, most of the stories are true. She wants money and power and she'll go to any lengths to get it. I figured that out about her just in time, but you're green, you won't see the truth until it's too late."

The guy might not mean to be condescending, but he was doing a good job of it. "Find him for me."

"What's the point?" he asked, gritting his teeth.

He still had her arms, so she couldn't move far, but she pushed her shoulders forward. "Save him, and I'll tell you."

"Tell me first."

"You think I trust you? The guy who knocked me out and abandoned me? Not a chance, buster. Benjamin first. I'll keep my word." He was still hesitating. "I'm the only one of the two of us who hasn't broken every written law, who's the more trustworthy here?"

Squeezing her, he pushed back and let go. "Not every law," he snarled. "Fine. I'll find your Benjamin for you. I'll drag his carcass out of wherever he's being held and you can have your happy ever after." Pointing into her face, he bared his teeth. "But if you screw me over—"

She grabbed his finger, pulling it down from her face. "I won't," she said. "Where do we begin?"

FIVE

FIRST THING was to get out of the city.

Strike took Rora to her hotel room and watched her stuff what little she could into the pack he gave her that fitted on his bike. Everything else was left behind. Rora had picked up her laptop, but he'd swooped in to take it from her and put it back on the table while shaking his head.

So her laptop wasn't good enough for him? Whatever. She had a cloud account and he had a machine, Rora was prepared to play nice with him as long as he played nice with her.

She wasn't a pro on a motorcycle, but he had no time or patience to ease her in, so she had to learn fast. Clinging to him, she clenched tight and closed her eyes when they began whizzing down the highway. The city streets had been tough enough to deal with, but when they got onto the open road, it seemed they were going so fast that they might take off.

Wishing for a car when it got dark, Rora was beginning to get tired, but couldn't relax. She had to keep hold of him, and her fear of falling asleep and falling off made her cling to him tighter.

When they slowed down, she lifted her head and was so relieved to see they were pulling into a truck stop with a diner, a gas station, and a motel in back. He drove around to the back of the diner, parking up in a dark corner that would be visible from the rear seats in the eatery.

Rora was forced to fumble her way off the bike when Strike got off. Her legs were like jelly and she had to grab for him to steady herself. It felt like her muscles had been through a vice and a grinder, she ached, all over.

His mood hadn't improved, he took her hand off the bike, like he was offended she was touching it, then pushed her other hand from his forearm. When they were separated, even though she was still wobbling, he grabbed his laptop from the bike and strode off, heading for the diner without even waiting for her.

It was amazing that this guy had ever had any kind of girlfriend at all if he dismissed women like this, even those in need. Maybe him and this Bella were a perfect match, she hated men, and it was seeming more and more like he hated women.

Without any other choice, Rora pulled herself together and scampered after him. By the time she caught up, he'd already gone inside and picked a booth with a view of his bike and the door of the diner. He was examining a laminated menu when she slid into the seat opposite him.

Glancing up, like he had timed it perfectly, he made eye contact with the waitress who came scurrying over. "Two black coffees, two ice waters, two burgers with everything and fries." The waitress breathed in to speak, but he cut her off. "That's all. Nothing else."

The waitress glanced at her, then turned to walk away and put in the order. "Ordering for me?" Rora asked, rubbing her thighs beneath the table, hoping to relieve some of their ache. "Aren't you prehistoric? Maybe I don't like meat or coffee."

Spinning his laptop around to face him, he flipped it open and cracked his knuckles. "You started drinking coffee when you were thirteen, stopped taking milk in it when you were sixteen and cut out the sugar when you were twenty."

She didn't have any idea how a person would know that. He was right. But that just made it all the more freaky.

But he was too busy frowning at his computer to bother noticing her surprise.

Pushing her lips to the side, Rora linked her fingers and straightened up to try peeking over his laptop. He put a hand on the top of it and pulled it an inch closer to him, scowling at her attempt.

So she sat back, chewed her lip for a second, then sighed. "You aren't a very good date."

"This isn't a date."

"Are you saying you'd be more attentive if it was?" she asked. "How did you bag Bella?"

His fingers paused for half a beat, then continued. "If I'd bagged her, I'd have tagged her," he said, and she didn't get it, which he must have realized because he stopped typing. "Like a toe tag. Body bag. Toe tag."

In a wide, silent, 'ah' her mouth opened. He was typing again. Rora squeezed her palms together beneath her joined fingers, hunching her shoulders at the same time. "Do you really think you could kill a woman you'd slept with?"

"Wouldn't be the first one," he mumbled.

"How do you do that thing where you distort your voice?"

"I carry tech, stops people listening in. Distorts video footage too."

It was a wonder that he was so casual about admitting his crimes and circumventing the law. "How did you get my license from me and put it back on the table like that? You didn't even touch me." He said nothing. "What about Benjamin's license, where did you get that?"

"It's a fake," he said. "And I took your license to prove a point."

"What point?"

"Carrying ID is an amateur mistake. If I could get it, anyone could, I learned everything about your entire life from that one card. And if you have ID and the cops stop you, that's it, over… For someone like you anyway."

"And you?" she asked. "You don't carry ID?"

"I don't have ID. Period," he said. "I'm not on any database either… not for long anyway."

Peering at him, she watched the intensity of his focus. This guy was beyond an enigma, all she had were questions. "I don't believe that," she said. "I heard you were wanted in a bunch of countries, that means you've travelled. You can't travel without ID."

"Says who?" he asked and paused to look at the ceiling as if he was considering something before he stopped working to look at her. "First, you don't have to be in a country to break their laws. Sitting right here at this table, I've added myself to—and erased myself from—at least three wanted lists, and none of them belong to the country we're sitting in."

"So, you're on their wanted lists without ever leaving the country you were born in? You've really never been out of the country?"

"Who says I was born here?" he asked.

"Oh my God!" she exclaimed, throwing up her hands. "Where were you born?"

"That's a question a lot of people would like answered," he said and went back to typing.

But she pushed the lid of the laptop down, almost trapping his fingers again. His hands balled to fists that he dumped on the table on either side of the computer, while he huffed through tight lips.

"Strike—"

"Stop saying my name in public," he said, but she glanced around and there were only three other people there; one guy at the counter, and another couple way on the other side of the room. "Get out of the habit."

"Are you an American?"

"Does it matter?"

"Yes," she said. "I don't get it. I don't get why you covet this reputation. Do you know what people say about you?"

"That I broke every one of the ten commandments the day I first walked your mortal earth? That Satan himself spat me out of hell for trying to take over? Yeah, I've heard what they say."

"And?"

"People leave me alone," he said, opening the laptop. "I like the stories."

"Didn't work on me."

Her lips turned up in a grin, and she hunched down to hide herself behind the top of his laptop, letting herself peek over it at him with glittering mischievous eyes.

"We've already established that you're… you know…" he said, little emotion in his words.

It was nice that he didn't say the word she hated so much. "Is any of it true? Any of the stories?"

"My father was Satan," he said, "that one's true."

"Maybe we're related," she said, thinking of her brother and his father.

"Could be."

He spoke without his fingers slowing or his expression changing, but such a statement buried itself into her consciousness. She wanted to know more but would save getting into parentage for a later date because the last thing she wanted to do was talk about her own.

"Isn't it lonely?" she asked. "How long were you with Bella? Does she know everything about you?"

"Giving Bella information is giving her power," he said.

Guessing that meant his ex didn't know everything, Rora thought if she gave a bit of herself, maybe he'd give a little back. "Benjamin is twenty years older than me. We met at—"

"Look, I'm sure you have a really incredible backstory. True Lifetime movies material."

"But?"

"I don't give a fuck," he said and closed his laptop when the waitress brought their food and drinks.

He kept the laptop open a crack while he ate his food and downed his coffee. He ate fast. Faster than she'd ever seen a person eat in her life. It wasn't uncivilized, just like he was afraid someone might take it away from him at any second.

Strike was back on his laptop, typing away, before she'd even half finished her burger. Letting him work, she did her best to eat quickly, just in case they had to leave in a hurry, but she was getting tired.

"Are we going to sleep?" she asked, pushing her cooling coffee aside.

"What?" he asked, his attention still on the computer.

"I don't want to drink the coffee if we're going to sleep."

"Sleep?" he said like it was the most insane idea he'd ever heard. He scowled at her like she was weird for suggesting it. "Do you want to sleep?"

"You probably shouldn't drive anymore, right? We've been on the road all day. Aren't you tired?"

Grabbing her mug, he downed the liquid, more like he opened his throat and just tipped it on down into his stomach because it was gone in a flash. "I don't get tired."

"Hmm," she said, earning herself a side glance. "I never considered that you might be dumb enough to believe the stories. You aren't actually immortal or inhuman; you're as frail as the rest of us."

"We'll get a room," he said, slamming the laptop. "I'll let you have a couple of hours."

"So generous," she said, sliding to the end of the booth.

"Get moving," he said, tossing a bunch of bills onto the table, way more than was necessary to cover the meal.

"Who knew Satan's son was such a good tipper?" she said, sliding her back across his torso when she passed him.

With his laptop in his hand, he rested his knuckles on her hip to push her towards the door. "Pay enough, you can be as rude as you like."

"Where do you get your money?" she asked when they pushed out into the cool night air to cross the parking lot.

"Tonight?" he asked, scooping her body in front of his so as they walked, he occasionally bumped her to keep her moving at his pace. "That diner's corporate account."

Rora gasped, tipping her chin up to look at him over her shoulder, but he kept them moving. "You can't do that! It's stealing."

"A couple of cents here, couple of bucks there, they'll never notice it. Even if they did…" he smirked, showing her the closest she'd ever seen to a smile on his face. "They'd never trace it."

"Because you're just that good," she said.

He shunted her forward with his hips to urge her toward the motel office door. "Get a room, I'm moving the bike."

Spinning around, she grabbed each side of his leather jacket, holding it so tight that the zip dug into her skin. "What's to stop you ditching me?"

"Nothing," he said. "If you're ready to tell me what I want to know."

As long as she kept her secret, she'd have him on the hook. Triumphant in that knowledge, she smiled and pulled herself closer. "I need some money." His teeth clacked when she widened her grin. "Cards are traceable and somebody emptied my bank accounts anyway… How did you do that by the way?"

"Let's get something clear," he said, peeling her fingers from his jacket before stepping back and pulling a roll of bills from his pocket.

"What?"

"We're not friends," he said. "And I'm not here to teach you anything or to share."

"You don't like to share?" she asked, teasing him. "That's a shocker. I'd have figured you to be a real open guy… Bet you're a crier too."

Twirling away from him, she took two steps toward the office. "Rora," he said, forcing her to pivot to face him. "If I smother you in your sleep, this is why."

For some reason, despite his deadpan expression and sincere delivery, she failed to contain the laugh that burst from her lips though she did squeeze them together for as long as she could. "Am I the first of your victims you've ever justified your crimes to?" she asked. "Does that mean I'm special to you?"

"You're not my victim yet," he said. Walking backward, he held up his hand. "But I'm just saying, I'm making no promises."

SIX

"I'M SAYING, a rental car would make more sense," she said the following day when they got off the bike at a gas station. "I mean, geez, Strike…" Bending over, she pushed her hands between her legs to rub her inner thighs around to her ass. "I'm working muscles I didn't even know I had… Don't you feel that?"

"Your ass?" he asked, waiting for the pump to start.

Standing up to stretch her back, she bumped him with her hip. "Do you offer massage?"

He glared, looking her up and down. "Did you just flirt with me?" he asked. She bobbed her brows, which only made his scowl deepen. "Don't do that."

"I'm learning that the number of things in this world that make you uncomfortable far outweigh those that make you comfortable."

He started to pump the gas. Rora had no intention of watching him do it, so she dipped a hand into his pocket to pull out his money, another thing that made him growl at her. But he didn't object, and he didn't break her arm, which was more than most people could hope.

Going inside, she was counting bills, wondering if they should get food here or if he planned to stop later.

Noticing there were fresh cupcakes on a stand across the store, she went to them and selected one, considering if Strike might be a cupcake kind of person. But it was getting late, should they have cupcakes now or wait until dinner? When was dinner?

Rora turned to seek out a clock and saw three guys approaching her. She didn't think she'd done anything to draw attention to herself; all she was doing was standing there… holding a cupcake in one hand and a bunch of bills in the other. Hmm, she might be more appealing than she'd realized.

Folding the bills, she stuffed them into her bra, but that seemed to intrigue the lead guy more. "That ain't gonna stop us, sugartits," he said, and the two that flanked him leered at her chest.

"What is it you want?" she asked. "The money or the breasts?"

"Oh, you hear that boys?" he said over his shoulder. "That there's an invitation!"

He grabbed her wrist and she screamed, trying to pull back, but his buddy grabbed her other wrist and yanked her. The third guy went around behind her to push her along. To Rora's horror, there was a fire escape propped open just feet from where they were and it took them no time at all to get her out into the rear service space of the garage.

They wrestled her along the wall and though she struggled and screamed, they weren't dissuaded. The lead guy pulled her away from the wall and threw her down to the ground. Fear pumped her chest, her breaths came out as huffs, and she eyed all of them, noting the interest and intent in each of their expressions.

"Take what you want," she said. With her arms extended behind her and her hands in the grass, she held herself up. "Ok? You want the money? I'll give you the money." They closed in around her as she tried to push away from them along the ground. "Please, you don't have to do this."

The guy to the left screamed and arched, his shoulders thrusting back as his body bucked forward. Still in a panic, Rora didn't know what had happened to him and didn't see anything, until the guy turned and she noticed a blade between his shoulder blades.

A knife. How would a knife—the guy to the right was next to call out. She heard the familiar crack of bones before he crumpled to the asphalt. Wide eyed, she was shocked to see Strike standing where the guy had been. Now the assailant was nothing more than a blubbering idiot on the floor.

Strike's cold eyes slid from her to the main aggressor who was trying to puff up. "Who the fuck are you? She's our party. Fuck off."

"Oh, I wish I had time to enjoy this," Strike said, and she believed he was really disappointed.

The two men circled each other. The way Strike had moved put more distance between her and her attackers, while at the same time putting her behind him.

"You're not gonna enjoy nothing!" the head guy said and charged forward.

Rora screamed and scrambled to her hands and knees, but Strike absorbed the impact of the guy smashing into him. He pushed him back, hit once, twice, and then ducked the guy's punch.

"Fuck it, I don't have time to play," Strike said and threw another punch, which sent the guy down to the ground with an undignified thud.

Strike breathed in so deep that his shoulders rose, he huffed the breath out and then turned to her. "Did you pay for the gas?" he asked. Managing a loose shake of her head, Rora was almost sure her thoughts jangled in her head. Was he… was this… "You gonna stay down there all night?"

Another loose shake and then she forced herself to climb to her feet. Swallowing to moisten her dry throat, Rora was quick about wiping the stray tear from her face. Strike went to the guy with the knife embedded in his back, who was still writhing around on the ground. Without grace, he put his boot on the side of his face, squashing it down into the asphalt as he bent to pull his knife from the prick's body.

Another swallow, this one to quell her nausea and her hand went to her mouth. "Did you touch anything inside?" he asked, pulling a rag from his back pocket to wipe the guy's blood from the blade.

"A… a cupcake." Which must have hit the floor during the struggle.

He nodded. "Walk round the outside and meet me at the bike."

In a daze either from the near assault or his nonchalant reaction to it, she stumbled forward, ready to do what he said. But his arm came out to block her route and she recoiled, though God knew why; the guy had just saved her life.

As if he'd sensed that instant second of ridiculous fear, he pointed his index finger and touched the underside of her chin to elevate it. "Chin up, Cupcake," he said. "Never let them see fear." Another slack nod from her and he opened his palm. "Money."

Digging it from her bra, she put it on his open hand. Once he'd folded the bills into his pocket, he gave her a shove, putting her body in front of his to walk toward the fire escape door, bumping her along as he had last night, his body shielding her from the mess he'd made.

But he pushed her past the door and walked with her around the exterior of the building to return to the front. "Anyone asks, we were making out. That's the line," he said into the top of her head and jolted her toward the forecourt. "Wait by the bike."

Strike went inside to pay for the gas and she crossed the forecourt to return to the bike. There weren't many people around, but enough that she was wary of what would happen if the guys out back made a scene before they made their escape.

A minute later, Strike came out of the store holding something behind his back. Hoping it wasn't a gun, she watched with interest when he came to a stop on the other side of the bike. Her head tilt was enough of a question and he brought his hand around to show her what he had.

"A cupcake," she said, taking it from him in two hands.

"I'll drive slow; you'll have to eat it on the move. Can you hold onto me with one arm?"

Her face melted into a grin. "You bought me a cupcake."

"Yeah, whatever, don't make a big deal of it," he said, getting onto the bike and steadying her as she climbed on too.

"You're a secret romantic, aren't you, Strike?" she asked.

"They had an offer on the stupid things."

They did have an offer, she remembered, but it was a two for one offer and he hadn't come out with two. "I won't tell anyone that you were sweet to me," she said, dipping her finger into the frosting and reaching over his shoulder to smudge it between his lips.

To her surprise, he sucked her digit clean without objecting. But he did it like it was a task to be completed, rather than anything more salacious. He can't have felt the same quiver she did when his tongue made it through the frosting to meet her fingertip.

"Doesn't fit with the legend," he said and put on his helmet. She was glad hers didn't obstruct her mouth. "And there's still time for me to change my mind about smothering you."

But she didn't care about that, she was too busy biting into her cupcake when he rose and descended to get the bike going.

Strike, the man who'd knocked her out, the man who'd held a gun to her head, the same guy who'd stolen from her, had bought her a cupcake. She'd never had a more valuable gift given to her in her life and she'd savor every bite.

***

"BUT WHERE IS it that we're going?" she asked, sitting in the middle of the motel room bed with the sheet pooled around her hips.

It had been two days since their run-in with those guys at the gas station and so far, no cop cars had pulled them over, there was no dramatic car chase to apprehend them. They were just driving for what seemed like ever.

Strike was sitting on the couch with his laptop open on the coffee table in front of him. "Get some sleep, Cupcake," he said, focused on whatever he was reading.

"I'm restless," she admitted. "I don't feel like we're making progress. Do you know where you're going? Do you know where Benjamin is?"

"I'm working on it," he grumbled. "Until I pin him down, it makes sense to keep moving. It makes us harder to pin down."

Something she hadn't considered was that this Bella might still be pursuing him. "Do you think she's after you? That she's sent more men after you?"

"After us," he said.

Alarm prodded her. "Why would she be after me? What do I have that she wants?"

Lifting his eyes, he asked again, "What's the point?"

Rora scowled at him. "Do you keep asking to aggravate me or because you think I'll slip up and blurt out what I know by mistake?"

"Either way, I win," he said, returning to his typing.

He never seemed to be off. He'd told her in the diner on the first night of their journey that he didn't sleep and she was beginning to believe him. "Do you ever lie down?" she asked. "I've never seen you sleep. How do you do that? What kind of person doesn't sleep? You must sleep. Do you sleep?"

"I grab a half hour here and there," he said.

So he waited until she was asleep before he went to sleep. But how did he know how to wake up before her? "I've never seen you lie down."

"You don't have to lie down to go to sleep."

Did that mean he slept sitting up? "You have serious issues, Strike," she said, plumping her pillow.

"You're just now figuring that out?"

"Tell me something about you," she said and he drew his eyes off her, his fingers never slowing. "I'm serious. It can be anything. Just something personal."

"Why? So we can bond?" he muttered.

He could be as condescending and aloof as he liked, she was going to keep prodding him. It wasn't like she had anything better to do with her time. "To distract my mind from thinking about whatever Benjamin's going through," she said. "Tell me something I wouldn't expect, something that's not just another part of the legend… Tell me something, Strike."

Sucking in a breath, he dropped from his starched upright seated position into the back of the chair. "Ok," he said, rubbing his hands over his face. "I tell you one thing and you'll stop bugging me?" Rora nodded. "Something you wouldn't expect…"

"Yep," she said, closing her fists around the sheet on her knees in anticipation of what he might reveal.

"Anything?"

"Yep, anything," she said. "Anything at all."

"I'm terrified of flying," he said and sat up straight to start typing again.

Shock opened her mouth, something she was getting used to around this guy. Drawing up her knees, Rora hugged them to her chest. "Really? I would never have thought that you'd be afraid of anything! Why flying? Is it because you're out of control? I guess, when you think about it, there's lots of reasons to be afraid. You're basically just toothpaste in a tube up there, waiting to be squirted out at God's discretion."

He stopped typing. "God?" he asked and sneered at her. "Don't tell me you're one of those people."

"One of those people? If you're asking if I believe in God then yeah, I guess I do…"

"Oh shit," he groaned, falling back into the cradle of his seat again. "You're not serious. After everything you've been through, after what your brother did. You still believe?"

"You can't believe in Satan and not believe in God," she said. "I don't spend a whole lot of time thinking about it to be honest. I don't think a lot of people do these days. I'm not pedantic about following the commandments or anything." She smiled. "I covet things I shouldn't. All. The. Time… Another thing a lot of people do these days."

"What about the others?" he asked, something like interest seeping from between his eyelids. "Worshiping other gods or taking the lord's name in vain."

"Oh, I do that all the time," she said. "I don't mean to, it just… I don't know."

Closing his laptop, he used his hand on it to boost himself onto his feet and started toward her. "Do you keep your Sabbath holy?" he asked, creeping toward her. She shook her head. "What about bearing false witness, you ever do that?" She nodded and he sank down to sit on the edge of the bed, his voice growing slower and more seductive, like he was talking to a lover about what he planned to do to her. "You ever steal anything, Cupcake?" She nodded and he hissed. "I find out you've broken one more and I'll believe there's hope for you yet…"

"That's all," she said, but couldn't actually remember all of them when he was leaning in like that, coming so close to her, making her forget her senses.

"Murder?" She shook her head. "Adultery?" Turning her lip into her mouth, she dug her teeth into it and shook her head. He'd put murder ahead of adultery, like the latter was worse than the former. "Do you honor your mother and father?" he whispered.

Inhaling, her breath hitched twice and like it was programmed, a tear slipped from her eye in the same moment she shook her head. "No," she breathed out, her heart shattering with the confession.

One corner of his mouth rose. "You're just the right amount of corruptible, Cupcake."

Was he going to corrupt her? Was that what he was implying? It seemed that he was fascinated by her mouth, maybe he liked to watch her chew her lip. It was a nervous habit she'd started as a child and not one meant to entice. But he looked more tired now than she'd ever seen him.

"Talking about breaking rules turns you on."

"Not as much as actually breaking them does," he said, but instead of coming closer, or trying to break rules with her, he stood up and went back over to his laptop.

He'd never shown interest in her like that. He never tried to touch her or to tempt her to touch him. In this situation, he'd had plenty of chances to join her in bed or force himself on her if he was that kind of guy, and he had to be that kind of guy because he'd broken every law by his own admission. That had to include the sexual ones.

But scaring her wouldn't get him what he wanted. He'd never find out what the point was if she hated him. And until they had Benjamin, Strike couldn't demand that she tell him. He could be biding his time until this was over, or nearly over, maybe he planned to make his move then, they couldn't call him 'Strike' for nothing.

It could be that he just wasn't attracted to her. If Bella was the type of woman he went for, he liked his women bitter and apparently vicious. Being with her wouldn't offer him any type of thrill; that was probably why he'd referred to her as 'vanilla.' It wouldn't be breaking any rules, she wasn't married and if he wasn't on any database, he couldn't be hitched either.

Flopping onto her back, she kept her knees bent and squeezed her eyes shut. Rora shouldn't be thinking this way about the man she'd basically blackmailed into helping her.

The fizz of attraction might have first touched her in the Last Resort parking lot, but it had been growing since. But that could just be because of the amount of time he'd spent between her thighs in the last few days.

Riding the bike from motel to truck stop to gas station, it was a long, arduous journey, though he didn't seem fazed by it. The man had no country, no home, no family. She wondered if he'd ever stopped moving or if this was his life. If it was, it explained a lot.

Letting her feet slide down the bed, Rora flattened her legs and rolled her head on the pillow to get a better view of him. Intent on his typing as always, she wondered at what was in his mind. What was he doing over there? What was he working on that he seemed so desperate to finish? All he did when he wasn't driving was type on that thing. Day in, day out, his laptop was his idol.

"Strike," she said, without teasing or expectation. But her softness got no response. "Strike, come and lie down with me." He stopped typing. Like he always did, he hung there in silence for a few seconds, doing nothing before he turned to her. "Don't fight with me. Just this once… Please?"

Lifting her hand toward him, she hoped he wouldn't just ignore her.

He examined her for half a minute, poked at something on his computer and closed the lid. With her lip between her teeth, she waited to see what he'd do when he stood up and started toward the bed. Fearful that if she spoke she might make him change his mind, she kept her lip between her teeth even after he sat down on the edge of the bed and bent over to unlace his boots.

Once he'd kicked them off, he cleared his throat and twisted, lifting his legs up onto the bed. But he was still sitting and from the movement of his head, she wondered if he'd forgotten how to lie down.

Though it was funny to see him unsure, she hid her smile, and sat up beside him. Picking up his arm, she lifted it over her shoulders and used her upper body to ease his back onto the mattress. He stayed tense, his hand hovering over her arm rather than relaxing.

Nestling closer, Rora put her head on his chest and pressed herself to him, reaching for his hand and lacing her fingers through his to keep his embrace tight around her.

"I can't reach to turn the light off."

"I got it," he said and lifted his hips to pull a phone from his back pocket.

With a few quick flicks, the lights went off and finally, she could let herself smile. "Is there anything you can't do?" she asked, but the question didn't seem so glib when he didn't answer it.

Confessing his fear to her was a sign that he did have insecurities, whether he liked to advertise them or not. He seemed so strong, invincible. Benjamin had a way with computers that left her in awe, but even he hadn't shown ability like Strike had. It was possible he could do all the parlor tricks that Strike had impressed her with, but he'd never shown them to her.

"When can I get up again?" Strike asked when they'd been lying in silence for a few minutes. "Is that enough?"

"Close your eyes for me," she said. He huffed. "Just close them and see what happens. Think of it as a challenge."

He muttered something to himself but moved enough that she guessed he was getting himself comfortable, inadvertently tightening his arm around her.

She took it as a good sign that he didn't just curse at her and shove her away. The phone was still in his hand, resting facedown against his thigh, she'd seen the screen light fade against the denim he was wearing.

All she wanted was for him to be rested. Whether he lay with her for ten minutes or two hours, it was better for his body to recharge than not. With a yawn, she closed her own eyes and turned her face into his tee-shirt, making the most of his protection while she had it this close.

SEVEN

A WHIMPER SQUEAKED from her throat when the first whisper of awareness stole into her slumber. Rora moved, testing her muscles, and smiled, her legs were wrapped around something long and hard, it felt good, solid. Pushing her hips forward, she found herself at the perfect angle to rock against it.

The smooth, hard warmth beneath her hand was nice too. Letting her hand move up and down, she thought it might be flesh, so she guessed she was still in a dream. The careful, constant rhythm of a heartbeat beneath her palm made her pause and press her hand down. Her hips were still moving. She tilted, pressing her clit into the stimulator she'd been writhing on.

Something tightened around the back and side of her neck, pressing her face closer to the hard thing she was wrapped around. When a masculine grumble drifted to her ears, Rora tried to open her eyes, and curled her fingers at the same time, but she scratched whatever was under her hand deeper than she'd meant to.

The grumble became a curse and whatever was around her neck clamped tight fast, closing over her throat and cutting off her breathing in an instant.

Her eyes flew open and she punched out. Strike! It was Strike! His arm was around her neck and he had her in a headlock.

Just as her panic rose and she punched again, his arm loosened. She coughed. "Shit," he mumbled. "It's you."

Sucking in a breath, she recovered from the few seconds of terror and sagged. Her hand was up under his tee-shirt, lying in the middle of his chest beneath the fabric. Both her legs were coiled around one of his and then… Oh, the bulge behind his fly was unexpected, but intriguing.

"Part of you was happy to wake up with me," she said, impressed by what she saw. "Shame another part of you wanted to kill me."

"I'm a conflicted guy," he said, stretching. But her fingers rose to thread between his, keeping one of his arms around her because her head was enjoying using his upper arm as a pillow. "Want to take your hand out of my shirt?"

Tipping her head up, she wasn't surprised to see him glowering down at her. Seeing him grumpy was par for the course, but she wasn't used to this. His hair was rumpled, his eyes heavy, and the masculine scent of him swirled around both of them. Waking up wrapped around each other was intimate, being here in the heat of his embrace did more to her than just keep her toasty.

"Do you wanna…"

He licked his lips though his scowl went nowhere. "Do I wanna what?"

Boosting herself upward, she lifted her pelvis toward the front of his thigh. With every increment closer to his mouth that hers got, it opened in anticipation. Kissing him would be a gateway to going further. They were alone, having spent the night sleeping together, there was no other way this could turn out.

At least that was what Rora thought until he grabbed her shoulder and at the last second, right before their mouths met, he pushed her away. "No," he grumbled. "I don't wanna."

Shoving her onto the bed, he got up and grabbed his phone from the mattress while he stuck his feet into his boots. "Strike—"

"Just because you're the proud owner of a sweet, slick pussy and I've got myself an overeager hard-on, doesn't mean the two will ever meet, get it?"

Sitting up, she gathered the sheet with her like she was naked beneath it, though she wasn't. "Eager?" she asked without thinking about how eager the question would make her sound.

"I'm gonna have a shower," he said. "Stay there."

Stay where she was so she wouldn't follow him? Because he sure as hell wasn't coming back to the bed. Her first night of sleeping with him was going to be her last; he'd sent that message loud and clear.

He was quick in the shower, she knew that from experience. Instead of staying where she was like he'd said, Rora got up and made the bed and then gathered her clothes for that day.

Except he took longer than normal in the shower, so she found herself sitting on the couch with her toes hooked on the edge of the coffee table, waiting for him to finish in the bathroom. This would be another day on the back of that bike. Her body was getting used to it and now that she'd pushed through the initial discomfort, she liked the freedom of the bike, liked being able to race anyone else on the road and win. The speed was exhilarating and somehow made her feel invincible.

But it had been days, racked with the vibrations from the engine, and her skin was itching to just be still. Considering whether or not she should ask Strike for a day off from their journey, she caught sight of his laptop on the table.

Having it lying around was a familiar sight, but it reminded her of the computer she'd left behind. It had been months since she'd heard from Benjamin. But if he was trying to get hold of her, it didn't help that she was off the grid. Rora had to be there for him and at the very least should check her email and the message board to see if he'd written anything.

Sliding off the couch, she knelt on the floor and tentatively let her fingers move toward Strike's laptop. She'd touched it before and it wasn't like it had ever bitten her. It was a piece of machinery, just like any other. Who cared if it looked different with its reinforced cover and the weird metal shielding that was almost like cladding. It was a computer.

Her nerves began to subside when she opened it and nothing bad happened. It was just a screen and a keyboard, just like she'd expect of any computer. Except it wasn't any computer. All of the keys were completely blank and it didn't seem to be accidental, there was no indication the characters had worn off.

There was at least one extra line of keys and there were some weird symbols above those that she didn't understand. But she didn't have to understand them to know how to type, that was something she could do blindfolded.

If she could figure out how to turn the thing on. Except… peering at the top corner of the screen, she saw a single line flashing. Was it on already? Ready for her? Now, if she could just remember how to switch from—she touched a key without thinking and a hot, sharp pain shot through her hand.

She yelped in time with the sound of his voice. "Aurora!" Strike called out.

With tears in her eyes she looked up to see him crossing the room in a flash wearing only a towel. "Strike," she said, pain quaking through the hand she was cradling. "I—"

"Damnit, damnit, damnit," he said, dropping to his knees and grabbing the top of the laptop to flip it around to him. "I got you, girl. I got you. Calm down. Keep calm. I got you."

His whispered words were meant for the laptop that he was battering on at a thousand miles an hour.

Here she was, an actual flesh and blood person, in pain, and he was focused completely on comforting the machine. "Strike," Rora said, tears of pain slipping from her eyes. "I'm hurt."

"You're lucky that's all you are," he mumbled. "She could've killed you. Next one would've."

Swiping at her tears, the shock of agony was subsiding. "She?"

"What were you thinking?" he snapped. "Don't touch what doesn't belong to you."

Oh, that was rich coming from the guy who'd been stealing from her since the second they met. "Strike!"

Crawling over the floor, she grabbed his arm, trying to pull him around to look at her. His fist came up fast, but he breathed through clenched teeth and extended a finger.

"If you don't let me fix this, you're going to be on every wanted list on the planet within the next twenty seconds. There will be a BOLO out, your location will be fed to the cops and they'll be here with a full SWAT team within five minutes. This might be a two-bit town, but I guarantee they still carry guns and they will have a shoot-to-kill order."

Unable to process the extent of what he was saying, Rora's hand slid away from his arm and she sat gaping at his fingers flying across the blank keys. "H… how?"

"She reads your fingerprint. Yours didn't match mine, so zap," he said. "Soon as you touch a key, she scans it and pulls up every detail of your life. Planting evidence isn't difficult, and everything is digital. If a cop has an order to arrest, that's what he'll do. She'll freeze your assets too, and those of every person you ever met, talked to, touched. Everything. 'Cept as soon as the cops start looking, they'll see your assets amount to exactly nothing since we've already wiped those."

So he was worried about the cops tracing a connection between her and Exile? "But… why?"

"You touched something that didn't belong to you," he said.

The bathroom door was open, the sound of the shower hammered away like he'd rushed from it without having a chance to turn it off and she wondered… "How did you know?"

Holding up his forearm for a brief second, he flashed his wrist at her. "I have a security chip in my wrist. Anytime she's in trouble. I know it."

"She wasn't in trouble," Rora said and then closed her eyes to shake her head. "It's a computer, Strike."

"My computer." He hadn't been wrong about not sharing. "What were you looking for? You think I just left Gallagher's address in a convenient little stick-it note for you?"

There was real anger in his voice and his lip curled like he was struggling to suppress his rage. "I wanted to check my email," she said. "That's all. I wasn't spying on you."

"Are you really dumb enough not to know I've been monitoring your email since this started?" he said. "Gallagher hasn't been in touch, is that how he did it? Emailed you? Primitive. I'm not as impressed anymore."

No, it wasn't email, it was the message board, and she had to interpret his message. Benjamin wasn't direct, they took precautions. "No, but I thought—"

"That message board is no better," he said, and she was surprised to hear that he knew about it. "Don't know if it's a reflection of your skills or his that he went for a place filled with kooks and crazies."

"Some would say I fit right in," she said. "That's what you're implying, isn't it?"

"I don't imply anything," he snarled. "If I have something to say then I say it."

But that wasn't true. Through all of this there had been something he'd held back from her and it wasn't any kind of information about Benjamin or what the goddamn point was.

"Then say it," she spat and was aggravated that he ignored her to keep typing.

Characters flew onto the screen's black background. Windows of different colors opened and closed, each movement of his fingers caused another ripple and she didn't understand anything of what she was seeing.

Grabbing the top of the laptop, she slammed it down and pushed it away. "Goddamnit!" Strike yelled out and tried to sweep her aside, but she dug her nails into his arm and yanked at him. "Get out of my goddamn way if you don't want to—"

"Go to jail, I know, you just said it! I'll go to jail. I'll do the time. Just say it!"

"Say what? What the fuck are you—"

"Say what you've wanted to say to me since the minute I walked up to your table in Last Resort and dropped Benjamin's license in front of you. Say it, Strike! Goddamnit!"

Lunging forward, he gave her no choice but to fall back and catch the weight of her upper body on her elbows. He pointed his finger into her face and snarled, "You have no place here! No place in this world!"

"Feel better to say it?" He sneered at her, eyeing her body and turning to straighten and reach for his laptop again. She sat up. "You hide behind that, behind her," she said. "You act like you're this big, scary guy with all these skills and maybe you are smarter than me. Smarter than everyone, who knows? But you're alone, hiding behind your screens and machines. Who would come for you if you were in trouble? You don't stand for anything, you don't have a cause, and you don't have any right to judge mine." With a hand on the coffee table and another on the couch, she pushed herself onto her feet, but stayed bent over to snarl in his ear. "You leave me alone with that bitch again and I'll put my new switchblade through her motherboard."

He blinked upward, his fury merging with a resentful hatred, but Rora smiled. That computer had tried to kill her and if she got the chance, she had no trouble returning the favor.

***

STRIKE WAS DRESSED when Rora got out the shower and there wasn't a sign of the laptop anywhere. "What's going on?" she asked, noticing that resolve was stiffening him.

"We're taking a day off from the road," he said.

Rolling her eyes, she folded her arms. "Is this about what I said about your computer? I promise not to touch her again, ok? I was hurt." Rora waved her fingers at him. "Still stings by the way."

"Then you've learned your lesson," he said. "But this isn't about that. You wanted a day off from the bike, right?"

She did, but she didn't think she'd said it out loud. "Ok," she said, taking a step toward him. "So, what are we going to do today?"

"You do whatever you want," he said, pulling a wad of money from his pocket to toss it over the couch onto the coffee table. "Just be back here tomorrow by check-out time if you want to keep going."

That seemed like an odd thing to say, why wouldn't she want to keep going? "Do you want to keep going?"

But he didn't say anything either way, just turned around and walked out, leaving her alone. Insulting his precious computer hadn't been intentional, but he'd obviously taken it to heart.

When she heard what sounded like rotor blades, her eyes traveled upward, he wouldn't have… would he? No way Rora was going to wait around to find out if he'd sent some covert international organization after her. Hurrying across the room, she grabbed the money, and her jacket, and ran out of the motel room.

***

THE TOWN WAS SMALL, but still had a shopping district. To her delight, she found a beauty salon and treated herself to a mani/pedi. She got her hair done too, choosing to get purple streaks through her auburn locks. The stylist was overjoyed by her choice, claiming she didn't often get to work with hair as thick and soft as hers. Rora was sure the woman was feeding her a line to get a better tip. Her hair couldn't be in that great a shape, she'd neglected all her beauty needs for the last six months. Not that she'd ever been much of a spa bunny.

The body scrub felt great and the massage even better. For one day, she let herself relax. It had been impossible to chill out since Benjamin was taken. But now, with Strike on the case, she wasn't as worried. Not only wasn't she alone anymore, but she had one of the world's most skilled men helping her fix her problem.

Walking down the street with her shopping bags, she felt freer than she had for a long time. He wasn't at the motel when she got there, not that she'd expected him to be. But she changed her clothes, took time to do her make-up, and began to feel like a normal human being again for the first time since all of this.

Even going to dinner by herself was a liberating experience. Strike was out there somewhere. She might not know exactly where or how to get in touch with him, but he was nearby, and that was enough to make her relax.

She was out walking in the moonlight when her pocket buzzed. Smiling to herself, she wondered if Strike was calling to check why she wasn't at the motel when it had to be after midnight.

Except when she took her phone from her pocket and saw that it had no number or identifier, she stopped walking and lost her smile. Hesitating for only a second, she held her breath, pressed receive and lifted the phone to her ear.

"Aurora," a voice said and although it was distorted, this time it was definitely female.

Rora knew she hadn't misinterpreted it the last time, whoever this was they'd either changed their voice or there was another party coming to the table. "Bella?"

A chilling digital laugh made her shiver. "Seems we have the same taste in men. You have mine and I have yours," Bella said. "I would ask what we should do about that. But I have no problem sharing mine with you... Do you have a problem sharing with me?"

Benjamin? Did she have Benjamin? Rora was confused. How could a woman hold a man as powerful as Benjamin? He'd be able to physically overpower her. Except, she'd seen the marks on Strike and remembered what he'd said about Bella's minions.

"Yes," she said, heated by anger. "I have a huge problem sharing. I want you to let him go."

"I would give him back, course I would. But your man has something I want, something he won't relinquish. Odd because Exile was once in the same position. Did he tell you how we met?" Rora said nothing. "He was a prisoner of my father and brothers. They held him for half a year. Tortured him. But that didn't make any ounce of difference to a boy who's been tortured since the day he was born. He was born hated. Conceived in evil. His mother killed herself on the day he was born because she couldn't stand to look at him. I'd say it was sad if it wasn't so tantalizing. It's difficult not to fall in love with a man like that, isn't it? A man so… unmoved and unafraid. So untethered. He's so broken and damaged that he doesn't have a thing in the world to lose. He revels in the pain, cares about nothing. He doesn't fear pain or death. His indifference… it's arousing. He's the epitome of freedom and I'd say that's why a girl like you would fall for him. You, a girl always concerned with what everyone else thinks about your past, must be drawn to a man so invulnerable."

"Why did you call me?" Rora asked. "Are you going to ask the question?"

"No. I called you to caution you," Bella said, and to her credit, she sounded sincere, like she had a grave warning. "Tread carefully with him, one day you think he's your savior and the next, he snaps, and he's like a stranger. I could handle it, before Exile killed them all, I dealt with the brutality of my father and brothers on a daily basis, but you don't deserve to live through another trauma."

"You don't care about me," Rora said, not falling for it. "What's this really about?"

"Men have ruled over us for too long. They believe themselves better, stronger. Only women like us can stand up against them. Fire forged us. We were burned, scarred by the men forced upon us. We owe it to ourselves and each other never to let them mark us again."

EIGHT

TRACKING DOWN STRIKE wasn't as difficult as Rora had thought it would be.

Without a phone number for him, or even an email, she had no way to reach out. But her desire to see him had reminded her of how she'd found him in the first place. In the darkest corner of the most rundown and terrifying bar in town.

There wasn't a biker bar around here, but she recalled overhearing a conversation in the salon about a woman who was upset with her husband for going to the seedy strip club near the highway.

The cab driver did a double take when Rora asked to be taken there, and she thought there was something ironic about the parallel of cab drivers not wanting to go to the place Strike coveted.

But he took her, and Rora kept her eyes open on the journey to the club. Checking out the corner near the rear exit as they drove by, she spotted Strike's bike. Bingo. He was always in a position to make a quick getaway. If his bike was here, with its special custom spot for his beloved laptop, then he wasn't far away.

The doormen didn't look any less surprised to see her than the cab driver had been, and she was let in for free even though she offered to pay. Descending the stairs into the dark club, she smelled the scent of a smoke machine and saw the flash of lights swinging in various arcs past the circular glass windows in the doors at the bottom of the stairs.

Pushing through, she felt a sense of deja vu. The large room with its various podiums was better lit than Last Resort and there were women in here, even if they were basically naked for the most part.

The darkest corner.

Scanning the room, she turned slowly, letting the flashes of light from the mainstage reflect off one of the mirror balls to light up the corners. But the curved walls didn't give much opportunity for darkness to fester in corners.

Her attention went past the bar and then back… There he was, sitting at a table at the end of the bar, tucked in a corner formed by it. He probably couldn't even see the main stage from there. Not just because he was so engrossed in his precious laptop, but because the bar was high and would block his view.

In her tight cocktail dress, she got a few glances. Rora guessed the patrons considered her too overdressed to work here and the only women around were employees. Some of the women followed her progress too, probably expecting that she was someone's wife or girlfriend, here to throw a hissy fit.

But there were more important things to consider than creating a scene for sport. Striding over to his table, she didn't even come to a stop before he was sliding a hundred over the tabletop.

"Not interested," he grumbled, tapping away on his keyboard. "Leave me alone."

Picking up the bill, she pouted at it and shrugged before tucking it into her bra. "No Buddy here to keep the masses away, huh," she said.

His fingers froze. She smiled, it was funny to literally feel the air around him begin to crackle with annoyance. "You're like a goddamn homing pigeon," he grumbled when she spun around and dropped onto the seat beside him, thigh to thigh.

"Or a cadaver dog. You are meant to be a ghost, right?" she asked, crossing her legs toward him and admiring the view. "You know, I wouldn't have pictured you in a place like this." He was quite happy to type and she was quite happy to keep voicing her opinions. "There are a lot of people here and most of them are happy." Rora made a dramatic show of shaking her whole body in a shiver. "Imagine the horror? They could infect you… Oh my God, what if they make you smile? Quick, we better get out of here fast or we might find ourselves…" She curled her fingers around her throat and swallowed down feigned fear. "Having fun! Strike, please, don't let it happen! You're stronger than this! Resist temptation! Step away from the light!"

"Did you come here for a reason?" he asked without reacting to her theatrics. "You didn't get yourself in trouble dressed like that, did you?"

Opening her arms, she admired her own dress. "Do you like it? I got my hair done too."

"I noticed," he mumbled.

"Do you like it?"

"No."

Well, ok, she had asked, but he really didn't get the point. "There's an implied right answer to that question," she said from the corner of her mouth. "Want to try again?"

"I told you, I don't do implied," he said.

"So why—"

"Color like that makes you distinguishable," he said. "Reason?"

She hadn't thought about how she might want to blend into the background. But he was right, she'd just given herself an identifiable feature. Damn it.

"Bella called me."

"I know, I ran a trace," he said. "She's on the move. Heading north."

"We're heading south," she said.

"Right now, we're heading nowhere."

Sighing again, she noticed one of the half-naked employees walking by eyeing them. Rora grinned and gestured her over. Plucking a couple of hundreds from her bra, she gave them to the woman. "Would you help me out with my boyfriend? We're experimenting with kink. Touch as much as you like. He needs a little boost to get him going."

The woman was happy to take the money. Strike had no opportunity to say a word. Rora grabbed the laptop, closed it and hugged it to her chest. The dancer pushed the table away, moved between his thighs and began moving for him.

Rising a fraction, Rora murmured in his ear. "A-sexuality is a recognized thing now, you should look it up." The dancer pushed her ass into Strike's groin. He leaned away, wearing a look of disgust when the blonde lay back on his chest and put her head on his shoulder. Running her hand through her hair, the blonde spread her shimmering locks all in his face. When the dancer licked his jaw, Rora had to smile. "Have fun for a night, just one won't kill you." The dancer spun and dropped to squat, her hands open on his knees. "I swear I won't tell anyone."

Smacking his chest once, she kissed his cheek and got up. Handing the dancer another bundle of bills, she widened her smile. "Make sure the girls treat him well," Rora said and flounced away, still hugging his laptop to her chest.

He'd taken her phone from her after the last Bella call. Maybe it made sense that he'd done something to it to ensure he was notified of who was calling. Figuring she should've asked if he could listen in too, she thought about what Bella had said.

Until now, she'd been so determined to find out where Strike was to tell him what had happened that she hadn't focused on Bella's words and what they meant about who he was. But if it was true… Had his mother committed suicide? Rora couldn't believe it, there was no way that a woman could do such a thing to a newborn… could she?

Strike had told her not to trust his ex, that she was a plausible person. Rora had been determined not to be drawn in, she wasn't going to be naive and prove him right. But she could interpret facts in her own way. And the more she thought about it, the more it made sense. He came from nowhere, he had no family, and he had a major chip on his shoulder.

What chance did any person have when they had that kind of start in life? Walking down the side of the road, back toward town, Rora was proud of herself. It might have started as a joke, but now she felt like she'd done a good thing. Strike did deserve to cut loose and have a bit of fun and he was in the perfect place to do that.

***

HER MOUTH WAS DRY when she woke up.

Rora yawned and turned her face toward the heavy warmth that had made her stir. "Strike?" she whispered, recognizing his scent and the texture of his palm on her face.

"Open your eyes before you say my name," he said. "The next time, it might not be me touching you."

His hand moved away, and she opened her eyes to see him getting off the edge of the bed where he'd been sitting. "What time is it?"

"Time to check out," he said. When she turned to blink at the curtains, she noticed daylight shining from the other side of them. Strike was grabbing up her things and stuffing them into her pack, and she realized he was wearing the same outfit as he had been last night. "Are you just getting back?"

"Yeah," he said. "You were right, that blonde was just what I needed."

Pushing onto her elbows, Rora didn't expect to feel a sharp pain in the middle of her chest above her breasts. "You slept with her?" she asked, her words little more than a breathy gasp.

He spared her just a brief glance and tossed her pack toward the door. "You gave her almost a grand. We don't let money like that go to waste, Cupcake."

She couldn't close her mouth, was he really using her pet name after admitting he'd been intimate with another woman? What was the sickness and the fever that was making her feel weak?

Rora had been fine last night, she'd slept fine, waking up with his hand on her face had been a pleasure. But now, she didn't want to move. Flopping onto her back, she pressed both hands to her face. She'd paid that woman to dance for him, not to…

Another pain hit her chest and heaviness filled her gut. It was wrong that she should feel betrayed, because she'd set it up, but she did feel disappointment, in him and in herself.

"Where's the laptop?"

"Under my pillow," she said, her hands still over her face. "I figured there was joking around and then there was a capital offense. If I let anything happen to your Precious, I'd probably pray for a smothering compared to what you'd do to me."

"Opal proved yesterday she can take care of herself. I'd never have let her leave with you if I didn't think the pair of you would make it through the night without killing each other."

Letting her hands slip from her face, his shadow crossed her and there he was, standing next to the bed, looming over her. "Opal?"

"Figured now you've slept with her, you should know her name," he said and leaned over to shove a hand under her pillow, displacing her to tug the laptop out, which also sent her switchblade skittering to the floor.

"You slept with the blonde, did you get her name?"

"The blonde's name's irrelevant," he said, bending over to retrieve the switchblade. Laying it on her chest, over the sheet, he turned to walk away. "Did you put the blade there just in case or did something happen?"

Pointing her toes, Rora stretched her hands over her head, pushing against the headboard to slide herself down the bed. "If someone had come to attack us, I'd have let Opal zap him… She taught me about pain without blood, and blood means evidence."

"Good tip," he said and opened the motel room door. "I'll give you five minutes and then I'm on the road."

"Are we heading back north?" she asked, grabbing the blade and leaping out of bed, pulling her tee-shirt down as fast as she could.

"No," he said. "East."

"I don't understand."

"No one said you had to."

He turned around, opening the door wider and taking a step out. "Strike," she said. He stopped to look at her. But the longer he stood there, the faster her nerve fled. She had no right to ask him about his night, about whether or not he had gone home with the blonde, her friend, or a posse of women. She smiled. "I'm glad you had a good night… Five minutes."

NINE

EAST BECAME NORTH became west, until five days had passed and Rora had no earthly idea where they were going anymore.

After having dinner and setting up camp at a city motel, Strike had told her to put on her fancy dress and pulled her from the room into the street, which they'd been walking on for at least twenty minutes.

Going up one block, they came down another, until her head was spinning. Though she couldn't figure out where they were in relation to where they'd started, Rora was sure she'd seen the same business names more than once.

"Where are we going, Strike?" she asked, her heels beginning to nip her feet. "I'm getting cold."

She wasn't really worried about her feet or the temperature, she just hated to be out of the loop. Tossing an arm around her shoulders, he pulled her close to him, but didn't slow down for her, which caused her a new set of problems.

He hadn't let her bring a jacket, she'd been wearing one when she got to their room door, but he pulled it from her and tossed it to the bed telling her it wasn't allowed. He was wearing a jacket, one with a leather hood that he had pulled over his face. It seemed like some bullshit that she wasn't allowed one. If it was just to present a better view of her breasts, she'd kill him. But given how little interest he'd ever shown in her body, Rora was confident that his motive wasn't sexual.

Since finding out about the blonde, Rora's playfulness had cooled. She hadn't minded pushing his buttons when it was just a joke. But her games had backfired big time when he'd actually followed through with the beauty. She still felt sick when she thought about him enjoying that perfect female form.

It was a double joke on her though, because it proved that not only was he fully able to enjoy a woman, it proved he had no interest in enjoying her. A stripper with possibly loose morals had probably been all kinds of naughty and that was what he liked.

Rora was no saint, and she'd enjoyed her share of sexual escapades, but when it came to flat-out being bad in a break-the-law kind of way, her experience was on the light side. Except aiding and abetting Exile, a known criminal, was adding a little weight to that file.

"Strike, why—"

She shut up when he grabbed her hips and turned her sideways to push her into a wide communal entrance. He urged her on, up the stairs, and onto the second floor. "Don't use my name in here," he said. "Don't ask any questions. Just go with whatever happens."

Knocking once on the first apartment door, he didn't wait for a response, and instead opened the door and pushed her inside first. Nice, so if they'd been shot at, she'd have been his human shield. Inside was a large room, sparsely furnished. The three suited men inside stopped talking to each other and turned to examine her and Strike.

An air of tense intimidation constricted her breathing. She'd never been in a meeting like this and didn't even know why they were here this time.

Doing as Strike said, she said nothing, and expected him to look after her. So when he nudged her forward with a shoulder, she stumbled and looked back at him. But he was looking over her head at the men in front of them.

While she was looking the wrong way, Rora didn't expect anyone to touch her, but someone grabbed her wrist and instinct made her pull back. "Hey!"

"Go with him," Strike said, still staring out one of the guys.

"Wha… what?" she asked, but the one who had hold of her pulled her across the room, and all she could do was let herself be dragged, glancing back at Strike for any hint of what was going to happen. But he gave her none.

"Torres," Strike said, stopping the guy who had ahold of her wrist. "You hurt her. You die. You know it's that simple. All I need is one word from her and I'll take down your whole organization."

Torres pulled her through a door at the back of the room. He yanked her forward so he could move behind her and lock the door. The sound of the lock sliding into place made her gasp, but he didn't reassure her. Thrusting her against the door, he opened her arms to press them to the door and kicked her feet apart to begin frisking her.

Panting to keep up with her quickening pulse, Rora wanted to tell him to take his hands off, especially when one slid under her skirt to check her inner thighs. Torres must have been satisfied because he grabbed her shoulder and pulled her into the room only to push her toward the bed.

"Get on the bed," he said.

Rora was horrified to see him open a drawer to pull out a set of handcuffs. "No," she said and tried to get to the door, but he sidestepped and got into her path. Seizing her arm, he slapped one cuff on and wrestled her backward, forcing her onto the bed. "No! Get off me!"

"Please," he said, trying to pull her other hand to the headboard. "Put your wrists together!"

"No," she said and fought harder, kicking at him and fighting against his strength.

With his hands on her arms, trying to pull them up to the top of the bed, she was trapped in a small space. Remembering what Strike had said about keeping her chin up, she elevated hers and took a chance to dig her teeth into Torres's knuckles when he got her other wrist into the cuff.

Screaming out, he leaped away, but it was too little, too late, her wrists were both in cuffs, around the top bar of the long headboard.

"You bitch," he said, cupping his bleeding hand.

"Come near me again and I'll skin you," she snarled, rattling the cuffs on the bed.

He wouldn't be the only one; she'd skin Strike when she got her hands on him too. A laugh startled her. The bleeding Torres stepped aside, and another man appeared in the doorway that she assumed led to a bathroom or a closet.

"We'd expect nothing less from Exile's woman," the new entrant said. Her eyes flicked from him to Torres and back. "You are a powerful woman, Kero." The name made her fixate on him, had he just called her… what had he called her? "Exile assured us we would be safe from you, but you understand that we had to take precautions… I understand that few women would appreciate being restrained on a bed. But you understand that with his history, we have to assume that you have the power to hurt us."

"I didn't come here to hurt anyone," she said and followed all other eyes that fell to the bleeding wound on Torres's hand. "He should've asked nicely."

"He should have," the stranger said. "Let me learn from his mistake. My name is Isaac Burke, and I have what Exile wants."

Burke nodded at Torres who went to the drawer where the cuffs had been and opened it to take out a metallic case, four inches long by about one and a half inches wide. The whole thing was less than a half-inch thick. Curious, she wanted to ask what it was, but Strike had told her not to ask questions.

Torres put it on the bed beside her, not that it was possible for her to pick it up. But she did shift, lifting her thigh to lay it over the item. Whatever it was, Strike needed it and as far as she knew, that meant Benjamin needed it. So she'd protect it in any way she could right now.

"Is that it?" she asked. Even though her heart was beginning to calm down, she was no less angry. "Are you going to let me go?"

"With Exile on the other side of that door, we have little choice," Burke said. "But we would be foolish not to take this chance, while we have you alone."

"Chance?"

The men exchanged a look and then Burke stepped toward her, becoming suddenly serious. "What's the point?"

It was so unbelievable that it was almost laughable and for half a beat, a laugh did threaten her lips. But her patience with presumptuous men who assumed she was an idiot was wearing thin. Her eyes dropped to focus straight ahead between the two men and her voice became an unfamiliar cold drawl.

"If I tell him that you hurt me, what do you think he'll do?" It was interesting that the men didn't respond. When she let her attention slink upward, she saw the fear in the look they were exchanging. "He didn't send me in here to answer your questions. Let. Me. Go."

"Kero, we're worried about the safety of the world," Burke said. "We have to know what—"

"If I scream, and you make him force his way in here, he won't kill you quickly. The word mercy won't exist to him."

"Kero—" She breathed in as if to scream. "Ok," Burke said, gesturing at Torres. "Ok, we'll let you go."

Torres dashed over to unlock the cuffs. As soon as she was free, she pulled back her fist and punched Torres on the jaw. Pain burst in her knuckles, but she didn't care. The prick had scared her; she'd probably never been so scared.

"Gentlemen," she said, scooping up the metal tin.

"You're his perfect equal," Burke said when she strode past him.

Rora had to pause to give Torres a chance to catch up and unlock the door, so she turned to Burke. "Exile has no equal," she said. "Underestimating him will be your downfall."

"We did it once before. The global economy hasn't recovered since," he said. "We won't make that mistake again."

She nodded once, just as Torres opened the door. Going back into the previous room, she kept her chin up, striding between the two suited men to head straight for Strike, who had zeroed in on her, probably trying to figure out what was in her head.

Rora decided she wasn't going to make it easy for her accomplice when she stopped in front of him, close enough that her chest touched his when she breathed in.

"What happened to you?" one of the guys said behind her, though they weren't talking to her or Strike.

Strike curled his fingers around the metal box she was holding. Rora wrapped her other hand around it and shook her head. "Not a chance," she whispered, and the slight curl at the corner of his lips seemed proud and… something else.

"Looks bad," another voice behind her said.

"She bit me," Torres said.

"Crazy bitch," the other voice said.

Her expression must have changed because Strike's did in response to whatever he saw on her face. "I've got this one, baby," he murmured and stroked a hand down the back of her hair as he moved past her.

Rora heard the cry and the crack and spun to see the speaker on the floor, his temple squashed into the floor by Strike's boot that was on his face. Strike put an elbow on his knee and leaned on it as he bent to address the man.

"When you think of Kero, I want you to think of one word: respect," he said, giving a polite tutorial. "Show her anything less than the utmost respect at all times, and I'll make you wish you'd chosen to piss on the President's wife during the inaugural address instead. My woman's a few rungs above that first bitch. You respect Kero. Show deference. And never, ever, call her names. You're on my shit list now, that's not a fun place to be. Expect all of your offshore assets to vanish before you get to bed tonight." Shoving his foot away, he stepped back and snarled at all of them. "And don't ever forget that biting isn't her only talent."

Marching away from the men, Strike came to her, threw an arm around her neck, and led her out of the apartment block. They got to the corner and turned before she spoke. "You know I don't really have any talents, don't you?" she asked, languishing in the buzz of adrenaline.

"Are you kidding? Two minutes alone in a room with the NSA and you got them eating out the palm of your hand," he said, tugging her closer to plant a kiss on her head. "I'm impressed, Kero, and more than a little jealous."

She didn't ask about the name or why he was jealous because she was too shocked. "The... the NSA?"

"Torres and Burke are NSA, the other two were DARPA," he said. "What you've got there in those hot little hands is a matter of national interest... or it was until we blackmailed it out of their vault."

"Black... you blackmailed them? And I... Oh my God, I assaulted an NSA agent! I bit him! I hit him!"

"Shit, now I am jealous," he said. "Open hand or closed?"

Stuttering, she couldn't feel any oxygen reaching her lungs. "Closed."

"Ooo," he said, hissing in appreciation. "A hot woman committing multiple felonies while absconding with state secrets... talk dirty to me, baby."

Forcing him to a stop with the whole strength of her being, she blinked her wide, terrified eyes up at him. "Strike," she said. "I could go to jail forever."

He smiled, a slight sinister sparkle met his eyes and he growled at her. "Yeah, baby," he said and lunged forward in a dip.

All of a sudden, his mouth was on hers. The hot hungry need of his tongue plunging into her mouth made her forget about the item in her hands, and everything she'd just done.

His mouth opened wide to lick and suck at hers with such force that it pushed her back a step and then another. He scooped his loose hands under her ears just as her back hit a wall and with his fingers curled at the back of her jaw, Strike kept her position steady while giving her space to respond under the constant movement of his lips and head that ducked to meet hers one way, then the other.

He bent his knees to come at her mouth from beneath then kissed her so hard that her chin rose until her head went all the way back, making her neck hurt. He was over her, his form dominating hers. Yet, their bodies never met, this was a meeting of mouths, his hands barely touched her, all he wanted to do was taste her.

"Mmm," he said when he backed off, leaving her in midair, panting, her body in need of his shield. "Don't think I'd let them hold you."

"You weren't wrong about being bad turning you on," she managed to breathe out.

He hummed at her again and grabbed her hand. "Business is good, Cupcake," he said, striding away.

Their arms were fully extended before she was yanked away from the wall and forced to run across the street with him.

His reaction to how she'd followed him into sin, the kiss, his attention, it was unexpected, and she didn't think she'd recover from it in a hurry. Rora hadn't signed on to be Bonnie to his Clyde, but his allure might be too powerful for her to resist.

TEN

STRIKE RUSHED RORA all the way back to the motel and pulled her up the stairs to return to their room. When they got there, and the door closed, she immediately turned to him, expecting… something.

But the first thing he did was put his hand around the box in her hand to try to take it from her.

Rora held onto it. "Is this all you want?" she asked, tightening her grip.

"Yes," he said, his brows snapping down in a frown.

"I risked my life for this, my liberty. I think I should know what it is."

Impatience was making him edgy. "It would take too long to explain," he said and tried to take it again.

Rora swung her arm around to extend it behind her. "Then I want something."

"Want something?" he snapped. "I could just take it from you."

"Hit me? Crack my bones? Do that squeeze thing and knock me out? Yes, you could."

"Then hand it over," he said, trying to reach over her, but she put her hand on his chest and pushed back. "Ro, don't fuck with me."

"Or what?" she said, smacking his chest with the heel of her hand. "What are you gonna do about it, big scary criminal? I'm not afraid of you."

"And that's been your problem from the beginning," he said, moving forward, pushing her deeper into the room. "You should never have made it this far."

"But I did," she said and smacked him again. "No thanks to you. You put me in danger tonight. You didn't tell me the truth. You set me up. I was so mad at you, Strike. So goddamn mad."

Showing his teeth for a second when her legs hit the bed, he leaned over her until her back was arched at an awkward angle. "Yeah? Show me," he said. "How mad were you, Cupcake? Show me. Give me what I deserve."

Fueled by arousal and caught up in adrenaline, she shoved him hard with both hands. The box fell somewhere to the floor before she brought her hand across his face in a cold, hard slap. His head snapped to the side, not far, but enough that she knew he'd registered the hit.

Immediately feeling regret, she sucked her lip into her mouth and worried it hard in her teeth. "Strike," she whispered, sliding a hand up his arm when he stayed in that position with his head tilted away and his eyes closed. "Strike, I—"

"Damnit," he whispered through his teeth. She held her breath, sealing it in with her chewed lip. "Even that didn't make me hate you."

She was still trying to figure him out when he yanked one arm out of his jacket sleeve and then the other. It seemed that he was mad at something, and all she could guess was that she was the cause. Tossing the jacket across the room, he kicked the box aside and grabbed her arms, his strong fingers biting into her when he suddenly flipped her around a hundred and eighty degrees.

Rora was lost, confused, drenched by the heat of the want pulsing through her body. His palms slid down her shoulders, down over her breasts to cup them in his strong hands.

"Strike," she whispered, pushing back against him.

But he didn't let his hands linger, he swept one arm around her pelvis and pushed the other between her shoulder blades, forcing her to bend over in front of him, planting her hands on the bed. The pace of her heart vibrated through her throat and down to her thighs, and only sped when he gathered her skirt, bunching it over her hips, pushing it higher, out of his way to expose her ass.

She didn't stop him when he took the elastic of her panties and drew it down her legs to her knees. "Open wider," he said, and she shuffled her feet apart.

The moment his finger slid into her, she breathed out. "Strike," she whispered.

Her bliss was broken when he smacked her ass hard. "No names," he hissed. "No words."

Having never made love in silence, she didn't know if she'd be able to do it, but she'd try if that was what he needed. Pulling her lower lip with her teeth, Rora whimpered and moaned when another finger slid into her. He kept fucking her with them for over a minute. Curling and bunching, varying pace, he tormented and teased her with his fingers, using a third and sometimes a fourth on her clit.

Those fingers she'd seen flying over his keyboard were dexterous. Strike knew how to twist and stretch them in just the right way to make her pant.

Struggling to contain her voice, Rora opened her mouth and yelped. She didn't even realize he was on his knees behind her until his tongue dipped into her.

"Oh, fuck me," she exhaled.

"Not a chance," he said, squeezing an ass cheek in each hand and sucking her clit hard until she screamed. He spanked her harder this time. "Enough."

"Oh, Strike," she said, her legs buckling.

She managed to turn as she collapsed and somehow, she got her hands on his shoulders and pushed him back onto the carpet. Climbing up him, she yanked off her underwear and grabbed for his hands, gripping his wrists tight in her fists using every ounce of her ferocious appetite for him to hold him down while she pushed her mouth onto his and sucked her own taste from his tongue.

Rubbing up and down, she was moving in the way she would if he was embedded inside her and it seemed such a waste that he wasn't.

Strike bit her lip hard enough to make her yelp and pull her mouth from his. "I said no, Cupcake."

Something was alight in him, it wasn't the hatred or anger she usually saw; he was challenging her. "But you didn't mean it," she panted. "I thought you never noticed me. All this time, I thought you didn't want this."

"I don't," he said. "But don't trust me not to use you if it suits me."

"It suits me, Strike," she whispered.

He pulled out of her grip to reach down and spank her. "Stop saying my name."

"Strike," she whispered, kissing him at the moment before he smacked her again. Her body jolted forward, pressing her mouth closer to his. "Strike."

The word was barely a vibration on his lips, but it was dare enough to make him spank her again. Then he crunched up and snagged her legs to twist her around so her body was draped perpendicular across his.

Rubbing a hand across her ass, he hit one cheek, then the other, and she flipped her hair to peek at him over her shoulder. He was watching his hand stroking her ass. Spanking and caressing in turn.

Bending her knees, she let her feet swing in the air. "Strike," she said, daring him to follow through.

He opened his hand and brought it down harder than he'd hit her yet. She hissed and her forehead fell to the floor. But it wasn't pain that zipped through her, it was the unmistakable zap of pleasure.

"Did I hurt you, baby?" he asked, squeezing his hand between her thighs to ease them apart so he could start to finger her again. "Does that make it feel better?"

"Oh," she panted. "Oh, my flame…"

"Better," he said, "call me that."

Just like that, he'd adopted another alias.

Rora could never have guessed when she'd called him her flame that first time in Last Resort that they could end up here, lying on the floor of a motel room together with his fingers sliding in and out of her.

Pulling the zip beneath her arm, she loosened her dress, and tugged it up, lifting only as much as she had to in order to shimmy it up over her head.

"Don't clench like that," he said, planting a hand on her lower back to hold her still. "Gives me ideas."

Relaxing her nude body, Rora propped her chin on her fist and squeezed her inner muscles around his plundering finger. His eyes leaped to hers; he showed his teeth when he growled at her.

"Bitch," he said, but it was such a light-hearted insult that she wasn't offended.

Moving an inch, intending to go back to his mouth, she was diverted when Strike grabbed her hips and pulled her around, this time turning her body on top of his, to bring her hips up to his face. Tucking her knees in at his shoulders, he curled his arms around her thighs and directed her pussy to his mouth.

"Oh, fuck," she said when he began to flick his tongue over her clit. "Mmm…"

It was so difficult not to push down into the pleasure he was delivering. He'd threatened to smother her, and here she was with her chance to return the favor.

Death by pussy for Exile, that would be one to add to the legend.

Thinking of returning the favor, she wriggled against him. Running her hands down the inside of his drawn-up thighs, she cupped his groin for a moment. He was hard. He was huge. She wanted him inside her. Now.

But she hadn't gotten very far with his belt when he picked up her hips from his face and planted his feet on the edge of the bed to push up, away from beneath her. She was still there, face-down on the carpet when she heard him pounce to his feet behind her.

Rolling over, Rora rose to her elbows, while watching him adjust his belt. "Strike?" she asked, wondering what had changed so quickly.

But he didn't even look at her, he went to the metal box on the floor and bent to pick it up. "That settles our tab," he said, turning the box over and over in his hands on his way to the bathroom.

Rora was on the floor. "If you're gonna jerk off, can I watch?" she called out, tipping her head back, but the bed was obstructing her view.

"Get ready for bed, Ro," he said. "I've got work to do tonight, and you'll need your beauty sleep if you're going to see your beautiful Benjamin tomorrow."

She gasped and flipped over, using the bed to help her scramble onto her feet. The bathroom door was open a crack, but she was so desperate to find out if he meant what he'd just said, that she probably could've bowled right through the thing even if it wasn't.

Running across the bedroom, she shoved the door back on its hinges. "Benjamin?" she asked. "We're going to get him tomorrow?" Strike had his shirt off and was washing his hands. She'd never really looked at his body. The only time she'd ever seen it was the morning Opal zapped her and she'd had other things on her mind then. "Strike…"

The marks on his back made her gravitate to him. Opening her hands, she wanted to stroke him, but was worried she might hurt him.

"What?" he asked, reaching across to grab the towel to dry his hands.

"Your back, what happened? Are they sore?"

"That shit's been there for years," he said.

The long straight scars varied in width and length; some licked right up to his shoulder blades, others disappeared beneath the belt of his jeans "Oh, baby," she whispered and made contact. Running her hands down his back, she leaned in to kiss him with a feather-light touch, tracing her lips across and down each of the scars.

"It's no big deal," he said.

"How did you get them?"

"Different times, different places," he said and twisted away from her kiss to lift his arm. "This one was my favorite." Showing her a long red scar that ran from beneath his arm down to his waist, he seemed almost proud of it. "It was so deep I could see ribs."

"Strike," she whispered, her eyes stinging when she stepped forward to wrap both arms around him.

"Cupcake, it's no big deal," he said. "You don't learn to fight like I can without scrapping."

"This isn't scrapping," she said. "Knives and cuts, and rib bones, that's not scrapping. That's serious. You could have died."

"I could have died a bunch of times," he said. "Most of the scars are years old, I haven't had a serious injury for a long time. I got these when I wasn't so good. I'm good now." Closing her eyes, she squeezed him tighter and his arm relaxed across her shoulders. "Your tits feel good, but back them off."

Rora had forgotten she was naked, now that he'd reminded her, she realized this was the first time they'd been skin to skin like this. Tipping her head back, she met his eye. When he didn't make a move, she reached up to cup his face, but he took her wrist to pull her hand away.

"I have work to do and that ain't happening."

"Why don't you want us to have sex?" she asked.

"Why do you want us to?" he asked. "Hmm?"

"Why? Because it will feel good. Because I'm curious. Because I like you. Because you're a man and I'm a woman and—"

"We happen to be in the same place at the same time," he said. "Tomorrow goes to plan, you'll get your Benjamin back, and this will all be over for you. Minimize your disruption. It would be a shame for me to come all this way just to have to kill Gallagher myself."

"Kill… why would you kill, Benjamin?"

"If he comes at me for touching his woman, I'll take him down. You've seen what I'm like when I have no patience. And if Bella's around, assume that my patience gauge is in the red."

"Strike," she said, but he urged her away and turned back to the mirror, scrubbing his hands through his hair and rubbing a hand over his stubble. "Benjamin and I aren't together." Bending over the sink, he ran the cold water and splashed his face. "Seriously, we're not. Why would I get physical with a homicidal maniac and then take him to meet my boyfriend?"

He grabbed the towel and dried his face. "Now who's calling names?"

"It's an expression," she said. "Can you deny that you've killed?"

He shrugged. "No. But, Cupcake, come on… nuance."

"Ok," she conceded and leaned against the edge of the shower stall when he went to the toilet in the corner to pee. "I'm sorry." He glanced over his shoulder to make eye contact with her in the mirror. "I'm not sleeping with him."

"Doesn't matter if you're having sex or not," he said, flushing and turning away from the toilet.

She squawked. "Lid." He twisted to put it down and then went to wash his hands again. "I'm not having sex with him. I'm not his."

"You might not have been having sex when he left, but no one does what you've done unless there's love involved. I'll get him back for you and in a couple of days you'll be banging like bunnies. Guy like that, with his own department, he'll marry you, knock you up, and it'll be happy ever after for the Gallaghers."

Strike wasn't that kind of guy. He didn't have a steady job—at least not a legal one—he wouldn't be getting married and settling down. But why were they even talking about that? They'd been talking about sex, not… fairytales.

"And you and me, we don't have the kind of genes that mix well," he said, tossing the towel onto the vanity. "Those are dice we shouldn't risk rolling."

Departing the bathroom, he left her standing there speculating on his meaning. Rora got with it and scampered out after him, finding him sitting on the short couch with his laptop on his lap and his feet stretched onto the dresser the TV was on.

"You don't want me to have your baby," she said, climbing onto the couch. Her statement earned her a brief glare. "What? That's pretty much exactly what you said." She touched her chest. "I said, 'Let's have sex because it will feel good.' And you said, 'Let's not because I'll get you pregnant,' like you have some kind of super sperm or something."

"What the fuck conversation were you listening to?" he asked. "I didn't say pregnant or sperm once."

"It was implied," she said and he side-eyed her, so she waved at him. "Right, ok, so you don't imply, but it was in the undercurrent. You think I have faulty genes because my brother is a… homicidal maniac." Another side glare. "But you don't kill because you're mentally ill, you do it to survive. I don't see you going out at night to stalk student nurses or staring at me wondering if my severed, boiled skull would make a good salad bowl."

"There's time," he muttered. Leaning over, she rested a hand over the top of one of his. His hand tensed, holding hers above the keyboard. "Careful."

"What happens if Opal reads my fingerprints and yours at the same time?"

He turned and they made eye contact. "She gets jealous."

"I've never had a threesome."

Bowing forward, she meant to kiss him, but he pushed her away and this time his scowl was deeper. "Quit fucking doing that… And why are you still naked?"

"You told me to get ready for bed," she said. "I always sleep naked and I figure now you've seen it, it doesn't matter." Huffing, he returned to his laptop. "I don't think you said what you said about our genes because of your crimes." Examining his profile, she hunched lower, resting the front of her fist against her temple when she put her elbow on his shoulder. "Is it true your mom killed herself?"

He stopped typing. Although his chin moved a fraction toward her, he didn't lift his head to look at her. "Who told you that?"

"Bella," she said. "That last time she called."

"What else did she tell you?"

"That she didn't mind sharing you with me… That you killed her family after they tortured you." He slammed the laptop. "That you've been tortured since the day you were born."

"Why the fuck didn't you tell me you knew all this before?" he hissed at her.

"I didn't want to push you," she said. "I can't imagine what you've been through, baby." Letting her fingers leave her temple, they drifted down the side of his face. "Why did she kill herself?"

"Because my father raped her," he said. "She knew the minute she saw me that she'd never be able to look at me without remembering how I'd been conceived."

"Oh, Strike," she breathed out and looped her arms around his neck to pull herself against him. "I'm so sorry. That's awful."

"I don't blame her for killing herself," he said. "Never have… I just… There's one thing I never understood, and fuck it, I wish I could ask her."

"Ask her what?" she asked, brushing a hand up and down his chest.

After twisting toward him so they could make eye contact, she saw the return of his anger. "Why didn't she take me with her?"

Stunned, she could do nothing but explore the determination that bled from him. Shoving the laptop onto the dresser, he got up, pulling away from her. "Strike, why would she—"

"It makes no fucking sense, I was the spawn of that devil, so why didn't she just put a pillow on my face and end it?" he demanded, clenching his jaw. "I was a baby, I wouldn't have fought back. I don't blame her for leaving, but what the fuck life did she think I was going to have? I never went to school. Never went to college. Never mattered a fuck. Why the hell didn't she just toss me out with the trash?"

Unfurling her feet from beneath her, Rora climbed off the couch. "Because she knew you were going to achieve great things. That you were going to be brilliant. You are brilliant, Strike… More brilliant than any man I've ever known… even if it's not in the traditional sense." She smiled, but he wasn't moving, so she opened her hand against his jaw.

"I'm so glad she didn't take you, Strike. I'm so glad that you are who you are and that you came into my life… that you let me into yours. Strike, you're… you're overwhelming and I… the way you make me feel, that's something no other man has given me."

"How can you say that? Knowing what I do, what I've done?"

"Easily," she said, sliding her hands to his torso. "My life was a mess, nothing but heartache and tragedy. I've faced one after the other. Every day I could feel the resentment growing in me, I was so tired of being afraid. So tired of always wondering when the next tragedy was going to strike or when I was going to be the one struck down and then… I met you and… you stole my license and trashed my hotel room and… saved my life." A blink of surprise on his face made his jaw twitch and relax a fraction. "You took my fear. The fear I've been running from all my life. It's gone. When I'm with you… I'm not afraid anymore."

"This is temporary," he mumbled, but was looking at her, into her.

"It doesn't have to be," she whispered.

"Everyone in my life is temporary."

"I won't be," she said, stroking his arms. "I promise, Strike."

When he scooped a hand up over her jaw and into her hair behind her ear, she expected him to bow and kiss her. While he did stoop a little, his lips didn't meet hers.

"Aurora," he murmured, pulling her up to the tips of her toes.

"Yes, Strike?" she sighed.

"What's the point?"

Jarred out of her emotional haze, she searched his face. "Seriously?" she asked, hoping more than anything that he was joking.

"You don't trust me enough to tell me?"

"But, I…"

"If you tell me, it won't be a barrier between us anymore," he said, brushing his thumb up and down her cheek. "We can really trust each other."

"You're manipulating my feelings for you," she whispered.

"No, I'm on your side," he said. The sinister twist of his lips made her shiver. "If I'd known my sob story would loosen your tongue, I'd have told you a week ago."

Shoving him with both hands, she growled and spun around to march away. "Go to hell!"

"Come on, baby! I haven't even told you about how my granddaddy beat me! I haven't told you how I gutted him when he slept!"

Hurrying around the room, she grabbed clothes and changed as fast as she could. "You're a bastard, Strike! Bella was right about you!"

"Yeah, yeah," he said, dropping onto the couch. "All men are scum and women don't need 'em for shit. Funny, 'cause when that shit hits the fan, the first thing you do is call up the closest dick you know."

"Well don't worry about me calling you or your dick," she called out.

"I won't," he said, retrieving his laptop. "You don't have my number... I don't have my number." Growling at him, she grabbed the door and tugged it open. Laying an arm along the back of the couch, he looked over at her. "You want to save your precious Benjamin, be at the Banton Field Airstrip tomorrow at two PM."

"Airstrip," she said, some of the bluster taken from her sails. "But I... I thought you were afraid of flying." Another sinister smirk, and he turned back to his computer. She exhaled. "That was a lie. You aren't afraid of flying."

"I'm not afraid of anything," he said. "But you fell for it."

"You are evil incarnate!" she screamed at him. "What the hell was I thinking? You don't have a decent bone in your body!"

He tipped his head onto the back of the couch. "We at Evil Incarnate thank you for your custom," he said. "Please come again. First tongue fuck's free, next one will cost your beautiful Benjamin his apartment."

Gritting her teeth, she hissed, unable to believe that she'd thought there could be anything redeemable about him. "Go to hell, Strike!"

"Or as I like to call it, home sweet home."

Rora just barely heard the last word as she stormed out and slammed the door as hard as she could. If he wanted to be a bastard and push her away, she'd let him. If he wanted to be all alone, if that was what made him happy, then who was she to stand in the way?

He'd accused her of being green. Bella had told her she wouldn't be able to handle Strike's vicious moods. Turned out they were both right. The only one who'd been wrong so far, was her.

ELEVEN

"DON'T BEAT YOURSELF up, men are just superior in general." Strike leaned over the cockpit of the tiny plane to flick a switch near her. "You didn't have a choice. You had to come. You rely on me now."

So far, Rora had managed to say very little to him. If she'd had any other choice, she would never have gone to the airfield. Rora had even considered that she could get in touch with Bella and try her luck direct. Except, she had no way to contact Bella and no way was she leaving Benjamin out there to rot another day if she didn't have to.

When Strike had said airfield, she didn't expect it to be so far out, or for Strike to be the one flying them. It was really aggravating how it seemed there wasn't anything outside his range of expertise.

"Do you know what my favorite part of today is going to be?" he asked. Rora gained a new appreciation for how her twittering probably annoyed him. It didn't seem to matter that her arms were folded and her nose pointed to the window furthest from him, he filled her in anyway. "The part where you realize you've got too much integrity to back out of our deal. I'll get your Benjamin back, you'll have your little fuck session to say hello and then it'll be you and me, baby.

You'll hate every second of it, but you'll have to tell me the truth because you promised you would."

So their fight last night would've been for nothing, that's what he was trying to say. But Rora disagreed. If she'd told him the truth last night then he'd have had no reason to bring her here today.

"I have no intention of backing out," she said, sliding down in her seat a little.

"Good."

"You asked one question. I promised to answer that one question, which I can actually do in as little as two words… I didn't promise to answer any follow-up questions."

"Wait," he said. "What?"

"I heard the guy at the airstrip tell you to fuel up before flying back," she said. "You have no choice now. We have to land wherever we're going to land… You have to take me to Benjamin."

He went from aloof to angry in a blink. "I'll take you and leave you there with him. Good fucking luck getting out."

"No, Flame, because we had a deal," she said, taking pride in using the name she'd used while they were being intimate.

"And you declared me evil incarnate," he said. "I don't have to do anything."

"Yes, you do," she said, pulling her legs up to fold them under her. "Because if you don't, I'll go to my other buyer."

"What?" he asked, doing a double take. "Buyer? What the hell are you talking about? You haven't sold anything to me."

"Someone emptied my bank accounts," she said. "You've been paid, by me, for everything we've been through."

With his hands on the control wheel thing, he looked proficient at flying. The headphones were kind of sexy; she just hoped no one was listening through that microphone right now.

"I didn't take your money," he said. "It's sitting in a fucking trust to be released to you whenever I feel like it… Remember that."

"Whenever you feel like it," she said. "Still under your control. It doesn't matter. I don't care about money."

"You care about Benjamin."

"And once we have him released and safe, I will answer your one question, and we'll be even."

They flew for a few minutes, and she was happy to have knocked him off his high horse. When he wasn't smug, he was quiet, and left her alone to her anxiety.

"I ate your pussy last night," he mumbled.

"I remember," she said, reaching over to rest a hand on his shoulder. "You were very good at it. I appreciate your effort."

"This is one of your stupid jokes, isn't it?" he asked. "You don't really have another buyer. You're for sure not talking about Bella, she'll raze the fucking earth."

He was right, though Bella was an interested party who Rora would hear out if she had a proposition. But the other buyer she was really thinking about was the NSA. If Strike left her high and dry, she hadn't eliminated the idea that she'd go to the authorities and give them what they wanted in exchange for her safety and Benjamin's.

No matter how much he annoyed her, Rora doubted that she'd be able to betray Exile; but as far as she was concerned, he didn't have to be part of the deal. Still, that didn't mean she wasn't going to taunt him with the notion he might have solved her issues by making the introductions.

"Bella doesn't say nice things about you either," she said, looking out at the ground below.

At first, all the trees had been nice and green. The mountains had risen from the horizon and she'd spotted the odd bit of movement that suggested wildlife, but Rora knew nothing about that kind of thing and Strike wasn't exactly a great tour guide who could fill her in either.

She didn't know where they were going or how long it would take to get there. But the verdant vista had faded, the trees were looking decidedly white and the mountains around them were covered with snow.

She wished she had her wool coat.

"Ro, you wouldn't really… Bella's not what you think she is. I don't know what kind of mood she'll be in when we show up unannounced. If she didn't need something, she'd shoot you in the head or keep you as her toy for a few months. But she needs something…"

"She took Benjamin because she needed something," she said. "But I'm still confused, what's the Black Jewel got to do with this?"

Looking from the front of the plane to her and then back, he lingered when their eyes locked. "Sometimes, when the light hits your eyes like that and your hair kinda glows, I think…"

Surprised to hear anything even close to romantic from his lips, she sat dumb for a few seconds, but then just had to know. "What? You think what?"

"You'll make a beautiful corpse."

"Strike!" she said, lunging over to smack him in the chest.

"Hey, whoa," he said. "Don't kill the pilot, then what would you do?"

Sulking, she folded her arms and slouched back. "Make a beautiful corpse apparently," she muttered.

"I'm just amazed sometimes that you're still here. I've been around cons and aliases all my life. You have to think fast and work on assumptions. Life is a risk. You've gotta be willing to be wrong."

"I don't work on assumptions," she said. "I don't ever factor anything in until I know it's a fact."

"Fact," he said. "You tried to get me into this because you said I had an interest in the Black Jewel."

"How do you know that?"

"Did you say it or not?" Short of lying, she had no choice except to nod. "I don't have an interest in the Black Jewel."

"Then why are you here if I was so wrong?"

"I used to be in the Black Jewel," he said. "A lot."

Squinting out front, she tried to figure him out. "You used to… But you said the Black Jewel had…" Rora gasped and grabbed for his forearm. "That's her alias. Bella, she's the Black Jewel."

"You got it," he said. "You're touching me again."

"Oh," she said, and her hand sprang away from his arm. "The Black Jewel has Benjamin… He doesn't have her, no one has her…" All the things he'd said began to click into place. "You could've just told me that, Strike. Why do you have to be so evasive all the time?"

"We've had this conversation," he said. "I like to be alone."

For the first time today, she started to feel a shift, like they were relaxing enough to maybe forget about the bravado and be honest with each other. "Strike, about last night…"

"Let's just forget it," he said. "You're getting stuck in the past again."

"I should look to the future."

"We can't change yesterday. Tomorrow's a whole new adventure."

For him, maybe, but not for her. As soon as she had Benjamin back, she was returning to her normal life, collecting his data, writing reports, running his department. Rora was good at keeping Benjamin's haphazard thoughts on track. Sometimes he got a new idea and wanted to go off on a tangent, but his sponsors didn't like that so much. Her job was harnessing the genius.

"What's next for you?" she asked.

"I've got a couple of projects on the go." Vague. Just like she expected him to be. "Buckle up, we'll be landing in five."

Adjusting to sit in her chair properly, Rora fastened her belt and watched him concentrate on his approach. "In case this all happens fast and I don't get a chance to say it," she said, focused on his determined profile. "I meant every word I said last night. Before, you know, you flipped the switch on me… I meant it all."

His gaze drifted around to hers and she caught her lip in her teeth. This was one of the many times she wished she could read his mind. It must be a terrifying place in there, so much going on, it would be easy to get lost.

"I didn't sleep with the blonde. I wanted to teach you a lesson about playing with me," he said, startling her, but the confession seemed to surprise him too. He frowned at himself, and his chin rose an inch. "I don't know why the hell I just said that." Something must have sounded in his ear, because he cast off his glower and adjusted the mouthpiece. "Roger that…"

Rora didn't care about why he'd told her or why he hadn't slept with the blonde. But she couldn't deny that a weight lifted from her shoulders when she learned he hadn't slept with any other women during their trip. He'd watched over her and pushed her away, because soon, too soon, this would all be over.

***

LIKE A PRO, Strike landed the plane.

They got out and she walked to the edge of the trees, turning in a full circle to admire the scenery. It was cold, no doubt about that. Icicles hung from the trees that were weighed down by snow. It crunched beneath her feet and the icy air nipped at her nose, but it was… invigorating.

"It's beautiful," she said.

Strike had been approaching her, but she turned away to peek into the trees, inhaling the new scents of their environment. A strong hand grabbed the back of her neck hard. He squeezed her tight, pulling her backwards, almost off her feet. Fumbling behind her, she tried to pull at his arm.

Terror burned her lungs, and she gasped a ragged breath that burned her throat.

"Don't fight," he said, closing a hand over her mouth and pulling her against him to talk into her hair. "Don't fight me, Cupcake. Relax. Don't fight it."

Her body got heavy, went limp, then she was out.

***

RORA HEARD STATIC and it took her a few seconds to realize the noise was just in her head.

Brilliant white light blinded her when she opened her eyes, so she closed them immediately. She couldn't remember where she was or what had happened. It was warm and the air was perfumed, but there was something new, unexpected… Where was Strike?

Gasping, she sat upright and almost said his name. She grabbed for the back of the candy-striped couch she had been lying on and blinked around the room. Strike was there, standing fifteen feet away in the arms of a woman she didn't recognize.

There was a wooden table and chairs behind the couple, in a rustic style that suited the wood-clad room. A fireplace burned somewhere behind where Rora was lying and to her other side were floor-to-ceiling windows that led out to a wide terrace. Beyond that were snow-covered trees and mountains.

Holding up her hand to block the sun that was reflecting off the snow, Rora chose to turn the other way and look over the back of the couch again. But that meant looking at Strike and the woman he was holding.

"She's awake!" the woman exclaimed and pushed away from a reluctant Strike.

He didn't want to let the woman go and Rora speculated they'd been doing a lot more than just holding each other before she woke up. It was sickening to think she might have been in the room while he was being intimate with another woman.

"You knocked me out," Rora said, her voice hoarse in her throat. "Again."

"Bella likes her privacy," he said. The beautiful brunette, who Rora assumed was Bella, was staring right at her, a wide smile on her face, her eyes glittering with excitement. "And you're less trouble when you're unconscious."

"Don't be rude, Ex," Bella snapped at him and then turned her smile on again. "She's so beautiful. A perfect little possum."

"I didn't bring her here for you to play with," he said.

Spinning around with her arms wide, Bella went to him and wrapped her arms around his neck. "Will you tell me everything? Every detail? Tell me everything, prince. What's it like to be inside her? What does she taste like?"

"Bell," he warned, taking her arms to ease her body away from his. "We'll play later. Just you and me." Seeing him brush the back of his fingers down her face, Rora wasn't surprised to see the eager woman tilt her head toward his touch. But, she was surprised to see how tender he was in his caress. "You're getting overexcited. You need to calm down and focus."

Focus, yes, that was something Rora had to do too. "Where's Benjamin?" she asked, trying to stand up, but she wobbled and sat down again.

"Working," Bella said, putting her back to Strike. "Dinner will be served in an hour. You'll see him there. I assume you'll want to change into something lovely…" The woman sprang forward a step and held out both hands. "Come and I'll show you a wonderland."

Strike stepped forward and took Bella's arm to pull her back. "Aurora doesn't want to see your wonderland or to change her clothes. Show me."

Bella huffed. "Really? Can't she come with us?"

Stepping into her, Strike slid his hands under Bella's bolero and pushed it from her shoulders, letting his fingers trace all the way down the back of her arms to her wrists. His body made contact with hers and he enraptured her with his laser focus.

"Show me, pretty dolly," he murmured.

Bella's sulk slid away until her grin returned. "Oh, my naughty prince," she purred and grabbed his hand to tug him across the room.

Strike barely spared Rora a glance. "Stay here," he ordered just before Bella pulled him out of the room and closed the door behind them.

Inhaling, Rora turned back toward the view of the snowscape. Maybe she'd pushed too far last night in their argument. Bringing it up again in the plane had certainly been a mistake. She'd thought they were here to rescue Benjamin, she hadn't really known what that would involve, fighting maybe, bullets, running. She didn't expect it would involve him sneaking off to screw his ex-girlfriend.

Strike said that he 'didn't do implied', but she'd thought he was over Bella. If anything, he'd suggested the break-up was bitter. But that wasn't what she'd just witnessed. She'd seen an established couple who knew how to entice each other, something she'd never managed to do with him.

Bella wasn't exactly what Rora had expected either; she had an air of innocence about her, except there was also an undercurrent of something far more sinister that Rora couldn't quite pinpoint.

After discovering all the doors were locked, she returned to the couch she'd woken up on and sat down. Benjamin was here, somewhere. She'd achieved the first step, now she just had to get to him.

TWELVE

MAYBE AN HOUR or so later, a man came to tell her it was time for dinner.

Rora didn't know much about the building she was in—they were on the second floor, that was about all she could tell from the view—but when she left the room to follow the guy who was leading her to dinner, she saw a few more doorways.

At the end of the corridor, a door was opened for her and she went in to find Bella and Strike already at the circular dinner table. Sitting at opposite sides, they weren't even looking at each other. Strike was doing something on his laptop and Bella was issuing instructions to a man standing beside her. She was pointing at the copious amount of food, directing one dish to be switched with another and certain bowls to be rearranged. Talk about OCD, Bella got quite frustrated when her minion didn't put one bowl in exactly the right place.

Shooting to her feet, Bella grabbed her fork and stabbed it into the back of the guy's hand. "Get out of my sight!" she screamed. "Useless cretin!"

The guy scarpered, Strike didn't even look up at Bella or at Rora while she stood there just inside the door, gaping.

Bella turned, perhaps seeking out another server because there were a couple of others dotted around the room.

But when Bella saw her, she gasped and grinned again. "Oh!" she said and turned to admire her. "Those hips, the curve of that beautiful waist. You are just delectable, Aurora, and what a beautiful name, you have a beautiful name. Did Ex tell you that your name is beautiful? Ex? Did you?"

Another door opened, a tray of food was brought in, and then before it could close another man entered.

Rora's heart stopped. "Benjamin," she said his name in a rush of breath.

Benjamin was so startled by her that she supposed he hadn't known she was here. "Morning Sun," he said, stunned. "No… it can't be." He took one step toward her, another, and then she was running to him and they were in each other's arms. "My Aurora… my beautiful Aurora." Gasping for her, he crouched, pushing her hair from her face to smile into her eyes though there were tears in his. She felt wet heat streaking her own cheeks too, but didn't care that she was weeping. This was the climax of the most intense journey she'd ever been on. "Is it really you?"

"Yes! Oh, yes, it's me," she said.

"Oh, Aurora," he said, so overwhelmed that he almost seemed in awe. "You actually came. You came here for me?"

"Yes," she sobbed and they hugged for a moment.

Benjamin pulled back and held her face again. "Did you find him?"

"I… Yes," she said, taking Benjamin's hand from her face and keeping it in hers. Rora turned to the table. "He's here."

Strike wasn't looking at them; he tossed something into the air, caught it in his mouth, then went back to typing. From the smudges on his plate, she guessed he'd already eaten. No one else had even sat down yet and he was finished. The food had been on the table, and she knew what he was like when it came to eating fast.

"Oh my God," Benjamin said. "You actually found him. I've heard of him, heard the stories, but… he's really here. I never expected to meet him in the flesh."

"Touch me or introduce me and this stirring reunion will be short-lived," Strike muttered, and kept typing.

So excited, Benjamin might not have heard Strike properly, or he just couldn't restrain himself to play it cool despite Strike's sour mood. "He's working, what is he working on?" he asked.

"He's not a zoo exhibit," Rora said, guiding Benjamin toward the table.

"A monkey in his natural habitat," Bella said, seating herself at the table. "Benjamin, you sit there next to Exile… Aurora, you come and sit by me."

Rora didn't really want to let go of Benjamin now that they were finally in the same room and she had him in her sights. She didn't want dinner either. It was late in the day, she'd noticed the sun sinking in the sky, but they needed to get out of here. Except if Strike was at the table, showing no signs of going anywhere, she guessed they were waiting until morning to fly out.

Letting her hand fall out of his, Rora offered Benjamin a smile, but glanced at Strike who was still working away. The large table put quite a barrier between the women and the men. With Strike so close to Benjamin, her friend was vulnerable… But wasn't Strike her friend too? Not according to him.

Bella was putting food on a plate when Rora went around to sit down. Her hostess put the plate between them and cut a piece of meat, which she then offered to Rora's lips. Was her hostess going to feed her?

Fearful of offending anyone, and confused by the bizarre setup, Rora opened her mouth and accepted the morsel. Bella beamed and cut another, taking it for herself this time. "You have a beautiful mouth," Bella said, giving Rora another mouthful. "Mm, that lip, so plump and juicy… looks delicious."

"Uh… thank you."

"What are you working on?" Benjamin asked Strike.

With Bella feeding her, Rora had leave to just watch the men, observing Benjamin's shimmering excitement contrast with Strike's complete indifference. Strike was slouched away from the table at an angle, his ankle propped up on his knee. Benjamin was the opposite, seated straight and properly at the table as he served food onto his plate.

"Read your code," Strike said, and she wasn't surprised that he'd ignored Benjamin's direct question. "Tweaked it."

"I'm honored."

"You're going to struggle with the kick," Strike mumbled. "Do you have a patch? What I read this afternoon won't do it."

"It's in beta. I have to run more tests—"

"Increases your chance of discovery… I wrote the inverse. A couple of them."

Benjamin stopped and sank back in his chair to gape at the typing man beside him. "You… My code's unlikely to withstand yours," he said. "And I don't need it to. No offense to the world at large, but I'm not likely to deal with an adversary as skilled as you because, well, let's face it, there isn't one."

"Don't suck my cock," Strike said. "Never know who you'll come up against. I like to take the opposing side in an argument, sometimes just for fun."

Rora stopped chewing and saw that Bella was glaring at Strike. "Are you threatening Benjamin?" Bella asked. "Exile, we are here to have a pleasant meal. Everyone here is friends. Haven't we all enjoyed each other's bodies? Pleasured each other? Been a crutch to each other in times of need? Rarely would anyone find such a close-knit group." She squealed. "Isn't it invigorating? We're a happy little horny foursome."

Rora didn't know who was more shocked, her or Benjamin. But her friend didn't seem shocked by Bella, the astonishment written across his face was aimed at her. And when his next glance went to Strike, Rora realized he was shocked by the idea she might have been intimate with the enigmatic criminal.

"Ben—"

"No one gives a damn," Strike said, interrupting Rora's apology with a glare, which he switched onto Bella. "I wasn't threatening him. Testing should be over. If he can code to withstand what I wrote, it will be ready, no testing required."

Bella and Benjamin went back to their food. Rora made eye contact with Strike who was fixated on her over the top of his laptop. They hadn't slept together. Except Bella thought they had; Rora had figured that out when she heard Bella's questions earlier. It made no sense to her why Strike would maintain the fallacy. If he just wanted to be seen as a stud, he could've actually slept with her before they got there, it wasn't like she hadn't given him the chance to be with her.

"You should see some of what I've achieved," Benjamin said, stealing Rora's attention for a second.

When it went back to Strike, she found him focused on his computer again.

"You've been working," she said to Benjamin.

For months, she'd worried about what he'd endured. She'd been so thankful to see him that she hadn't considered his condition. His weight was good, his pallor warm, there were no obvious signs of abuse, and here he was seated at the hostess' dinner table.

"Yes," Benjamin said. "I have achieved some quite incredible things. I think you would be surprised to hear about some of the things I've done. And now that Mr. Exile is here, I'm excited to see what will come next."

"Exile," she said, looking at Strike and then at the grinning Benjamin. Bella put a wine glass into Rora's hand and urged it up to her lips to make her drink. "I don't understand."

Strike blinked his hateful scowl up to her. "No one said you had to."

"But, I... We didn't come here to work."

"You didn't," Strike said.

If he wouldn't be forthcoming, Benjamin might be. "I thought I needed him to help find you. I thought..."

"He did help you," Benjamin said. "And now he can help me."

This didn't feel right. This wasn't why she was here at all. Luring Strike into the open, bringing him back to his ex-girlfriend… Rora hadn't considered for a second that it might be some kind of set-up just to get Exile here.

"All of this talk has made me eager for results," Bella said, pushing Rora's wine up to her mouth again.

The red wine was good; she'd drunk more than half the glass and would be happy to drink the whole bottle.

Strike didn't usually choose to look at her for any reason, but he'd been really glaring at her earlier and now she understood why if he'd been coerced into doing something he didn't want to do. She'd thought he could use his physical skills to bust them out; the last thing she'd expected was that he'd have to work for Bella in any way.

Bella took her wine glass and she heard it fill, but Rora was fixated on Strike. What she wouldn't give to be alone with him, even for a minute. She had to ask questions, but he hated her questioning him at the best of times. He sure wouldn't want to be questioned in front of other people.

But right now, she'd settle for him looking at her.

Benjamin rising from the table made her turn. "I should get back to work," Benjamin said, taking an apple from the bowl in the middle of the table.

"Excellent idea," Bella said. "Off you go."

Benjamin went to leave. Watching him move away from her made Rora push up from her seat. Bella caught her wrist and pulled her back down. "Benjamin," Rora said when it was clear that her hostess wasn't going to let her go.

He smiled at her. "I'll see you at breakfast," he said. "You are a formidable and determined woman, Morning Sun. I didn't doubt you for a heartbeat."

His sweet words touched her, but he faded from the room and she didn't even bother to swipe the tear from her face. Sucking on the center of her lower lip, she tried to quell the fresh tears that threatened to form. She'd just gotten him back and now he was gone again.

Rora had been right about the air around here, there was something sinister in it. This wasn't a happy place. Appearances might be designed to suggest the opposite, but

Benjamin was a prisoner, no doubt about that. A prisoner who'd been forced to use his skills to do goodness knows what for the woman at her side, who was now stroking her arm. And now that Rora had brought Strike here, Bella had it in her power to do even more evil.

The sensation of Bella's fingernails on her forearm made Rora turn. It didn't feel nice to be stroked by the woman who was fascinated with her skin. "How do you feel, Arousing Aurora?" Bella purred, leaning in to kiss her shoulder. "Relaxed, duckie?"

Why was she stroking her and kissing her? Bella pushed her hair back and the slight movement made Rora's head fall, giving the woman access to slide closer and kiss her neck.

It didn't feel good. She frowned and tried to push her away, but her body was heavy, her mind slow. Rora heard a sigh, but her vision was blurring, her eyes wouldn't focus. "Bell, what did you do?"

"What?" Bella asked, exuding pure innocence. "I just helped her to relax."

Something, or someone, was caressing her breasts. Rora tried to open her mouth, but her voice was gone. There was nothing she could do to defend herself. A hot hand slid up the front of her dress and she felt lips on hers.

"You roofied her." Rora recognized that voice: Strike. He was in the room, but… he was far away, too far away. The scent in her nose was too delicate to be his; he wasn't the one touching her.

The rasp of a zipper met her ears and Rora tried again to speak. "I'll share her with you, prince," Bella purred, and a tongue slid across Rora's throat. "She's so sweet, Exile… Come and taste her with me…"

The feminine voice came closer to her ear, a mouth nuzzled her there and then there was a pain just behind, so sharp it made her yelp.

"This one isn't a toy."

"Our Aurora doesn't count against your ridiculous rule," Bella said, pulling Rora's dress strap away from her shoulder. "You've had her. She's accepted you. She wants you, prince. Let me watch you take her… I'll lick your seed from her skin, drink it from her pussy… Tonight, you'll rule us both."

That was the last thing Rora remembered hearing before she lost the last thread of grip on her consciousness.

THIRTEEN

"I THINK SHE'S waking up."

Rora heard the voice but couldn't open her eyes or lift her head. She was lying down on something soft… in a bed, maybe… and there was a hand on her belly, sliding up toward… Gasping, she grabbed the hand that was between her body and the blanket laid over her.

Bella was there, lying beside her, looking down at her. Yes, she was in a bed, a large bed, near the edge. Bella was in it with her and Rora was… not naked.

"Where's Exile?" Rora croaked.

"Right here, Cupcake."

Staying on the pillow, her head snapped to the side and she saw the back of his. Ten feet away, he was seated on a couch that faced away from the bed; no doubt he was working on his laptop.

"She's awake, now can we make love to her?" Bella asked and sat up. The blanket fell from her body, revealing that she was naked. "Let's shower together! He's magnificent in the shower, isn't he?"

Bella grabbed her hand and pulled it out from under the covers, but Rora slid her palm out from between both of Bella's. "I…"

"She can probably barely stand," Strike said. "You get your ass in there, Bella. Ro's going nowhere. I've got shit to do today; I don't have time for your crap."

Bella grumbled something, tossed the covers away and climbed over her. Rora tensed when Bella brushed their lips together. For Rora's liking, it took too long for her hostess to get off the bed and stomp across the room into the bathroom.

The sound of the shower made her eyes close. If Bella was in there, she could relax. Her head was spinning, heavy and sore. Putting a hand on her forehead, Rora let her lips move.

"What is that?" Strike said, making her eyes open. "Are you telling me a story?"

"Myself," she said, lifting her legs to push the covers away from her body. "Little Red Riding Hood. I tell myself stories when I feel like I'm falling off the edge of the earth… Started when I was in the police cells waiting to tell them my story."

"After they caught your brother," he said.

She and her brother had been arrested by the cops at the same time because they were both found in the bloodbath and no one was sure of the truth. Those hours in the police station had been some of the worst of her life. After what immediately preceded them.

Even though she'd only been a child, the cops had said they had nowhere else to put her, so while they'd been trying to get their shit together, she'd been left alone in a room staring at bare walls. She'd needed some way to comfort herself and stories were it.

Her stomach clenched when she forced herself to sit up and turn her legs off the edge of the bed. "Last night… did we…"

"No," he said. "You slept. So far, I've resisted committing that particular sin."

Which made sense if his mother had been raped. Strike probably believed himself capable, but she didn't believe it. "Bella tried to make a convincing argument. She thinks we've had sex… everyone thinks it."

He offered no explanation for why he let them believe it. Pressing her fists into the mattress, she pushed forward and got her feet into the thick pile of the carpet. She wobbled for a minute, and had to close her eyes against the heaviness in her head, but she took her time about shuffling forward toward the couch. When she could reach it, she used it for balance and its support to help her around.

She slunk onto the couch, using the arm as a backrest against her shoulders, and tucking her dress around her legs when she pulled her knees to her chest.

"Why is Bella… Why did she…"

"She's attracted to you," he said, working on his laptop. "She didn't have a conventional upbringing, she doesn't know how to express that in any other way."

"Is that how you got together? Did she drug you?"

"More than once," he said.

But there hadn't been anyone there to protect him against her violations. "Thank you," she said. "For not letting her…"

"Don't start thinking it means anything," he said. "I need you sweet until you tell me what I want to know. If you'd been anyone else, I'd have let her do whatever she wanted to you."

"She wanted you… She wanted you to be with me."

He paused for a second but didn't look at her. "Yeah, well we both know that wouldn't have happened."

"No," she murmured, tucking her chin onto her knees.

"Quite the reunion you had with your Benjamin yesterday," he said. "Why does he call you Morning Sun?"

"It comes from my name, from light and dawn. He used to work so late that he wouldn't know it was daylight unless I walked in. Didn't really matter if it was the morning or not. He said I was his sunrise. His morning sun."

"Poetic," he scoffed. "And you still think he doesn't want to bone you? Fuck, you're naïve."

She folded her hands under her chin. "He never bought me a cupcake," she murmured.

He stopped again. This time his chin did move and they made eye contact. Sometimes it felt like he forgot who she was or forgot who *he* was. They'd been through a lot together in the last few weeks.

"I didn't know they wanted you here to work. If I had—"

"What?" he asked. "You'd still have brought me up here, you had to. You can't fly a plane. I found Benjamin, that's what you asked me to do. What I do after that is my business."

"Do you think she planned it this way? Gave out just enough information so that I'd bring you here believing you were my only hope."

"I was," he said. "No other guy would've brought you this far. We're in the middle of nowhere. Anything could happen out here and no one's getting out without her say so. But yeah, I think she planned it this way."

"So, what's our plan?" she asked. "How do we get out of here?"

"We don't," he said. "You're leaving tomorrow with Benjamin."

Surprise made her knees fall to the side. "What? No. What about you?"

"One of her guys is flying out to bring supplies back," he said. "You'll be on that plane with him."

"Strike," she said, falling forward to grab his arm. "No. I'm not leaving you here."

He lifted his arm up, out of her grip and gave her a push back to the end of the couch again. "You're useless to her. She'd play with you for a while, but she'll get bored with fucking you, and when she gets bored with one game, she moves on to another. And trust me when I say, the second game is a lot more painful than the first."

"We came here together, we're leaving together. I'm not going to let you sacrifice yourself for me."

A smirk twisted his lips and he glanced at her. "This isn't about you," he said. "We had a deal. You're going to tell me what I want to know and once you do, it doesn't matter where on the fucking planet I am. Here is just fine."

"I don't understand."

"No one said you had to."

Rora had had just about enough of this smug, sneering bastard. Moving onto her knees, she socked his shoulder hard enough to get him to turn to her. "Then I void it," she said. "I won't tell you."

Twisting around, he grabbed her arm, his grip so tight that it bit into her. "You fucking will, Aurora. I've played nice so far. Think about this, there's one reason and one reason alone that Bella didn't fuck you last night and it's got nothing to do with my skills of speech or seduction."

Wincing against the burn of pain in her arm, she felt the tingle of her fingers numbing. "You… you hurt her?"

"Threatened to," he snarled. "That's all I have to do with her because unlike you, she knows exactly what I'll do to her if she messes with me."

"You… you can't hurt me."

"Oh, I can, Cupcake," he said, tightening his grip and forcing her arm behind her. She yelped. "The sound of your bones breaking will be like music to me if you screw me over."

He pushed harder. With her knees bent and her legs squashed under her, it wasn't only her arm that was in agony, but he didn't move his weight, he loomed closer, pushing her into a more painful arch.

"Flame," she whispered.

He blinked and for a fraction of a second his anger died.

"Looks like I'm missing the party."

"Bella, get the fuck out of here," he snapped at the woman who must have returned from the bathroom.

"My house. My prince. I get to play too."

He bared his teeth, and Rora recalled what he'd said about his patience gauge around Bella. "I'm not going to fuck her. I'm going to kill her."

"Either way, I love it when you perform for me."

He swore under his breath and sat up, shoving away from her. He slammed his laptop and glared at Bella. "Don't do it again," he said to her. "You upset me one more time and I'll tear your kingdom down."

"You'd sign your own death warrant."

"Mutual suicide is your ultimate fantasy, isn't it, Bell?" he asked.

Rora was rubbing her arm, trying to steady her breathing when he spun on her and grabbed her chin to pull her toward him. "What's four plus two?"

"What?" she asked. "What are you—"

"Answer the question."

"Uh, six."

"Two to the third power?"

The math quiz was unexpected, she felt like she was foundering. "Eight."

"What'd you do to Torres?"

"I bit him."

"Lucky Torres," Bella muttered.

Isaac Burke had said that she was Exile's perfect equal, he wouldn't have been so sure if he'd met the Black Jewel.

Strike let her go and stood up, tucking Opal under his arm. "Unconscious twice in twenty-four hours is enough," he said to Bella. "No one messes with her today. We still need her."

The quiz was a concussion test or something? His vehemence might have suggested concern until he said that last sentence. Riding on the confusion of the morning and the drugs in her system from last night, it occurred to Rora that maybe she hadn't led Strike here like an innocent lamb to the sacrificial altar. Maybe she'd been played all along.

Listening to him leave the room, she stared at the table. Maybe his refusal to have sex with her was nothing to do with her, maybe... maybe he was being faithful to his mistress.

***

HER CONFUSION LINGERED while she got ready for the day. Bella gave her clothes and insisted that she left the bathroom door open while she showered. Though Rora didn't actually see her hostess, she was sure the woman was watching her in some way. She just couldn't shirk the feeling of ickiness that coated her skin, no matter how much she soaped her body in the shower.

When Rora was dressed, Bella took her to the lower floor to another dining room. This one had a terrace and the doors were wide open, letting the nip from the outside air come inside. All kinds of food were laid out on the table, almost every breakfast food she'd ever heard of. There was no way that both of them could eat all this food.

Bella went to the head of the table and pulled Rora down into the perpendicular place. While her hostess seemed oblivious, she felt more than a little awkward being watched by the half-dozen men dotted around the room. Either this woman was paranoid or she liked to be surrounded by men, which contradicted what Strike had told her.

"Wonderful, isn't it, duckie?" Bella asked, pulling off a piece of bagel to pop it between her lips.

"Wonderful?"

"All of these big, strong men completely under my control," she said. "I love to watch the way they squirm for me."

Presuming that Bella had caught her looking at the men, Rora did her best to keep her eyes on the food. "You must pay them well."

"Oh, they're not here for money," Bella said. "They're under my control. They get everything they need and they're grateful for it. They run around after me like the little puppies that they are."

How did that make sense? These were big guys, and at least two of them had guns. "Why?" she asked.

For a moment, Bella looked affronted, then she laughed and bent over the table to take fruit from a bowl. "Each and every one of them was recruited by Exile. He gave me the means to hold the lives of their loved ones over the edge of a cliff. Exile made all of them swear complete allegiance to me. I have their loyalty for life. Fear is just the greatest motivator, don't you think?"

Speechless, her next look around the room took on a different perspective. Scary as these men were, they were scared too. "Wow," she breathed out.

"Right? Him over there," Bella said, waggling a finger toward one of the men. "He's got the biggest dick in the room, want to see it?"

"Oh, no, I—"

Bella clicked her fingers. "You! Drop your pants!" Shading her eyes with her hand, Rora couldn't believe it when he actually unbuckled his belt. Bella leaned in to giggle. "I never bothered to learn any of their names. Damn us and our primitive needs. If I didn't enjoy them so much, I'd demand they become eunuchs."

She'd never been easily shocked. Rora's hand fell in surprise, she hadn't meant for it to, but with her unobstructed view, she was suddenly compelled to look at the guy on the other side of the room standing there with his pants around his ankles, his dick in hand. Yeah, it was quite the monster, even from here it was making her eyes water.

"You can have him," Bella said, popping a cherry between Rora's slack lips. "Isn't this fun, duckie? I haven't had a girlfriend in a long time."

Rora was still being rude, staring at the guy, and Bella stroked a hand down her face. "Do you want him to come for you?" Bella asked, still stroking her. "He can do that. All of them can. They'll come on you. On me. Anywhere you want… Just don't ask them to touch Exile's precious laptop, last guy I asked to jerk off over that did become a eunuch… he never even got to finish. My sweet prince is so protective of that thing. You know he refers to it as a female? It's nuts! He has a name for it. He never told me what it was, probably knew I'd laugh right in his face. Who cares about a hunk of metal?"

Strike did. Sensible or stupid, he did care about that hunk of metal, probably because it was his way to enter, and conquer, the world. Opal had been through everything with him. Bella snapped her fingers at the half-naked guy. "You'll spend your day pleasuring our guest. You'll be a slave to all of her sexual needs."

"Oh, no," Rora said, grabbing for Bella's hand. "No, no, I don't want that."

Panic made Rora take her hostess' hand. Bella looked down, her smile widening when she noticed the grip. "What would you like, duckie? If he doesn't appeal to you, you can have any of the others, or all of them... You can have any man in the building... or woman," she said, drawing a fingertip up the inside of Rora's sensitive inner arm. "But I'm the only one of those here... Did I come on too strong last night? I only wanted to help you relax. I promise I meant you no harm. You believe me. Don't you believe me, duckie?"

"I... Yes," she said because she didn't want to end up like the guy who got a fork in his hand yesterday.

"There are a dozen men in the building, at least, and I chose to share you with the one you've been intimate with most recently. I care about your comfort, Aurora. In fact, right now, it's about the only thing I care about," she said and pulled herself nearer. "Tell me about Exile, when did you first kiss him? Did he kiss you? He knows how to kiss, how to set a woman on fire, doesn't he?"

Squirming in her chair, Aurora couldn't take her hand from Bella because the hostess was holding it so tight. As Bella spoke, her excitement grew and her grip increased. "I... I suppose."

"And Benjamin," Bella said. "He's such a... peculiar lover, isn't he?"

All discomfort left her; in fact, every emotion fled Rora in deference to surprise. "You... you were with Benjamin?"

"Of course," Bella said, brushing a finger up and down the swell of Rora's breast. "You don't mind, duckie, do you?"

"No... no, I don't mind. Benjamin and I aren't... we weren't..."

"No," Bella said, pulling Rora into her arms and stroking her hair. "But you used to though, didn't you? I know. He told me all about it. About your affair and how you ended it. You're such a strong woman, Aurora... So strong and beautiful."

Easing back, Bella stroked Rora's face again and tipped up her chin. Her sultry eyes moved in closer. There was something fascinating about this woman and her confidence, the way she was so wrong and yet so enthralling. Beyond her obvious beauty and sinful figure, she seemed invulnerable in a way Rora envied.

The first touch of Bella's plump lips startled her, but there was no time for her to pull away. A door opened and she turned in time to see Strike there at the entrance scowling at them.

"Can we help you, Exile?" Bella asked, capturing a length of Rora's hair and letting it run through her fingers. She nuzzled the side of her neck, kissing her jaw and her cheek.

"I told you to behave, Bell," he said, marching across the room, clocking the pant-less guy at the same time. "Pull your fucking pants up."

"This is a private party," Bella said, surging to her feet when Strike grabbed Rora's arm to haul her up. "Let her go. We're not finished!"

"You're finished," Strike said, tugging on her.

But Bella grabbed Rora's other arm and tugged back.

"I thought you were going to the gym," Bella said, sounding juvenile in her petulance. "Trot along and do your workout. We're enjoying ourselves."

"I'm done in the gym, and how many times you gotta be told she's not a toy?"

"If she's not my toy then she's not yours either!" Bella said.

"Hey," Rora said, startling even herself, but maintaining her anger. "Stop fighting! I'm no one's toy, and I do not need to be pushed and pulled all over the place!"

When her surprise cleared, Bella grinned and let her go, reaching over to shove Strike's hands away from Rora's other arm. "Should we give her first shot of the whip, prince?" Bella asked, sliding over to his side to cling to his hand with both of hers. "Do we deserve to be punished?"

Strike was still scowling. Rora stared at him for a few seconds and then exhaled, she wasn't going to get anything from him, no apology, no acknowledgement of being wrong, and certainly no comfort.

Storming forward, she didn't even care when she hit his arm with hers on the way past. Maybe she was a prisoner, maybe there were places in the building that she wasn't allowed to go. But until someone came and stopped her, she was going hunting for Benjamin and Rora was grateful for the purpose when she slammed out of the breakfast room. She had to know what was going on here and right now, he was her only hope of making sense of this situation.

FOURTEEN

RORA HAD ONLY STORMED down about fifteen feet of hallway when someone grabbed her arm and spun her around. Registering that Strike was the one who'd grabbed her, she didn't hesitate to slam both hands onto his chest and shove with all her might.

Growling in frustration, she shoved him again and again. Grabbing her shoulders, he rushed her back, thumping her body to the wall. Looming over her, he grabbed her wrists and jolted them upward, pinning both to the wall far above her head with his own against them. Their bodies were like jigsaw pieces molded together, her head tucked beneath his chin without space to go anywhere else.

Her chest was heaving, her eyes burning, and her heart aching. She couldn't do this anymore, she just couldn't. With his hands planted against hers, she had an anchor point, and didn't have the energy to fight anymore.

Letting her knees buckle, Rora gave him responsibility for her weight and sagged there, letting her head drop to his chest.

"No," he said, gripping her wrists tighter to pull her higher. "No. No. No. Don't you fucking do it, Ro. Don't give up on me."

"I can't do it," she whispered, her face squashed to him, her adrenaline fading to exhaustion. "If you're going to kill me, kill me, or let her do it. I can't… I can't fight anymore."

"Yes, you can," he said, his hot breath in her hair. His lips lost in her locks. "Stand up, Cupcake. Get that chin up."

"No," she whispered. "I can't." This was ridiculous. She'd thought for half a second that she could actually do this. That she could come here and get Benjamin out. But it was crazy. "I am crazy."

"No, you're not," he mumbled. "You are not crazy. Get with it, Cupcake. Stand up. Now!"

She had made him hold her up for too long, ever since she'd dragged him into this by saying his name on the phone to Bella.

Strengthening her legs, Rora took her weight. Strike exhaled something that sounded like relief when she tipped her chin up. But she wasn't following his orders, she was resolved to the truth that he'd been right all along.

"I don't belong here," she said. "I never should have made it this far in your world. I don't understand it. I'm confused. I'm scared."

"No, you're not," he said, sliding her wrists down the wall until he held them just above her shoulders. "You're not scared. You're not afraid with me."

"You're not with me," she muttered, her head swinging on her neck. "You don't care if I live or die. This is you working your magic. Again." Her voice drifted off. "I thought we had something, thought at the very least that we were friends and now I… I just want it to be over. I'm never going to make it through this. You were right. I'm going to die here."

"You are not going to die here. You're going to get on that plane tomorrow and leave all this behind," he said.

"Do you think she'll let me live that long?" she asked. "Either I give her my body or I die. I don't want the whip. I can't stand anymore pain."

"There won't be any pain," he said. "Get through one more day. Just stay with it. Keep your wits. Be smart."

Gazing up into his steely, determined eyes, she was in awe of his strength, of his ability to keep going, to keep fighting. His whole life had been a fight. "I'm so confused. I'm so tired of being alone, Strike," she whispered, wishing she had someone to lean on who'd help her figure out the smart thing to do. "Nothing makes sense to me anymore. I think… this truly is Wonderland."

Up was down. Benjamin was sleeping with a woman who wanted to sleep with her. A woman who commanded men that Strike controlled. Everyone was fair game. No one could be trusted. Everyone had their own agenda. Did Strike come here to save her or did he come here to support Bella? Did Bella want her or was she playing a game that she'd get bored of? What happened when the game was over? Why was Benjamin healthy? Why was he in no rush to leave this place? Why had she come here? Why had she thought that she could make a difference?

"Ro—"

"What's the point?" she whispered. Surprise flashed in his eyes. "I should just tell you. I should just get it over with. Strike, the point—"

Swooping down, he captured her lips with his. Pressing her into the wall, his kiss grew deeper as he nestled her closer. One of his forearms eased down behind her head, around the back of her neck, holding her at his mercy.

Pinning her between him and the wall, he held her to him, the girth of his forearm acting as a cushion at the base of her skull.

"Don't you dare," he hissed, running his tongue along the inside of her lip. "Do not give up your only bargaining chip."

"I can't fight anymore, Strike," she whispered, her fists tightening in his tee-shirt. "It's the only reason you're with me. The only reason you have to be near me."

"Then dangle it in front of me," he said. "Keep it to yourself… keep me."

Searching his gaze, she felt him trying to tell her a truth he couldn't dare utter. As long as she had this secret, he had an excuse to be with her. "I'm scared to believe you might…" she whispered. "I don't trust you."

"Don't," he said. "Don't trust anyone."

"What difference does it make if I tell you today or tomorrow?" she asked.

"Tomorrow's the future," he said. "The future is the only thing we should be concerned with. Anything could change before then."

The future, she wasn't sure she had one of those. She was relying on catching a ride with a stranger, but if what Bella had said was right, the men around here were Exile's puppets. Except that didn't mean she was safe around them.

Whether it was right or not, Exile had shown real commitment to his ex by staffing her crusade. "Are you in love with her?" Rora asked, terrified of what the answer might be.

Yes, it turned out that she did have one fear when she was with him. But it wasn't fear for her life, it was fear of what he might do to her heart.

"No," he murmured. "No, Kero, I'm not in love with her."

"You never told me why," she said, opening her hands to press them against him, but the pressure of her palms only tightened the grip of his arm around her neck. He kept her like this, her knees buckled, her head tipped back, her lips just a breath beneath his. "Why did you call me Kero?"

"You called me your flame the night you first tried threatening me," he said. "The first time I tasted your lips."

For all the fraction of a second that lasted. "So? I—"

"It's short for kerosene. Kerosene ignites a flame," he murmured, letting his lips sink a fraction lower so that they moved on hers as he spoke. "Seeing you on the ground behind that gas station… You've never been afraid of me, but you were afraid of them… I don't get it. What do you want me to be, Aurora? What is it that you think you see?"

"I don't think it, Strike. I know I see it."

"You're naïve," he whispered, but closed his eyes to kiss her again.

"And you're stubborn," she said, scrunching his tee-shirt and giving him a tug though there was nowhere he could go, he was as close to her as he could get. "If I get on that plane tomorrow, will I ever see you again?"

"No," he said. "But you are getting on that plane tomorrow, whether you like it or not. Conscious or not."

Knowing that their association was coming to an end was probably the only reason that he was being this open with her. Not that she could be sure that any of this was true.

"You remember how I asked who'd come for you if you were in trouble?" she asked, and he brushed his lips over hers without responding. "I'd come for you."

"You won't."

There was no sorrow in his words, but his doubt strengthened her. "I'm your homing pigeon, remember? If hell is your home, then it's mine too. I'm drawn to you, Flame."

"Just the right amount of corruptible," he grumbled.

"I've broken another," she admitted and smiled, rising onto her tiptoes. "I worship a new idol. You, Strike, are my one and only Lord."

Opening her mouth, for the first time, she was allowed to kiss him. He didn't push her away, didn't refuse her tongue when it slid over his lip to meet his. He smudged the warmth of his own against hers. She hummed with pleasure, keeping her squashed bent elbows close together against his chest while she fingered his jaw to tempt his mouth lower, begging it to stay longer.

"Will you pray for me, baby?" he asked, tracing his lips up over her nose. "Pray for my eternal soul?" She shook her head and he blinked. "No?"

Grabbing her lower lip between his teeth, he growled at her, making her laugh.

"Because I don't want anyone else to take it or judge it," she said. "I want it, Strike. I want your soul and I'm not beyond stealing it if I have to."

"Naughty," he said. "But you don't have to break any of your commandments for me, Cupcake. My soul, my spirit, my conscience, my decency, they've been dormant so long, I don't need 'em. You can have them all."

"For a price?"

"Yeah," he said. She arched a questioning brow. "Don't ever stop fighting. You keep that chin up."

Elevating her chin now meant kissing him again, but there was no time to enjoy it or to wonder where this new side of Strike might lead them because a sound at the other end of the hallway made him turn away, taking his lips from hers.

Following his line of sight, she saw Benjamin at the other end of the hallway. With the flanking pillars in the way, it didn't look like he'd seen the couple. Benjamin went into a different room without acknowledging them in any way.

She didn't expect Strike to back off, but he took her hand and tugged her away from the wall. "Go," he said, looking at the door Benjamin had used. "Bella will be about done; I'll hold her off if I have to."

"Done with what?" she asked.

"The guy with his pants down, she was fucking him," he said. "She can't see a cock without riding it."

Of course he knew her habits, and how long it would take her to reach climax. "Oh… ok."

Strike nudged her down the hallway. "Hurry, if you want to talk to him, this might be your only chance."

"Strike…"

Taking her hips, he spun her around and swatted her ass to get her moving. "Go," he said and turned his back on her to walk the opposite way down the hallway.

She hoped his way of holding Bella off didn't include doing what the pants dropster did. Grabbing her lip in her teeth, she spun around and made a beeline for the door Benjamin had used. She had no idea what kind of room she was walking into or if there might be anyone in there. But Strike had implied—if he was the type of guy to imply things—that Bella was the only one they had to worry about. With her in the breakfast room, Rora had a clear shot.

Entering before she could psyche herself out of taking the risk, Rora found herself in a large room much like the one on the floor above that she'd woken in yesterday. This room had darker décor, more furniture, and was homelier, but there was no sign of Benjamin, or anyone.

The terrace doors were open and she went to them

to find Benjamin seated at a table in the middle of the curved space that had to be twenty-five feet across.

"Benjamin," she said and went outside.

Leaping to his feet, he didn't seem as jovial today as he had last night. "Aurora," he said, looking left then right. "What are you doing out here?"

"We don't have a lot of time," she said, glancing over her shoulder to check that no one had followed her.

"No, you have to go," he said, rushing to her to grab her elbow. "Go back to wherever you're supposed to be."

"No," she said, pulling her arm away from his grip. "We have a few minutes alone. We have to take advantage of that."

"If they catch us talking without Jewel's authority—"

"She's with Exile," Rora said.

Benjamin was already shaking his head. He grabbed both her elbows. "I'm sorry I got you into this, Rora, I really am," he said. "For weeks, I was kept in a hole, and they kept asking over and over, the same question."

"What's the point?" she said.

His expression slackened. "Yes," he breathed out and grabbed her tighter. "Yes. Exactly. She asked you too?"

Rora nodded. "She's not the only one."

"You can't tell her," he said. "You can't tell the Black Jewel anything. You can't tell anyone."

Pulling away from his grip, she went past him, heading across the terrace toward the snow. "You should've destroyed it when you had the chance."

"I tried," he said. Turning to lean on the wooden railing at the edge of the terrace, Rora folded her arms. He ran a hand over his hair. "I did."

"We both know that's not true."

Coming to her, he opened his hands, beseeching her. "You don't understand, Ro. Asking me to destroy every trace would be like asking me to murder my child. It's my magnum opus."

"It doesn't work to its full potential."

He seized her shoulder. "And that's why she needs Exile. He'll fix it if he gets his hands on it."

Benjamin seemed to be clinging to optimism, but Rora was more realistic. "He wouldn't give it to her."

"You don't know that," he said. "You can't trust him. We can't trust either of them."

If Benjamin knew what kind of woman Bella was, it made no sense to her why he'd choose to share himself with her. "You slept with her," she said, though why she had blurted that out, Rora had no idea.

Who he slept with was his business. But to sleep with the person responsible for your capture and torture was fathomless.

"You slept with him."

Looking to the decking just behind Benjamin, Rora warred with herself. Confessing the truth that she hadn't actually had sex with Strike would contradict what Strike had led the others to believe. Because she wasn't exactly sure why he was doing that, she didn't want to betray him by correcting Benjamin.

She also couldn't deny her feelings for Strike or her willingness to be intimate with him. It might never happen, they may never have the opportunity to consummate their feelings, but if she did get the chance, she'd take it.

Not that Strike had directly admitted to having any desire to be with her. But it seemed pedantic for her to reject the accusation of sleeping with the man when she had every intention of doing it if they found themselves alone.

"Exile isn't like her," she murmured.

"You don't know what either of them are like," he said. "They manipulate people, that's what they do, all of them. This is… it's a world without morals or loyalty. She tortured me, had her men do horrific things to me, for weeks. I begged for death, Rora, begged for it. She chained me up, whipped me, starved me…"

Her chin wobbled, she'd been right about his pain, about his horrific treatment. "Oh, Benjamin," she said, looping her arms around him to hold him. "I'm so sorry."

"All the time, always, over and over she asked me the same question."

"What's the point?" she said, burying her face against

him though she couldn't stop the tears. "Why didn't you tell her? You could've told her and saved yourself."

He held her close. "No, she would've killed me as soon as she had it. I couldn't re-write it, it's been months, and you know what my memory is like, especially under pressure. I've been trying to hold her off. I couldn't tell her what, or where, it was, but she wants it… She wants it bad and as she got more frustrated with me, the torture got worse."

"What changed?" she asked, looking up at him. "Why did she let you free?"

"She wanted Exile; I overheard her talking about it. I'd already told her that my work wasn't enough, so she knew we needed him. I convinced her we could get him here… that you could get him here. All you would need was a crumb and you'd find a way to track him down… and I was right, you did it… I'm amazed."

Anger tensed her. Benjamin had a heart of gold—she couldn't believe that he'd changed so much in six months, no matter what he'd endured.

"We're not trading his life for ours," she said.

His next statement shocked her. "Why not? Who cares about him?" Benjamin asked, cupping her face and crouching to her eye level. "We need to get away from here. You don't know what it's like, what she's like."

"I care," she said, pulling his hands from her face. "And you can't think she'll let us leave here. The Black Jewel won't allow us to leave without answering her question."

"We can't," he said. "I prayed that Exile would come here and she'd see that he could do so much for her that she might be satisfied. I had no idea they had a previous relationship. You have to believe me. I thought he would be enough, that maybe she'd forget everything else. You can't tell her. Do you hear me? You can't tell her, him, no one… You haven't… said anything about it, have you?"

Thinking about the hallway, just a few minutes ago where she had almost told Strike, Rora couldn't deny that she would have told him if he hadn't cut her off with that kiss. When they'd been fighting in the motel he'd broken her heart by asking the question. He might just have mended it by preventing her from making a mistake he'd somehow known she'd regret.

"No," she said, but didn't exactly feel proud of that right now. "But how do you expect us to get out of this if we won't give them something? The Black Jewel holds all the cards. You were desperate when you told her I'd find Exile. You bought yourself time, I understand that. But now we're all here, she'll want the truth, and if we don't give it to her..."

As sorrowful as he looked, Benjamin didn't retreat from his position. "We can't, Aurora. You and I are the only two people in the world who can answer their questions. You have access to everything, absolutely everything. Whether I brought you here or not, you'd always have been at risk because... I will sacrifice myself for this secret. You have to make your decision, be willing to sacrifice yourself or endure their torture. The third option is unimaginable. If either one of us gives them what they want, they will own the world." Her gaze was drifting again and to get it back, he captured her face in both hands again. "You remember what I told you. Don't you?"

She nodded, recalling every conversation they'd ever had. But that didn't mean she was ready to give up. There was another option.

"I can destroy it," she said.

Frustrated, he exhaled, and shook his head. "You can't. You don't understand. There's no way that they won't be able to retrieve it. They have skills, technology. Exile has access to resources you can't even imagine. He has skills that you wouldn't believe... Their eyes will be on you now. Wherever you go, they'll find you. They'll follow you. You'll lead them right to it."

She knew something about Exile's skills, and about his connections, she'd met the NSA for goodness sake. "I can talk to him," she said to herself, but Benjamin gave her a shake.

"You can't trust him."

"I know," she said. "He told me not to. But I don't see what else we can do."

"For now, we play along," he said. "You promise me

you'll never breathe a word. Promise me, Ro." She nodded. "Until she asks for it, we have time to think of something else. But if we don't come up with a plan B, you know what we have to do, right?"

The resolve in his eyes was humbling and terrifying at the same time. She nodded once and he reciprocated. Without a plan B, there was only one course of action to ensure success and to save the world.

FIFTEEN

THE LODGE WASN'T LARGE, two floors with some additional space in the attic and basement. Rora imagined it would be a beautiful place to spend some time, if the company was better.

Before sneaking off the terrace, Benjamin told her how to get to the library, explaining that it was one of the few rooms he was allowed in. Working on the assumption that if he was allowed in there, she would be too, Rora used the space to regroup.

There were no phones lying around anywhere or computers outside the office he was required to work in. While telling her that, Benjamin didn't reference Opal, but he probably assumed Exile was exempt from Bella's rules, which may be why Benjamin assumed he couldn't be trusted.

Lunch was brought to her in the library, but she ignored it and spent most of the day gazing out of the window at the falling snow, trying to come up with a strategy.

Plan B.

She understood Benjamin's desire to protect the secret at any cost. It just wasn't one she'd considered paying. Strike had told her that he took risks based on assumptions. Until now, she hadn't realized that was what she'd done too.

Rora had assumed that Benjamin would do nothing to hurt her and that Strike's role in this was as facilitator to get her to where she needed to be. Turned out, neither of those things were true.

Benjamin hadn't meant to hurt her by revealing the secret to her. She'd worked with him for a long time and knew a lot about his work. She didn't understand much about it, and some of it was gobbledygook, but Strike would understand it. Except Benjamin was sure the hacker was untrustworthy, and Strike himself had told her not to trust him.

Bella loved games. Maybe that's what this was, a game. Rora didn't know what to believe of Strike or what was in his heart. If he cared for her, her perspective on trusting him would be clearer. But he could spin on a dime. One minute, she was sure he saw her, and the next, she felt like nothing more than a tool for him to wield.

Benjamin had been in such pain that he'd been willing to do anything to save himself. Some part of him believed she'd be his saving grace, even if it was just to offer him some comfort for a while, and she had. But now she was here, the timer was back on and the onus was on her to figure a way out.

Without any clear idea of what they could do to get out of here and protect the secret, she was still considering options when she went upstairs to the bedroom she'd shared with Bella and Strike the previous night.

Strike had always made it clear that survival was everyone's primary mission and no one should focus on the past. Benjamin had told her that any sacrifice was worth it to protect the secret. Both men, in their own way, had told her what she needed to do.

Knowing that Bella would want to change her clothes before their main meal like she had last night when she'd gone to some effort to dress for dinner, Rora had chosen this position to intercept the hostess.

When the bedroom door opened and Bella came gliding into the room, Rora was resolved. "Aurora!" Bella declared, closing the door and opening her arms. "My duckie!"

Rora rose from the seat at the end of the bed and smiled. "Hello," she said. "I haven't seen you all day."

Bella pouted. "No, I'm sorry, I had men to keep in line. You know what they're like, dirty animals who'd be lost without their mistress."

Crossing to her, Bella gathered her into her arms and held her close. "You… you feel good."

Bella seemed to freeze and then she relaxed to draw Rora back down onto the seat. "Duckie," she said, stroking her face. "How could I forget… we were interrupted at breakfast." Pushing out her lower lip, she simpered. "My darling, have I neglected you today?"

"No, I… I didn't mean to imply that—"

Bella put a finger to Rora's lips and smiled. "Don't you worry, we're together now," she whispered and leaned forward.

Sliding her finger off Rora's lips, Bella's mouth quickly replaced it. Kissing her was different to kissing any man; her lips were softer, confident, but slick with gloss. Pulling back when Bella's tongue touched her lip, Rora let her eyes drop. "I haven't ever… with a woman, I mean."

"Duckie," Bella said, opening her palms on her face to hold their eyes on each other. Her simmering need was recognizable; some things were no different no matter the gender. Desire was desire. "I'll look after you."

Pulling her to her feet, Bella was first to slide off her shoes and unzip her dress. When she was in her underwear, she leaned in to kiss Rora again, seeking the zip on the back of her dress to pull it down. The dress cascaded onto the floor and she stepped out of it when Bella began to advance, easing Rora around the bench and the end of the bed.

Rora had no choice except to lie down when Bella stroked her hands up and down her arms and then took her waist to boost her onto the mattress. She didn't stop stroking. Bella's hands went down her sides to her waist, her hips and then up over her breasts.

"You're so sweet," Bella said, bowing to kiss the mound of each of her breasts.

Her hands went to Rora's thighs and Bella's lit eyes met hers when she slid her hands between them to urge Rora's legs apart.

Her heart was pounding. A quake of anxiety shook her gullet. Her lips were dry too. But Bella didn't seem to notice Rora's discomfort when she bowed to kiss her again. So far, she'd avoided doing any touching of her own. Rora wasn't really sure what she should be doing. Not that she didn't know what felt good; as a woman, she had the inside track on that. But she worried that Bella might be able to tell her touch wasn't genuine.

"What the fuck…" Strike's voice startled her. Bella tossed her hair to look over her shoulder. The break in the kiss let Rora see he was storming up the length of the bed. "What the hell is this? What did you do to her?"

"Nothing, our prince," Bella said, pouncing to her knees to lunge over and grab Strike's hand. "Join us."

Pulling his hand to her mouth, Bella began to kiss his knuckles and tugged him closer to cover the back of his hand and wrist in kisses. Bella kept advancing up his arm, but he didn't seem to notice because he was focused on the woman laid out on the mattress and ignoring the kissing woman.

Staying on her back beneath Bella who was kneeling between her thighs, Rora said nothing when Bella lay across her thigh to pull up the front of Strike's tee-shirt.

"No," he said, pushing his ex's hand away, but she fought to reach his fly. All the time, he stayed fixated on Rora, lying on the bed. "She doesn't want this."

"Of course she does," Bella said, grinning and running a hand from Rora's chin down to her cleavage. Tugging him once again, Bella squashed his hand down onto Rora's breast. "Just like you've done with her a thousand times." But they hadn't. Strike didn't acknowledge where his hand was even when Bella sandwiched it between hers and Rora's breast and began to massage. "She's so soft, isn't she?"

Bella squealed and lowered to kiss Rora again, but it wasn't as easy for Rora to do this with Strike's hand on her body, or with his disapproving glare looming over her.

Strike grabbed Bella's shoulder and pulled her back. "No," he said. "Get your hands off her, Bell."

Snatching Rora's wrist, he dragged her off the bed with such a fierce tug that she tumbled to the floor. "No," Rora said, using his leg to pull herself onto her knees. "I want this."

"No, you don't," he said, pulling her from his leg to toss her to the floor again. "You're being manipulated."

"Maybe I'm manipulating her," Rora argued.

Bella laughed, her face appearing off the edge of the bed for a brief second before she pounced to her knees. "Yes, if you don't want to play, go away, and leave us to manipulate each other."

"You are not putting your hands on her again," he snarled, shoving Bella back onto the bed and lunging down to grab Rora to pull her onto her feet. "Put your fucking clothes on."

"Who the hell are you?" Bella called, flying off the bed onto Strike.

Scratching and screaming like a banshee, Bella locked her legs around his hips while punching at his shoulders. She attacked without restraint, and after opening her mouth to shout, she tossed her head forward to latch her teeth to his lip.

Strike swore and threw her onto the bed so hard that she bounced twice. "What the fuck, Bell!" he said, touching his lip to then look at the blood smudged on his finger.

"Flame!" Rora said, rushing to his side to touch the lip Bella had bitten. "Baby."

"I'm ok," he said, and tried to push her aside.

But Rora slid in between him and the bed and cupped his face running her thumbs over his lips. "My baby, you're hurt," she whispered. "You're bleeding."

Putting an arm around her, he kept his forearm tucked at the base of her skull and with his finger still on his lip, he looked down at her. "What'd I tell you about scrapping, huh?"

"Baby," she murmured, still stroking him. "This was my fault, this was..."

But it wasn't her who'd hurt him. Fury burst inside her and she spun around, not caring for a second that Bella was stunned and probably angry too. Rora opened her hand and swung hard, slapping Bella across the face so hard that the beauty fell to the side.

Bella screamed and leaped up, grabbing for Rora's hair and hauling her onto the bed again. But Rora grabbed her hair too, pulling and kicking, wrestling the woman on the mattress.

"Hey! Whoa!"

Strike was still somewhere nearby, but Rora was too consumed by the anger caused by the sight of his blood. This bitch had caused him to bleed! Her formidable Strike was hurt because of this evil wench and if he wouldn't fight back, Rora would fight for him.

Forcing Bella to her back, Rora straddled her, ignoring the woman's hollering even after she slapped her again. But an arm too strong for her to fight came around her waist and she was hauled away backwards.

"No!" Rora screamed, reaching forward.

But it didn't matter, Strike dragged her off the bed, his solid arm locked around her ribs, he pinned her back to his torso beneath his arm.

With her hair tangled across her face, Rora couldn't see anything, but she could feel Strike's tension. "Move and you get one in the head," Strike snarled.

Tossing her head back, Rora did what she could to get her hair out of her eyes and when she thought it felt like Strike had loosened his hold on her, she tried to leap on the bed again. But it was futile, he was ready for her and she sprang back against him when his arm tightened.

He turned his body to twist her further away from the bed and it was that move that revealed the gun he was holding in his other hand, aimed at a huffing Bella who was on her knees in the middle of the mattress.

Strike turned his mouth into Rora's hair. "Would you calm your goddamn jets, Cupcake?"

"Are you… comforting her?" Bella laughed. "Well that's no fun! You want to beat me, Exile, do it. I'll still expect you to fuck me and her."

"Not gonna happen," he said, squeezing Rora so hard that her lungs tightened. "We're done, Bell. You're not going to lay another finger on her. Not one."

"I'd say that's up to me now, isn't it?" Bella said. When she slid one knee closer to the edge of the bed, he took a step back, taking Rora with him. "Are we playing a game, prince? Do you want me to beg for her? To fight you for her?" Curving her hands around to her back, Bella unhooked her bra and dropped it to the floor. "Maybe you want us to fight over you? You should worship the ground we walk on. You and your kind, all of you. You think you can take what you want from us, that we work for you. We don't. Your life should be dedicated to serving us…" With a sultry tip of her chin, she smiled. "Should we take this to the basement? I had no idea she was so adept in the sexual arts, you've taught her well in such a short time."

But Strike wasn't playing. "I've taught her nothing and this isn't a game."

Bella wasn't dissuaded. "Everything's a game," she said. "You taught me that when you turned the tables on my family and slit their throats in front of me."

"I should never have done that," he said, his focus staying on Bella though he kept Rora tight against him. "I told you that was wrong."

Something so perverse crossed Bella's face that Rora was taken aback, then the woman tossed her head back and laughed. "I begged you, Exile," she called, opening her arms like she was reliving some kind of release. "I begged you to kill them. I promised you freedom if you destroyed them and you did. You did everything I asked of you and more."

"It damaged you."

"No!" Bella snapped. "It freed me! Freed me from them and their disgusting hands! Their disgusting bodies! You gave them what they deserved. I welcome the debt I owe you if it frees me from their bounds."

"Repay that debt now," he said and her eyes narrowed. "Repay it by letting Aurora and Gallagher go. Send your guy out tonight, my plane is right there, fueled and ready to go. Send them away… You can still have me."

Rora gasped and clawed at his arm, trying to pull it from her body so she could turn around, but he was too strong.

"No," Rora cried. "I'm not leaving you here."

His mouth bumped her head. "I told you, consent or not," he snarled down at her.

SIXTEEN

PICKING HER FEET from the floor, Rora tried to use her whole body to shake his arm loose, but he barely bent an inch, he simply took the weight she gave him and held her to him.

"So you can violate her, but I can't?" Bella asked. "You never had a problem sharing me, or sharing any woman. What's different about this one? What does she do to you that you don't want me to see? You can't get it up for her? You last three seconds? Never been a problem for you before. Maybe it's her ass you like, I have no problem with her eating my pussy while you—"

"Enough," he snapped.

"No," Bella said, dropping her hands to her hips and arching her back, thrusting out her breasts. "I want to know what you're so scared of me seeing." A mocking smile threatened her lips. "Are you sweet with her? Is that it? Do you expect me to believe that you take it all slow and vanilla with her? Does she go crazy nuts when you make her come... or maybe that's it, you can't make her come? Don't worry, prince, I'll take care of that, you just do your male thrusting thing and I'll take care of our innocent cherub."

Bella leaned forward, but Strike twisted, hauling Rora back again, out of her reach. "You don't touch her. Make me say it again, Bella, please. I fucking dare you."

Her brow came down when she fell back to sit on her feet. "I have never seen you like this, Exile. You don't want me to start worrying my pretty little head, do you?"

"I don't give a damn about your head, Bell. I haven't given a damn about any part of you for a long time."

"But you give a damn about her," Bella said, nodding at Rora without looking at her. "I want to know what her pussy does to your dick that's so special."

"It's nothing to do with her pussy."

"You're a man, everything's about pussy," she said, her hand loose on her wrist when she waved it. "Obviously something about sex with her is spectacular and you shouldn't keep that treat to yourself. Would you let my men have her?"

Bending his elbow, Strike put the gun to the side of Rora's head. She gasped and squeezed her eyes closed. "I'd put a bullet in her head before I'd let them near her."

Squealing with delight, Bella clapped. "Now that's more like it, I can work with that. How many of them would you kill for touching her? I can have all of them here in a minute… Let's play and find out!"

"Flame," Rora whispered, turning her face away from Bella and the gun to hide her tears in his upper arm.

Hauling her up again, he pressed his mouth into her crown. "I got you, baby. You're safe. No one will touch you. No one. You know your body's safe with me. It's safe from every man, including this one."

"Wait a minute," Bella drawled, and the gun moved away from Rora's head. "You have fucked her, Exile… haven't you?" He didn't respond. Her tone got more angry and urgent. "Tell me right now that you've had sex with her!" Still he didn't say anything. Bella shrieked. "No! You bastard!"

The sound of a gunshot made Rora scream. When she turned back to the bed, she saw Bella clutching a wound on her shoulder. "Do not move!" Strike shouted.

Bella didn't even appear to be in pain, her face was a picture of seething rage. "You bastard! You fell in love with her! Goddamn you!"

"Fuck you, Bella!"

The door opened and men poured in. "Bring Benjamin here, this minute!" Bella screamed. Strike pushed Rora behind him, blocking her from the half-dozen security men who'd just stormed the room. Cowering behind Strike, Rora didn't know what would happen next, or how they'd get out of there. "We need more men to take Ex down! We need all of them! It took twelve guys, a heavy shot of ketamine and a near fatal knife wound to capture him last time."

"You know what happens if I flatline, Belladonna," he said. Rora didn't know what would happen, but if there was one thing Strike was good at, it was contingencies. "And you need me."

"Your precious Aurora is expendable," she barked. "Get her! Strip her! String her up!"

Another gunshot sounded, making Rora jump. "One minion down, who's next?" Strike barked. "Take one step over here and I'll gut you bastards… All you gotta do is let her go, Bella, and all this will be over."

"No," she snapped. "Not until I get my answer."

"The answer," he said, and some of the tension left his body. "Tell her, Ro, tell her what's the point?"

And then what? She'd get to walk? But she couldn't break her promise to Benjamin, and there were goodness knows how many people in the room. Too many. She couldn't see anything around Strike because she was pinned between him and the wall with the nightstand blocking her right side. But she couldn't tell all these people the secret.

"Aurora!" Strike snapped.

She eased away from his back. "I… I can't."

He sidestepped, keeping the gun on the guards at the foot of the bed, but twisting to frown at her. "What? Yes, you fucking can. Tell her."

But she shook her head. "I can't… I promised Benjamin."

"Benjamin," Bella said.

The men at the door spread, putting Strike back on guard, but he relaxed when Benjamin was brought to the head of the pack. "Oh my god, Aurora, what's he doing to you?"

"Benjamin," she said.

When she tried to rush forward, Strike put an arm out to block her. "Answer the question, Rora."

"The question?" Benjamin asked, searching those he could see. "No! Don't! She'll never let us go."

Bella leaped onto her feet on the bed and thrust a finger toward Benjamin. "Keep him away from her!"

"Benjamin!" Rora called when the security men pulled him back into their throngs.

"Aurora!" Bella barked, bouncing to face her. "What's the point?"

Lost, she had no idea what to do, no idea what was right. Her gaze darted to Benjamin who was stuck surrounded by security. "You promised me, Morning Sun. You promised not to!"

Strike leaped forward a step. "You shut your fucking mouth, you fuck!" he snapped. "She's here 'cause of you. Let her save her life!"

That glorious optimism had faded from her friend. "Jewel will never let her leave," Benjamin said. "We're all doomed. We're at her mercy, locked in this hell until she ends our lives."

Bella laughed. "Oh, I love that! The truth is pure!"

Benjamin was right, the only way they were getting out of here was without their bodies. "Ben," she whispered, her eyes locking onto his. "Please, Benjamin."

"I'm sorry, Aurora," he said.

Less than a breath passed. A tear slipped from her eye. Benjamin pitched sideways, grabbed something from the belt of a guard and then there was a pop. It was that fast. The world didn't slow down until his body began to fall to the floor.

"No!" she screamed and ran toward him. Something stopped her from getting there; both of Strike's arms had locked tight around her waist. "No! Benjamin!"

Pushing at Strike's arms, she tried to free herself, tried to get away from the man restraining her. With her feet off the floor, she curled her legs up to her stomach, the pain of grief a weight of horror in her chest, making her stomach heave.

"Damn him," Bella hissed.

Going limp, Rora was ready to give up, ready to admit defeat. Benjamin's body was there on the floor, lifeless, blood seeping from the hole on the side of his head, trickling down his face. Her great, brilliant, kind, wonderful Benjamin was gone. A bullet was his freedom. A final chance to take control. His death was meant to save the innocent people of the world from falling under Bella's control.

Strike turned around, putting his back to the guards to put her onto her feet. Before he could turn back to the room, her hand slipped over his, over the gun.

"Give it to me," she said, her weak voice barely a whisper.

"What?" he said, his attention leaping from her to the gun and back, but she barely saw it or registered his angry horror.

Sliding her fingers around the butt, her finger curved around to the trigger. "I need it."

"No," he snapped, pulling the gun away from her grip. "No, fuck that. What the hell are you thinking?"

"Mutual suicide," Bella drawled, the thump of desire in her voice. "I want to know what she knows so badly, but this is almost too hot to resist. Someone give her their gun. Let's see if she'll really do it."

"No!" Strike said, thrusting an arm up toward Bella, his hand open wide, but kept his eyes on Rora. "I am not going to let you hurt yourself, Aurora. You don't take the coward's way out like he did."

An invisible weight on her chest made it hard to breathe. "I made him a promise," she said, finding herself unable to look into his eyes.

But it wasn't out of guilt that numbness was creeping through her. She didn't want to live here under Bella's torture and that's the only thing she had to look forward to. Strike was always telling her to look to the future. For her, there were two choices, torture or death.

"A promise to kill yourself?" Strike snarled. "Fine." Loading the gun, he slapped it into her hand and grabbed her wrist, yanking it up hard. Instead of putting the gun to her head, he used his strength to point it at his own. "Take out the trash first."

The venom in his words complemented the anger burning from his eyes to hers. His mother had killed herself. Rora didn't know how she'd done it. But Strike had admitted how he wished she'd taken him too. Now he had his chance to be taken by someone else before their suicide.

"I need him as well," Bella said, from somewhere in the room. "But triple suicide?" She squealed. "If they go, we're all going with them… Can you just imagine the horror? Hell will be crowded tonight!"

Strike's eyes got closer to hers, his gaze so intense that Aurora believed he was unaware of anyone else being in the room. He had his hand around hers, holding the gun to his temple so tight that the metal pattern from the grip was imprinting itself on her palm.

"Pull the trigger, Cupcake, what are you waiting for?"

"I… I don't want you to die," she said.

"Then put the gun down," he growled and dipped even lower to get into her face. "Because there isn't anywhere you can go that I won't follow."

She felt how deeply he meant that, his determination made her shiver. "Flame," she whispered, tormented by his vehemence, her promise, and Benjamin's sacrifice.

"Send me first. I'll scare the demons into their holes, clear your path home. Death's no obstacle to the devil."

Her finger tensed, and he didn't even blink as it tightened around the trigger.

But she faltered. "No," she said, taking her finger from the trigger. "I can't do it."

Without acknowledgement of her admission, he clicked into action mode. "Go out the window," he said and spun around, pulling his phone from his back pocket.

The window in the corner was behind them, and a better option than trying to go through the guards to get to the door, but they were on the second floor. "You think we'll just let you walk out of here?" Bella said.

Halfway to the window, Rora noticed Opal on the arm of the couch. Strike had his back to her, blocking her from the aim of the others, and still holding the gun on the guards while doing something with his phone.

Diverting, Rora grabbed Opal and ran to the window. The latch wasn't locked, and it was starting to get dark out, but she didn't remember about the cold or about her partially nude body until she pushed the window open as wide as it would go.

She gasped, but had no choice now. Strike was backing toward her, obviously meaning to come the same way. With Opal tucked under her arm, she grabbed the frame and hauled herself up onto the sill. Stepping over the lip of the window, she put a hand over her head, balancing herself on the fixed pane above.

"Flame," she said, waiting for him to get closer.

"Out," he called over his shoulder. "Go now."

Beneath this window was a drop of just a few feet. The roof over the lower floor provided a landing. Forgetting the cold and her lack of outerwear, Rora put her other foot over onto the outer sill, dipping her head to exit at the same time. The narrow ledge didn't offer much safety, but she crouched, and just at that moment something sparked inside.

Whipping around to see what it was, she saw sparks leaping from every electrical socket and appliance in the room. The carpet flamed, going up in a blaze just a second later.

Strike spun around to head for her, the flames rushing up behind him. Rora looked at the roof four feet below, measured the distance in a blink, and jumped.

Her feet chilled in the snow, but she went into a crouch and scrambled toward the wall, pinning herself to it to give Strike space to jump down. Peeking upward, she saw him come out onto the upper windowsill. But he didn't jump straight away, he pulled the window closed and did something to the outer latch, then he dropped down. The jump barely registered to him as anything more than a step.

Scooping an arm around her, he urged her to the corner near them. "Down onto the tank then to the ground," he said. "Good girl, go."

Her butt froze in the snow when she sat on the edge of the roof to dangle her feet over. Sliding down onto the top of the tank as he'd said, she got her footing and then sprang to the ground. Strike wasn't a breath behind her.

"Come on," he said, grabbing her hand to pull her around the building, tugging her arm to speed her up. The first gunshot startled her to a stop, but when she saw it was Strike who was firing at the wheels of the truck closest to them, she breathed a sigh of relief.

He pulled her to the second vehicle, opened the door and shoved her inside. "All the way across, go," he said, shoving her ass and leaping in behind her.

Speeding away from the house, he kept his focus on the road ahead and she blinked at his profile, amazed and speechless. Light out the back window made her turn and she gasped. Scrambling around to press herself against the back of the seat, Rora gaped at the view of the orange flames leaping from the lodge they'd just left.

"Strike," she whispered. "Oh my God, how did you do that?"

"I've been laying accelerant all day. My tricks do have a purpose," he said, doing a double take when he noticed what she was hugging to her chest. "Is that…"

"Opal," she said, keeping her fingers curled around the edge of the laptop as she twisted onto her knees and laid it on her lap. "Wouldn't have felt right to leave her behind."

He exhaled what might have been a vague laugh. "Get warm," he said. "Look in the back for a blanket or a shirt, anything."

"I'm not cold," she said, unable to take her eyes away from him.

He reached over and rubbed her upper arm. "You're like ice," he said. "You're shivering."

"Strike," she said, her heart so overwhelmed that she didn't feel anything but its mass dominating her chest. "You saved my life."

"We're not out of the woods yet," he said, using the dials on the dash to turn on the heat. "Literally. We've got two more miles before we reach the plane, and without headlights…"

She hadn't even noticed that they were bouncing

around off the beaten track without any light to help them find their way.

"You're brilliant," she breathed out.

She'd said it before, but tonight proved beyond any doubt that his abilities went beyond basic skills or theatrics.

"Cupcake, don't make me stop," he said. "Look for a blanket. There will be one in the back."

She didn't want to leave him, but she climbed over into the back and pulled a heavy flannel blanket from the back of the truck. Tossing it into the front, she climbed after it and wrapped it around herself, tucking her feet up against her butt when she laid down, putting her head on his thigh.

His hand rose from the wheel, unblocking his view of her. After he looked down at her, he put his hand back on the wheel, looked again, and then squirmed.

"Ro, you're touching me," he said.

She smiled and closed her eyes. "Get used to it."

No way was she moving. He might not be used to having her at this proximity, but she wasn't going anywhere, she was staying right where she was.

Focusing on the adrenaline, she didn't expect to feel his fingertips touching her forehead, but they did. Tentative though they were, they slid to her temple, and then returned to her forehead. Next time, he let a fraction more of his fingers touch her and when they reached her temple, the heel of his hand relaxed onto her head and she smiled, he was getting used to it already.

SEVENTEEN

FROM WHAT RORA could tell, they hadn't been pursued. They got into the plane and took off, but Strike hadn't relaxed even after they were in the air.

He took them into land at a different airstrip than the one they'd taken off from though she didn't realize that until they'd landed when she found that she didn't recognize anything. At first, she'd thought it was because it was dark, but Strike had taken her hand and pulled her back to the plane to stop her from wandering too far and that's when he'd told her they were in a different state.

Strike put her next to a hangar, dealt with everything, and then came back to take her hand. Rora was getting used to blindly following him and so didn't think much of the car he put her in until they were a few miles down the highway.

"Strike," she said, her eyes going left then right. "I didn't see a rental car place."

"This is Ad Hoc Rentals," he said, glancing at her. "They're up and coming, great future."

"Strike," she whined, but laughed. "You stole this car!"

He shrugged and lifted a hand to put it on the back of her head rest. "Least I didn't steal a bike," he said and nodded at her legs. "You're not wearing pants."

"And how did you explain that to the guy at the airstrip? He noticed that I was half-naked by the way."

Strike had some supplies in the plane, but not many. He'd given her a shirt and it hung almost to her knees, so she was warm enough with her hands tucked up in the sleeves. But he was right that a bike might have been too much, especially since she didn't have shoes either.

Covering her yawn with her hand that was lost in his shirt sleeve, she twisted and snuggled into the seat, tucking her feet up under her. "I told you a car was better," she said.

"You're tired," he said. "Let me put some distance between us and the plane, I'll switch out the car and then take you to a motel."

"With room service?"

Again, he turned to steal a look at her. "You're hungry? Of course you're hungry."

"I haven't really eaten today," she said. "I didn't think about it. But I skipped lunch, and breakfast with Bella was—"

"Ok, ok," he said, cupping his jaw to rub his stubble. "I can't go to a drive thru. Their security cameras will—fuck it, we'll go to the drive thru."

Leaning over the console, she folded her hands on top of his thigh. "I don't want you to get into trouble. We're in a stolen car and..." Straightening, she peeked out the windshield to see he was pulling onto the shoulder. "What are you doing?" He stopped the car and reached into the backseat. A second later, he was typing on his laptop. "Updating your TiVo?" she asked but received no response. "Strike?" A minute later, he leaned back and put the laptop in the back again. "What was that?"

He put on his blinker to merge back onto the highway. "We are now the proud owners of our very own Honda."

"You hacked the DMV?" she asked.

He shrugged. "There's no stolen report on the car yet. Cops would be crazy to take one when the owners can't prove ownership. But I've put a bug in their network, if they try to put the report in the system, it'll bounce and never stick."

"Strike, you—"

"Don't worry," he said. "I put ten K in the owners' account, and no way is this car worth ten K. This is a good day for them."

Her smile twitched before it spread. Pride welled up inside her. "You do the most despicable things and then you... fix it."

This time when he tipped his attention to her, he didn't look happy. "You're a bad influence on me."

"Because I provoked your conscience?"

"Because I knew you'd bitch at me, so I slid in a contingency to deal with that."

"Contingency," she said, settling down again and folding her hands under her head. "Is that what I do? Provoke you into contingencies?"

"You provoke something," he muttered.

Her playfulness dwindled, and her focus began to wander. He was a handsome guy, smarter than most people on the planet, ripped, and he could turn her on with a glance. And he'd saved her life. He'd saved her life.

"I remember what it was like," she murmured. "I remember every detail."

"That fades with time."

"Not about tonight," she said, fixating on a point on his door. "I remember watching my mother die, watching the blade slice through my father's chest... the terror in Markie's voice when he begged Kyan not to hurt him... I remember it all. The smell, the sticky air, the panic. I couldn't move."

"You were thirteen," he said. "You weren't supposed to stop him."

"They were dead. There was nothing but blood, soaking into the carpet, pooling on the floor, splattered on the walls and ceiling. And Kyan was... he was so happy, he turned to me with this big grin on his face and I was sure he was going to come for me and then... he crumpled. He started sobbing.

The knife fell and… I held him, Strike. We sat on the floor, surrounded by their blood, saturated by it, and I held him while he sobbed. He talked about the pain, the release, the ache… I didn't get it, but… I cried with him, Strike. I cried because he was in pain. He was. I don't know if he knew why he did what he did, but there was a part of me that felt pain for him."

Listening, he kept his hands on the wheel, but glanced at her. "He was your brother."

"He is my brother," she said. "He's rotting in jail… I don't even visit."

"Do you want to?" he asked. "Is that what you want?"

"I don't know what I want," she said. "But tonight… when I saw Benjamin fall to the floor…"

"It brought it back."

Lifting her head, she tried to figure out the root of her feelings. This wasn't about grief, though it might have been provoked by it. Rora was affected by what she'd seen in a much more profound way tonight.

"I felt what you felt… You said you didn't understand why your mother didn't take you… I didn't understand why Kyan didn't take me like he took them, and Benjamin… why didn't he take me?"

"He almost did," he said. "Or did you forget asking me for my gun?"

"I would've done it if you hadn't stopped me," she said, clarity making her sit up. "I would've, Strike."

"That's the closest you'll ever come to hurting yourself. That's it, that's your one. I've turned maintaining liberty into an artform, but that works in reverse too, Cupcake. I can have you locked up so fast your head will spin."

He seemed so certain and there was still an edge of that anger in his voice. His stepping in had saved her life, but she still didn't understand why he'd done it. As far as she knew, he felt nothing more for her tonight than he had on any of the previous nights they'd spent together.

"Strike," she said, loosening her worried lip from her teeth to locate her gumption. "What's going on with us? Are we together now?"

His slow blink took his eyes from the road to hers, but they didn't linger. "Drive thru is ahead, buckle up."

Turning into her seat, Rora put her belt on, and sat up straight. They didn't want to draw attention to themselves more than they had to. He was driving around with a half-naked woman in his car, after all. If the cops did choose to pursue them, the car would be one thing Strike could explain away with his digital magic. Her lack of clothes was a more complicated problem.

***

AFTER EATING, Strike told her to lie in the backseat to get some rest. It didn't take Rora long to fall asleep and she only briefly woke up when he picked her up to carry her somewhere. She'd thought they were going into a motel, she was wrong.

When Rora woke up, she was in the backseat of a car, but it was a different car to the one she'd fallen asleep in.

The sun blaring in all the windows took a minute to adjust to, but she eventually figured out that they were still moving. With one eye closed, she lifted her head to see that Strike was still behind the wheel, but he only had one hand on it because the other held his phone to his ear.

"Couple of weeks, that's it," Strike said into the handset. "Yeah. Yeah, man. Soon as I stop moving, it's done."

He hung up the phone and lifted his hips, presumably to put it back into his pocket. She lay still for another minute before doing her best to stretch. Then sitting up, she yawned and wriggled to the edge of the seat.

There were no headrests in this car, and the seats were lower. Rora took the opportunity this presented to press her face into the back of his neck. Rubbing her face against him, she hummed with satisfaction and tossed her arms around him to pull herself closer, opening her hands flat on his hard torso.

"Good morning, Flame," she whispered and kissed the back of his neck.

"It's the afternoon," he said, catching her wrist in a pincer of two fingers and lifting it from his torso. "And you're touching me."

"What are you going to be like when we have sex?" she asked, letting him go so she could clamber up front. "Are you a germaphobe? I'm clean, I promise. And anyway, I've been everywhere you've been for two solid weeks at least. If I've got it, you've got it already. I think if we survived the Last Resort, we can survive anything. Something tells me they don't have a professional cleaner on payroll."

"I'm not a germaphobe," he said, and she was surprised to see shades on his face. "And we're not having sex."

"Not right now, we're not," she said and scooted closer. "Where did you get the shades?"

"Glovebox," he said. "There are power bars in there if you're hungry."

"Not yet, but I would kill for a coffee," she said, then slapped a flat hand to the middle of his chest. "I didn't mean that we should kill for the coffee. I didn't mean that. That wasn't like a request, or a suggestion… or an order."

"I don't take orders from you, Cupcake, and I'll stop when I'm ready to stop."

"Wouldn't expect anything else," she said, hooking her arms onto the back of the seat and extending her legs onto the dash where she pointed her toes. "I still have all my fingers and toes. Guess a night in the snow wasn't so bad."

"You spent less than ten minutes in the snow."

"We're going to work on your ability to sympathize," she said. "Did you sleep at all?" He shook his head once. "It would be some kind of ironic if you drove off this road and killed us after what we survived last night." Pulling her feet from the dash, she crossed her legs and leaned over to put a hand on his forearm. "Do you want me to drive for a while?"

He picked her hand off him again. "You don't know where we're going."

"Does it matter?" she asked, looking at the strip of highway stretched out before them. "It's not like I can get us lost when our destination is oblivion. We're together, the zip code we're in doesn't matter." Rora wasn't really thinking about much when she caught him looking at her. "What?"

His lips parted and she noticed his tongue curled in his mouth. Eventually, he exhaled. "Ireland."

"What?"

"I was born in Ireland."

Rora gasped. "You were?" she asked, pouncing onto her knees. He nodded once. "Your parents were Irish?"

"I didn't say that. But the physical process of birth, it happened in Ireland. I was born and she died on the Emerald Isle."

Rubbing his leg, Rora let her hand push up to his inner thigh. "I always thought Irishmen were sexy."

"I don't have a birth certificate," he said. "It's true that I have no nationality. My birth wasn't registered anywhere. Ever."

This show of trust invigorated her to the point of arousal. The great and powerful Exile was handing her his past, showing her that he trusted her in a way far more intimate than any sex act could convey.

"How do you know? If there was no one there?"

Another breath in, she could tell he was uncomfortable and her stomach flipped. "My father," he said.

"You knew your father," she said, exhaling her clarity. "Oh my God, Strike."

"He was a… a super professor, genius guy… After my mom got pregnant, he withdrew from the world, most people thought he was dead. Wasn't easy to track him."

"Not for a mere mortal," she said, and bowed to trace her lips on his wrist, her breath prickling the hairs on the back of his forearm. "You found him?"

"He never claimed me. Obviously. She worked in his department, she was his subordinate." So, it wasn't like a back alley, middle-of-the-night rape. His mother had been raped by a man she knew, one she probably trusted. A revered man of superior intellect, she probably didn't see the violation coming. "He paid my grandfather a fortune to keep quiet. Old man went through that money fast, extorted more, he had an easy life. He took me from Ireland to India, Thailand, Moscow, we never stopped… Made it easier for me to kill him. I don't remember much about him beyond that."

"Did he love you?"

"The old man?" he asked and scoffed. "Nah, I spent most of my life on the street, I was looked after by neighbors, or whoever walked by… he disappeared to blow through the cash, and he'd come back to switch countries and beat me some until my father sent more dough. Rinse, repeat."

"Do you think he was punishing you for your father's crimes? He lost his daughter and maybe he wouldn't have if…"

"If I hadn't been born?"

"I didn't mean that," she said, curling her hands around his forearm to rest her head on it. "You weren't to blame for your grandfather's hatred, or your mother's death. Your father was. He did this. To all of you."

Pulling his arm out from beneath her hands, he rubbed his own thigh in a sign of discomfort with her touch and with what he was confessing. "I've never talked about any of this stuff."

"I know," she said, folding her hands in her lap. She wasn't going to push him when he was proving he'd come to her on his own. But it was obvious he'd never been able to trust anyone. He hadn't even trusted Bella enough to reveal Opal's name to her. "I'm honored you chose to confide in me and I won't ever breathe a word to anyone."

"I know," he said, glancing at her. "Smothering is still on the table."

She smiled at him and he did his best to reciprocate, but it seemed his lips just couldn't figure out what they were supposed to do. "You can always tell me anything, but… why did you choose now?"

"You were fearless last night," he said, fixating on the road. "For a girl who says she's always chased by fear, you didn't hesitate when I told you to move. I told you to jump and you jumped."

Because she trusted him, probably more than she should, given some events of their past. But it wasn't easy to accept feelings like the ones he provoked in her. Chances were, he was going through the same things she was because they weren't that different in many ways, even though there was no doubt his journey had been harder than hers. But that just meant he'd need a little more time to accept that she wasn't going anywhere.

"I don't want you to change, Strike," she said, letting him know that he didn't need to prove anything to her. "I don't need you to be anything other than what you are. I won't ever judge you for anything."

"Did you just pluck that straight out of my head?"

He must have been thinking about her judgement or about what she wanted from him. "I wish I could read your mind, Strike," she said and took a deep breath before twisting to slump against the back of the seat. "Then I would understand why I haven't gotten laid since we met."

He didn't look at her or respond, but when she peeked at him, she was sure there was a hint of a smirk on his face. He enjoyed her, in his own way, even if she didn't completely understand it.

EIGHTEEN

"YOU'RE GOING TO STAY here," Strike said when he dropped his hand from between her shoulder blades.

"I'm going to stay here," she repeated, scanning the rundown apartment he'd brought her to.

It wasn't in a block she knew, but it was in a city she recognized because it was the one their story had started in.

"That's what I just said."

Strike turned away from her and she grabbed for him, bounding around to get in front of him. "No, I mean, if I'm staying here, where are you going?"

"Business, baby," he said. "You're going to be safe here."

A toilet flushed and the door on the right opened to allow someone to come into the room. "Buddy," she said and the hulk of a guy smiled at her.

"You look real pretty in daylight."

It was barely daylight still, and she wasn't sure if he was implying she didn't look pretty in the darkness around the Last Resort, but Rora chose not to fixate on that. "Ok, settle down, Bud," Strike said, putting his hand on her back to push her toward Buddy. "Buddy has clothes and stuff for you; he went out and bought a bunch of women's things."

Buddy was about a zillion sizes bigger than her, so he didn't exactly have a model for the apparel, and she'd never seen him in anything more than jeans and leather vests, so questioned his taste level. But… ok. Some clothes would be better than nothing, Rora just hoped she didn't live to be proved wrong.

Trying on a polite smile, she didn't want to be rude. "Uh… thanks, Buddy," she said.

"Everything's set," Strike said, but he wasn't talking to her, he and Buddy were exchanging something significant through their eye contact.

"Yep," Buddy said.

Strike turned and got to the door before she caught up with him. Pushing the door with her weight, Rora tried to get in front of him again, but he kept hold of the door, so she had to battle to stop him from leaving.

"Flame," she said, giving the door a hard nudge.

"What?"

"What?" she asked, astonished that he could think he could just walk out and abandon her here. "You just… you're just going to walk out on me?"

She stumbled when he let go of the door, but he caught her with a hand between her shoulder blades and pushed her back into the room. "You're going to stay here. Buddy will look out for you. He has a lot of friends around here. You'll be safe."

Twisting around, she managed to curve herself into his body and curled her arms against his torso. "That's not what I'm worried about," she said. "What about… us?"

His brow dropped, deepening his frown further. "Don't use cards. Buddy will give you cash. Lay low. You don't exist anymore anywhere, I erased you. Everything. Kyan's little sister died in childbirth, never went to school, and was never at that crime scene. Bud will get your new IDs. This is your fresh start."

She didn't even know what to say. It wasn't fair of him to drop this on her like this, seconds before he wanted to abandon her. "Strike," she whispered.

Touching his index finger to the underside of her chin, he pushed it up. "Chin up, Cupcake."

He spun around and walked away, out the door, and then he was just... gone.

Rora didn't know what to do, she wanted to run after him, but her feet were planted to the floor, like they were lodged in concrete. She'd thought they were starting something, that they were going to be a part of each other's futures, yet all the time he'd been concocting this plan that severed all ties between them.

"No," she said and took a step forward, but Buddy caught her arm and pulled her back. Rora hadn't even realized that he was so close behind her. "Let me go, Buddy."

"You have to stay, Aurora," he said and for a big guy he managed to soften his voice quite considerably. But after a brief glance at him, she returned her focus to the door. "I tried to tell you, he doesn't exist."

But he did. He did exist and she wanted to scream it from the rooftops. Detaching himself from the world was his way of surviving. He hid from the law, kept himself closed off to protect himself and his liberty. Making sure that he had nothing to lose was his way of limiting his vulnerabilities; no one could hurt him if he had no weak spots.

But... she'd thought she was different, that somehow, they were different.

The legend lived through stories. Those who came across him in the real or digital world, told another person their story, it was exaggerated and twisted until he became an untouchable enigma. Now her story would join theirs. Except, she would never tell anyone what he'd told her. She was different. But no matter how much he confessed to her, he wouldn't accept her, he wouldn't accept them.

"I love him," she breathed out.

"Who?" Buddy asked. "There ain't no one here but you and me."

His hand slid away from her shoulder and she was left cold, alone, and deeper in grief than she ever had been before.

***

FOR TWO WEEKS, Rora stared at that door.

Buddy wasn't a bad roommate. He had a tendency to drink too much beer and belch too much, but cooking and cleaning up kept her busy. Buddy insisted that she stay in the apartment most of the time. He wouldn't let her think about getting a job or socializing beyond the times he took her into Last Resort, which she'd actually come to see as a comfort.

Although Buddy usually put her at the end of the bar while he went to shoot pool, she'd sometimes stare at the corner where she'd met Strike. She resented anyone else who ever sat there and often wanted to go scare them away just in case Strike came back and wanted his table.

He didn't.

It was evening in the apartment and she was sitting in her armchair, fixated on the front door, as she often was when she was here. He'd left her. He'd turned his back on her and walked out that door like she was nothing, like she was the kind of woman who'd just lay down to be walked over.

But the woman who walked into Last Resort that first night wasn't a pushover. The woman who'd been ready to take an insane female as a lover wasn't squeamish. The woman who'd jumped from the window of a burning building wasn't easily scared.

And damn it, he'd bought her a cupcake. That meant something whether he would say it aloud or not.

"You hungry?" Buddy asked. He was seated on the threadbare couch perpendicular to her chair. The beer in his hand was propped on the arm of the couch, his attention stuck on the TV.

"No," she murmured, letting her feet slide down from the seat.

"I feel like Chinese… or pizza… what do you think?"

"That I'm not done," she said and stood up.

He looked up at her. "What?" She started across the living room. "Where you going?"

Snagging the baseball bat that stood in the corner by the front door, she tossed it up onto her shoulder and marched out, determination in her gait. She was halfway down the stairs by the time Buddy caught up to her.

"Hey," he said. "Hey, Rora, what's going on? Why do you look all… edgy and angry like that?"

Stopping at the communal entrance, she twisted to snarl at him, "Because he's not allowed to walk away from me."

Kicking the door open, she ran down the stairs, widened her grip on the bat and swung at the windshield of the car parked on the street. "Hell!" Buddy hollered.

Smashing a headlight on the same car, she moved to the next one to swing the bat at its quarter panel. "What are you doing?" Buddy asked as car alarms began to blare. "Oh my God!"

Taking out a parking meter, she went on to smash the window of the storefront on the corner. "Yo! Bitch!" someone screamed.

But there were plenty of voices rushing toward her, all angry, all looking for a piece of her. Rora grinned and swung at the back window of another car. After pulling the bat from the hole she'd just left in that window, Rora walked out into the street, looking straight ahead, ignoring the blaring horns, not caring that she was stopping traffic.

One car screeched to a halt and she turned to narrow her eyes on the driver for getting so close to her. "Get the fuck out of the road!" the driver screamed out his window. "You crazy, bitch?"

The corner of her mouth curled, and she lifted the bat up over her head. "You bet your ass I am," she said and brought the bat down in the center of the hood.

The guy started cursing and swearing at her. He leaped out of his car, but she propped the bat on her shoulder and sashayed across to the opposite street without slowing for him.

Buddy had his work cut out holding back the crowd coming after her, baying for blood. Beating the crap out of another car, and another, she didn't slow down even when she heard the sirens blaring.

Police cars screeched down the street and stopped all around her, one even bumped onto the sidewalk, blocking her from turning the corner. She didn't even pause; she swung hard, putting her bat through the police car headlight. Half a dozen cops jumped out of three different cars, pulled their guns and demanded she drop her weapon.

Letting the bat fall from her hands, she locked her hands behind her head and smiled when a cop ran up behind her and threw her down on the hood of the cop car she'd just trashed. He grabbed her wrist to turn her hand down against her lower back.

"I was just getting warmed up," she said when he clamped the cuffs around her wrists. "Can I request a cell with a view?"

She was hauled up. The cops struggled to hold back the masses who wanted her head. Every uniform looked at her like she was insane, and she didn't doubt that she was.

Just before she was pushed down into the cop car, she saw Buddy at the edge of the group. The poor guy looked terrified, but she smiled and winked. As far as she was concerned, there wasn't a thing to worry about.

NINETEEN

"DO YOU WANT TO EXPLAIN your actions?" the first cop asked.

Turning her lips into her mouth, Rora struggled to contain her smile. Blinking her wide eyes down to the table, she touched the edge of her paper cup with the tip of her finger, resting her cuffed wrists on the tabletop.

"You're in a lot of trouble," cop two said. "You caused thousands of dollars in property damage."

"The owners will be compensated," she said, taking a drip of her water to her mouth with a fingertip.

"By you?" cop one asked. "We can see to that, if you give us your name and address."

Squeezing her lips between her teeth, she shook her head and for a flicker of a moment, she understood the seduction of insanity. It felt good to be free of all fear. The cops certainly thought she was nuts and she considered that they may be right.

Rora wouldn't give them any of her details. She had no ID on her, no fingerprints in the system. They'd demanded a DNA swab, but she refused to give one, even though she was confident that they wouldn't link her to Kyan, even if they did run her DNA.

The door to the interrogation room opened and the cops turned. They might not have been expecting anyone to interrupt, but she had.

When she saw her old friend Torres there, just inside the door, she smiled.

"Who are you?" cop one asked, leaping to his feet.

Torres flashed a badge at him and the cop looked staggered. His partner got up, amazed. "You've got yourselves quite a prize here," Torres said. Rora turned her smile down to the table. "I've got this from here."

The cops faltered like they might consider objecting to this intrusion by another agency, but one nudged the other, shoving him to the door, and they gave up the fight.

"Go," cop two said to his partner.

Torres stepped forward to let the guys past, but just before they exited, he turned and held up a hand. "Guys," he said, getting their attention. "Do me a favor, update your wills and secure your assets. Tell anyone you ever met to do the same. Friendly advice."

The cops exchanged a baffled look, but shuffled out and closed the door. Torres took something from his pocket, pressed a button and put it on the desk. "Blocks all audio and visual recordings," he said, pointing at the small device before he sat down. "No one can hear us in here, Kero. It's a neat piece of tech."

"How's your hand?" she asked, linking her fingers.

He held it up to show a shiny new scar forming and she winced. "Occupational hazard," he said and she slouched back with a shrug. "But I guess you know that what we do sometimes involves sacrificing a little blood."

"Men usually ask nicely before putting their hands up my skirt and forcing me into bed. You should think about that every time you look at your scar."

"Par for the course," he said.

She drew her eyes from him. "For you maybe. My blood you can have. My body doesn't belong to you."

"No, we both know who has ownership of that," he said. Inhaling like he was cleaning the slate, he drummed his fingers on the table, and rolled his shoulders. "Want to tell me what today was about?" Rora shrugged. "Where's your boyfriend?"

"We're in a fight."

"Does he know that?"

Smiling, she turned her eyes up to the corner. "I think he's probably figured it out by now."

"Am I going to find his fingerprints in the system here? Erasing your little mishap?"

Her smile became a grin and she flattened her forearms on the desk to pull herself upright. "He doesn't have fingerprints," she said. "And he doesn't leave evidence… but you know that, Torres, so why don't you tell me why you're here."

"You're banking on him making this go away, aren't you?" he said. Leveling her eyes on his, she was doing her best to give nothing away while making it seem that she was assessing him. "I can make this go away too." He opened his arms. "And I'm the guy here for you. Don't see him around."

No, and that had been exactly the problem. She needed him around. "Then make it go away," she said and his brow rose. "Oh, wait, let me guess, there's a catch."

"Testify," he said, leaning over the desk. "Tell us everything. You must have witnessed—"

She laughed. "Do you really think I'd roll over on him because you wipe a little property damage from my record?"

"How about inciting a riot? Aiding and abetting a felon?" he asked. "How about accessory to murder? Extortion? Fabrication of evidence? Misappropriation of funds? I could go on all day, but you get the point."

Pointing her fingernail down into the table, she peeked up at him and down before holding his focus. "Are you married, Torres? Is your mom living? Have you always craved destitution? Is poverty a fantasy of yours? How about life in a supermax?"

He exhaled a grunt of disbelief. "Are you threatening me, Kero?"

"Tit for tat," she said and eyed the device on the table. "Gathering evidence against me won't help you… For one thing, I'm going to bet your bosses aren't wild about you handing over that little DARPA toy." His hand moved over the device and her smile grew. "You want something I have."

His fingers slid away from the tech and he leaned closer. "What's the point?"

She tilted her head. "You know, there was a time that question upset me. Now I think it's just hilarious."

"We can offer you protection," he said. "A new life. A new identity. Anything you want. Money. Is that what you want? You answer the question and—"

"What?" she asked. "You'll make all my dreams come true? Only one man is capable of doing that for me and it's not you."

"What would make you turn on him?" he asked. "There must be something. Everyone has a price. Everyone."

Sucking a breath in between her teeth, she considered his statement. "I will tell you absolutely everything you want to know," she said. "I'll give you everything, every detail."

His eyes flared and she was sure he began to salivate. "What do you want?"

"Lifelong immunity," she said. "For me and for him, from every law enforcement agency on the planet… Military protection from every single criminal with a bone to pick… or you could just off them for us." He sagged back and glared at her. "Oh, and you can throw in a private island… with wi-fi, of course… In fact, if you could just transfer every cent in circulation into an account for us and allow us to figure out how it should be distributed, that would be great… And cupcakes, we want a lifelong supply of those… We want everything from the DARPA vault… and the White House, that could be our holiday home… And, we'd like—"

"Do you think he loves you?" he asked, getting her attention. "He doesn't. A woman will be loyal to the man she loves to a fault, until he screws her over. Exile will screw you over."

"I don't know anyone by that name," she said, feeling the fire of anger licking her belly again.

He banged a fist on the table. "You don't know the forces you're playing with here."

Lunging toward him, she extended her arms until her chest was pressed to the table. "I think, out of everyone in this equation, I'm the most educated," she hissed. "Don't insult me. I know the answers, all of them! All of the answers you want, I got 'em!"

"What's the point?" he asked.

She knew the answer to that question; she was the only one alive who did. "Yes."

"Who is he?"

That was another thing she knew, and a truth she was even less likely to give to anyone. "Yes," she said, sliding back into her seat.

"Where we can find him?" he asked. She averted her gaze. "Ah, not that one. Maybe I'm just a little early, you haven't reached bitter yet. Ditched you already, has he? Do you think he doesn't find comfort with other women? You're nothing special, Kero."

"You don't know what you're talking about," she said.

But he'd found her raw nerve because for the last two weeks, she'd had nothing but time to torment herself with questions about what she meant to Strike.

Rising from his seat, he rounded the table and crouched beside her, forcing himself into her eye line. "You know what I think? I think he got bored with you. I think he left you and he's not ever coming back."

"That's not true," she said, but her confidence was wavering.

He smiled and put a hand on her shoulder. "You're worth more than that, Kero," he said. "What kind of life can he offer you? A life on the run? Always moving, never settling down? You can't marry a man who doesn't exist. You'll never have children… Would you give up your natural right to be a mother just to be with a selfish man who thinks only of himself?"

Hearing him disparage Strike wasn't easy. "You don't know what he thinks of," she said. "I owe a debt that has to be paid."

"A debt?" he asked, looking into her. "You think you owe him something?"

"No," she said. "I think I asked for something, and it came with a cost, and I think I'm willing to pay that price every minute."

This guy was good at false sympathy because she didn't believe for a second that he gave a crap about her or her future. "What was the price? What did you promise him?"

Leaning down, she whispered, "To never stop fighting… and that's exactly what I'm doing."

His certainty vanished in a blink and he rose to his feet. "So that's it? You won't tell me anything? You won't save yourself or let yourself have any chance of happiness? He's worth giving up your life for?"

Shifting in her seat, she sat straighter. Finding her confidence again, she set her gaze on him. "I would put a bullet in my brain before I'd ever think about betraying my god. Who do you pray to, Torres? How many commandments have you broken?" Scanning his body, she leaned back, settling her hands on her lap. "I think you're practicing a little coveting right now."

A smile became a whisper of a laugh and he took a step back, holding up his hands in accepting surrender.

"Burke was right about you and him," he said, heading for the door. He opened it an inch and paused to toss something to the table, the cuff key. Rora didn't move to take it. "You're free to go."

She nodded once expecting him to leave. "Nice seeing you again."

Torres turned, but then twisted back to nod at the device on the table. "Oh, and by the way… that isn't mine," he said and she caught sight of his quick smile before he departed.

The bastard. Though she tried to restrain her smile, it didn't stay hidden for long. Grabbing up the key, she freed herself, took the device from the table and slid it into her cleavage. Clipping the cuffs onto her belt, she dashed from the room.

No one stopped her.

She slowed her pace in the hallway, keeping her eyes fixed straight ahead, offering a half-smirking smile to the cops and perps who watched her strut through the precinct and straight to the front door.

Just before she went out, she spun to face those she'd just left behind. And blowing them a kiss, she bobbed her brows and then burst out into the night.

TWENTY

THERE WAS ONLY ONE destination on her wish list tonight, but she took her time about getting there.

Rora wanted to be sure that she wasn't followed. Being paranoid was starting to become part of her makeup. For better or worse, Strike had had an impact on her, and she was realizing that contingencies weren't such a ridiculous notion. Course, he was her main contingency and she'd make sure he spent his life cleaning up after her if she didn't get what she wanted from him: an apology for ditching her.

The Last Resort had added a special feature for her, a notch in the underside of the door. It meant she could get access whenever she wanted it and tonight, she wanted it.

Striding through the men she'd come to be familiar with, ignoring the music and the smoke, she kept her focus on one corner. Try as she might to quell it, she did get a rush when she first saw the faint outline of Opal through the shadows.

Straightening her face, she marched over, tugging the device Torres had left with her from her cleavage. Tossing it onto the table beside his keyboard, she waited for him to stop typing before she planted her palms on the tabletop and leaned over.

"Apologize," she said.

It took half a beat, but he blinked, and his growling eyes ascended to hers. "A private island?"

"With wi-fi," she said. "Apologize."

"Keep dreaming."

Rora gritted her teeth. "Apologize."

But he had the gall to remain rigid. "Next time you get yourself into trouble, you're on your own," he mumbled, typing on Opal.

Breathing in, she spun around and examined the room. "Let's test that theory, shall we?" He grabbed her arm and she turned back to see he'd closed the laptop and was bent over the table to keep his grip on her. "Strike, honey, you're touching me."

Yanking her arm free of his grip, she made short work of getting out of the bar and into the alley.

"You're testing me," he called out and she didn't bother to turn. "Rora!"

Spinning around, she walked backwards, her arms rising at her sides. "I learned from the best," she said. "Hope you didn't forget that doohickey you gave Torres... You know, if you wanted to know if I'd roll on you, you could've waited 'til I was approached for real. You know it'll happen... Maybe we'll wait and see how that works out for you if you don't apologize for walking out on me."

Returning to her path, Rora slipped into the parking lot to head for the bike by the entrance. She tossed her leg over it just as he came around the corner.

He paused, examining her position. "Where did you get that?"

"Ad Hoc Rentals," she said, grabbing the helmet from the back.

He said nothing for a second and then blinked. "You stole it?"

She shrugged. "Guy left his keys in it. He'll never do that again."

Turning the key, she was about to click it into gear, but he marched over and turned off the engine. "Did you go to all this trouble just to walk out on me, Cupcake?"

"Doesn't feel good, does it?" she asked and pushed his hand from the key. "Get out of my way, Strike."

"No."

The pulse in her throat had to be from the beat of her heart, but the bass of it was racking her whole being. Every hair on her body rose when he edged closer and leaned in, fascinated with the pout of her lips.

Just before his met hers, she leaned away. "Apologize," she whispered.

"You're something else, Cupcake," he breathed. "You were a very bad girl."

Smacking his chest with her helmet, she persisted. "Apologize already, Strike!"

"I'm sorry, ok," he exclaimed. "I'm fucking sorry."

She smiled and hung her helmet on the handlebars. Then, curling her fingers around the edges of his jacket, she gave him responsibility for the weight of the bike. "I missed you, baby," she purred and pressed herself to him.

After breathing him in for a second, she pushed away and climbed off the bike to stride from him.

"Now where are you going?" he asked, following her progress through the parking lot.

Peeking over her shoulder, she tapped a finger on her lip and scanned around. Identifying where she wanted to go, she pointed and followed her finger, stopping next to a bike with its own custom Opal pouch. "I prefer riding bitch."

He didn't argue, just came over to join her. Getting onto the bike, he held it while she climbed on. "That's 'cause you are one," he muttered,

Rora smacked his arm with the side of her fist, but smiled. He'd come back to her. Maybe not in the most romantic way, but they were together again.

***

STRIKE RODE INTO an alley and parked the bike beneath a fire escape.

Rora let him take her inside the dilapidated industrial building and up the cracking, broken stairs. Dampness bled through the walls. There was water dripping from various places in the ceiling and weeds growing from random cracks.

But when they got to the top floor, he pulled her into a dark, but wide-open space that was a little cleaner than the rest of the place. The walls were grey, the floor the same cold concrete. The windows were covered with moss and grime, and there was a chill in the air.

There was little in the room except a mattress on the floor with a flashlight beside it and a chest behind it.

Seeking Strike, Rora turned and found him up close, glaring down into her. He'd discarded Opal at the top of the stairs and come to crowd her. Adjusting his jacket, she smoothed her hands on his tee-shirt beneath.

"If those are your bedroom eyes, we're going to have to work on those too."

"You stole that bike," he snarled, his eyes narrowing further.

"Yeah, I did," she said. "What you gonna do about it?"

Hauling her against him, he forced the air from her lungs. "You trashed all those cars."

"And took out a parking meter," she said, scratching a finger along his jaw. "And a few store windows… One guy called me crazy."

"Don't you worry about him, baby," he murmured. "Turns out he owes the IRS and stashes illegal porn."

Dropping her weight, she sagged, hissing in her arousal. "My Flame," she purred, boosting up to graze her teeth on his chin. "I knew you'd have my back."

Ripping off his jacket, he tossed it away and grabbed her arms again. "I'm gonna have all of you," he growled. "I'm done playing nice."

Need and hope and passion boiled her blood. "Say it first, Strike," she exhaled.

Holding her up, he began to walk, forcing her backward one slow step at a time. "What you want me to say now, Ro? You're naughty? You've been a bad, bad girl who better get used to misbehaving?"

"No," she said, digging her nails into his tee-shirt. "Tell me why you came back for me."

"Because you were naughty," he said, pushing her back another step.

"Not that."

His arousal was filled with pride. "You're fearless. You acted out on purpose to drag me back to you."

"Because I love you," she said and grabbed his arms before he could think about running away from her. He stopped, but didn't let her go. "There's an implied response, Strike."

Pushing her back another step, she was encouraged when his grip tightened, that meant he wasn't looking for an excuse to retreat. "I don't imply."

"Then tell me," she said. "Tell me you love me, Strike."

His eyes were still probing hers, enamored with her need. "And if I don't?"

"Tell me or love me?" she asked, pushing her nail into him. She gasped when he yanked her up higher, onto the tips of her toes, bringing their mouths closer. "We both know that you love me."

"Maybe," he murmured.

But there was no maybe about it. She tried to push up to kiss him, but he tipped his head out of the way, making her grin. "Don't tell me my daunting devil is afraid of telling little innocent me the truth."

"You're not innocent," he said. "You're corrupted, Cupcake."

Bending her knees, she leaped up onto him, forcing him to catch her with one arm under her ass. He pulled her higher and drove his other hand through her hair, trying to pull her lips to his.

"Not yet, Flame," she breathed into his mouth.

"I can take what I want from you. Don't underestimate my need. I've been holding onto it, ignoring it for too long. I'm about ready to snap and you don't want to be in my path when that happens. You know what's in my blood, what I'm capable of."

But she didn't want to stop him, just to hear the words. He might think that he was trying to warn, or threaten her, but she wasn't afraid. "Tell me the truth and we can spend the night in the darkness together."

Curling his hand around her skull, he pulled her mouth onto his, consuming her with the power of his crushing kiss.

"Aurora," he whispered when she pressed her forehead to his, breaking their kiss.

"Do you? Do you love me, Strike?"

"Yes," he said, squeezing the back of her head, pressing her face to his. "I love you, Aurora."

Relief and ecstasy filled her, bleeding from her heart to spread throughout her body. He laid her on the mattress, taking her down carefully before rising to his knees to strip her and himself of their clothes.

Threading his fingers through hers, he laid over her, pressing the backs of her hands together forcing his own palms to merge with hers. With every nuance of his kiss, he squeezed and loosened his fingers between hers, moving his hips to use the thick length of his erection to stimulate her clit.

Moaning and writhing against the pleasure of how his naked body felt on top of hers, Rora kept her legs around his body, sliding them up and down his sides, letting her feet move over and around his thighs. She wanted him inside her, wanted him like this forever, the length of him protecting, soothing and stimulating all of her.

His hips rose and she loosened her legs enough to let him angle the head of his dick against her opening. Easing forward, he was just about to enter her, but she clenched her hands around his.

"Stop," she said.

It took him a second, but he managed to recover enough to focus on her eyes. "Seriously?"

He wasn't pissed, he was panting and incredulous, she blamed him for neither. "Once we do this, that's it," she said. "You can't walk away from me ever again… and no other women."

"For either of us," he said, making her smile with his rough exhale.

"Strike," she said. "Whatever happens, however this works out... I'm not temporary."

"You're not temporary," he said.

Satisfied with his word, she was ready to be his in every way. "Then hurry up and fuck me."

Thrusting forward he filled her up and she called out, arching into him. Well, she'd asked for it and he gave it to her, all the way, hard, and long. Moving inside her, he kept his eyes on hers. They didn't kiss or talk, he just looked down into her, engulfing her with his devotion.

Time didn't matter, there was no hurry to speed their way to climax, they just enjoyed being joined, their bodies learning what would become their new normal. Coiling her legs tighter, she used his endurance, his strength, to move with him. Lifting her hips to meet his, she took him into her body and begged for his heart.

Strike bowed to kiss her, slipping his tongue between her lips, giving his trust to her. Releasing her hands from his grip, he kept kissing her when he slid them down her body to take her hips. Guiding her leg around his hip, he rose higher over her, pumping into her harder and faster.

When he pressed his thumb to her clit, she exploded and bucked up, screaming her approval. The sinister smirk on his face when she opened her eyes made her sit up to hit his chest, but he grabbed her wrist, pulling it high to steal her mouth in another kiss.

His other hand scooped around the back of her head and he directed their kiss, keeping their mouths in contact when he moved to his back and put her on top. Taking her time to enjoy the new position, Rora moved her hips, and maintained their kiss. Reaching to the back of her head, she slid his hand from her hair down her body, closing it around her breast.

He massaged her and pushed her hair from her other shoulder, gathering it into his fist and bunching it at the back of her neck. Rocking and rising, she stimulated his dick inside her, doing her best to squeeze and roll, moving herself around him, but she wanted to feel more of him. Grabbing his shoulders, she stroked his chest, his back, and down his powerful arms, unwilling to forget a second.

Drenched with the dedication of her desire, she leaned back on her next climax, gritting her teeth to try not to make too much noise, but when he held her ribs and bowed to kiss her cleavage, Rora couldn't keep his name from her lips.

Strike flipped her to her back and propelled himself into her so hard and fast that she couldn't keep up with the power of his hips moving on hers. The beating force brought her to another climax on the back of the last one. On her next, she felt the bite of his fingers gripping her hair tight, pulling her scalp with stinging force. She hissed and a burst of endorphins made her open her mouth in a scream.

Spots were dancing in front of her eyes when he released her. She flopped onto the bed. The chill of the night swept over her damp body, but she just lay there, panting in recovery, wondering what had just happened and if she'd ever be the same again.

Pressing a hand to her heart, Rora blew out a breath and lifted her head, which was at the foot of the bed, and found herself alone on the mattress. Well she had told him that she didn't want him to change, now she had to prove it.

Sitting up, she reached for her panties on the top of the pile of clothes next to the mattress. Hooking them onto her feet, she lifted her hips up to pull them on and then stretched to snag her bra.

She became aware of Strike on the other side of the bed before he sat down in the middle, against the chest that formed a kind of headboard. Smiling, she wondered if he slept that way, sitting up, not that he regularly slept.

"Didn't take you long to bring another woman to bed with us," she said, staying on her back when she threaded her arms into her bra.

"Hmm?" he asked, looking over the top of Opal, who he had propped on his drawn-up knees.

"Nothing," she said, shimmying over the bed to snag the end of her shirt.

"You're getting dressed."

She stretched her neck while trying to uncoil her shirt. "Figured I should get back to Buddy, poor guy's probably freaking by now. You should've seen the look on his face when the cops put me in the back of their car."

While she could smile about it, Buddy probably didn't find it so funny.

"Bud knows I have you," he said, his fingers moving over the keyboard.

"You didn't…" When she didn't finish, he looked over the lid of the laptop at her. "You know… hurt him, did you? It wasn't his fault. He was talking about Chinese food and I just… snapped."

He didn't assuage her concerns about Buddy's well-being. "Fixing that mess came out of your funds, Cupcake," he said and went back to typing. "I routed it through a few dummy accounts first, but your bad, you pay."

"Ok," she said, "I can accept that." Rising onto her knees, she crawled toward him and knelt facing him, dropping her lips to his shoulder. "Are we teaching me a lesson?"

Seemed while their verbal communication wasn't always up to par, they could sure show the other how they felt, and what they thought, through their actions.

"You're a quick study," he said and opened his hand. "Give me your hand."

Without hesitating, she put her hand on top of his. But when he turned it and lowered it toward Opal, she tensed and tried to pull back.

"What are you doing?" she asked, panic kicking up her heartrate again.

Her worried eyes landed on his calm ones. "Trust me," he said and she relaxed.

She gave him her trust and let him lower her fingertips to the keys. Rora expected pain and squeezed her eyes shut in anticipation of it. But there was no pain, though it took her a few seconds to recognize that her hand was on the keyboard, all the way on the keyboard, with his above it.

"She doesn't hate me anymore?" she asked, relieved and kind of overjoyed.

"She'll protect you," he said. "If you're in dire straits and I'm not around."

Rora didn't want to think too much about why he wouldn't be around and chose to keep the mood light.

"Does this mean I can check my emails when I stay over?"

Letting her go, Strike pushed her hand away from the keyboard so he could begin to type. "You never get anything except junk," he said.

"Sometimes junk is interesting," she said, sliding down to rest her head on a pillow.

"No, it's not," he said. She smiled, exhaling her disagreement. Strike stopped typing to frown down at her. "What does that noise mean?"

"It means that not all your assumptions are accurate," she said and traced a fingertip up and down his thigh. "Can I ask you something?"

"You don't answer my questions, why should I answer yours?" he asked and was already typing again.

"That's sort of what I want to ask about," she said. "There's one particular question that you've stopped asking. I think... I thought you'd come back to Buddy's for me because you didn't have your answer. Why didn't you demand I tell you after we left Wonderland?"

"I didn't hold up my end of the deal," he said. "The deal was, I get you and Benjamin out alive, and you'd answer my question... I didn't follow through."

Propping her temple on her fist, she let her hand drift between his body and his thigh. Strike caught her wrist and put her hand on her own hip, never taking his attention from Opal.

"That wasn't your fault. You couldn't have known what Benjamin planned to do."

"Did you?" he asked.

Rolling onto her back, Rora gazed up at the ceiling, running her hands up and down her stomach. "I did that day. I mean, I didn't know he planned to do it that night. But I knew he would if he felt cornered... I didn't mean to be the one to force him into it."

"Why'd you get into bed with Bella? You thought you could make her fall for you? Bella isn't wired to love that way."

"I didn't care about love," she said, tipping her head toward him. "I had to buy time. You said she'd play with me. I figured if I was sleeping with her, she wouldn't be thinking about asking the question."

"And you thought I'd be ok with it?"

"I didn't know what you'd think," she said. "You'd be a hypocrite if you had a problem with it. You'd refused to sleep with me and *were* sleeping with her."

"When was I sleeping with her?" he snapped, offense in his tone and his eyes when they jumped to hers. "I didn't fuck her in Wonderland."

Pulling herself up, she straightened an arm to take her weight. "Oh yeah? Then what was all that pretty dolly stuff about?"

He returned his focus to Opal. "She likes to play dress up and be admired," he grumbled.

Resting a hand on the back of the laptop, she eased it down. "You were kissing her when we got there," she said. "And that night I was out… I don't know what you were doing with her."

He gave her his attention to reassure her. "My relationship with Bella was ugly," he said. "Rotten through to the core… I don't want to go back there."

"I understand that," she said, appreciating his attempt at comfort when he scooped a hand around her jaw. "But you still cared for her… she wouldn't have been able to do what she did without her crew. You gave them to her."

"The guys?" he asked. "Yeah, I got them for her. I wanted out. I needed to be away from her. Her poison was too much for even me to swallow every day. But I don't know if you missed the part where I killed her whole family, I couldn't leave her alone. It was that or kill her—guess I should've just gone with the latter from the start."

"So, her crew was a substitute for your relationship?" He shrugged and tried to open Opal again, but Rora caught his hand. "Do you think she's dead?"

"I went back up there," he said. "There's not a whole lot left, but Bella… I don't know."

"You went back to Wonderland?" she asked. "When I was with Buddy? What if she'd been there? What if something had happened to you?"

"What does it matter? You were safe."

This time when he tried to open Opal, Rora took the computer away from him. After closing it and setting it on the floor with great care, she climbed over his leg to kneel between his thighs. "I can't be safe without you."

Holding his forearm between them, he pointed to the back of his wrist. "You remember the chip?" he asked and she nodded. "If I flatline for more than a minute, Opal gets a signal, and she sets off a chain of events."

"What kind of events?" she asked. "Another global financial crisis? Nuclear winter?"

"Let's just say it's my life insurance policy; good for beneficiaries, not so good for those who owe me."

Reaching past him, she gripped the top edge of the chest to lean in and kiss him. With her body suspended over his, she could enjoy the flavor of his mouth, the texture of his lips, the slick warmth of his tongue.

Strike unhooked her bra and she let go of the chest to pull it from her arms as he scooped her onto her back and lay down on top of her.

Conversation was over, business was done, now it was time to appreciate the kind of action she'd been craving since she first made eye contact with the man she planned to dedicate the rest of her life to.

TWENTY-ONE

YAWNING, Rora sat up, running her fingers through her hair. Snagging her nails on the knots caused by Strike's rough grip last night, she opened her mouth in a silent scream and winced. Smoothing a hand over it instead, Rora twisted and stretched her legs to the floor at the side of the bed.

Glancing over her shoulder, she smiled at the sleeping man lying on his front, his arm stretched out toward her. She hadn't known that love could be as deep-seated as this. Just looking at him provoked so much sentiment and such a rush of hormones that she didn't know which to process first: love or desire.

Leaning back, she brushed the back of her fingers over his temple and sighed. When his hand shot up to grab hers, she gasped. He yanked her down onto her back, then he was up in a crouch beside her with a hand locked tight around her throat.

It took him a second to process who she was, but when he did, he let go. Releasing her, he sank back to bump against the chest at the head of the bed.

Rubbing her throat, she coughed. "Every minute with you is an adventure, Flame," she croaked.

"I'm going to kill you one day," he murmured, lunging over her to grab his boxers from the floor.

"Probably," she sighed and began to gather up her own clothes.

Given his demons, she expected that he had some bad habits. Knowing what she did of his past, she guessed he'd probably picked up his routine of not sleeping through necessity because he'd lived under threat for so much of his life.

Since he was a kid, he'd trained himself to respond to danger, to expect it at every juncture. In time, she hoped he'd become accustomed to her touch and maybe then he wouldn't lash out at her every time they woke up together.

But even if he didn't, she wasn't going to be scared away. Yes, he reacted on instinct like she was going to hurt him, but as soon as he regained his senses, he always let go before doing serious damage. In fact, he'd done more to hurt her when he was conscious and awake than he ever had in slumber.

"You can't be ok with that. You know I'm capable of it."

With her clothes on her lap, she twisted to look at him. Laying a hand on his face, she ran her thumb along his lip. "There's nothing I wouldn't give up for you, Strike," she said, but he didn't look reassured. Tilting her head, she wondered. "Is Strike your real name?"

"Would you believe me if I said yes?" he said. "My mom called me Stryker, don't ask me why, I don't know. I never really had a last name, so I always just made 'em up if I needed one." Taking her clothes from her lap, he tossed them away and she thought maybe they were going to have some fun. But he pulled her onto her feet. "There's a shower downstairs, the water runs cold, but it's there, and the toilet flushes."

"Ok," she said, rotating her palm on his to link their fingers and push her body into him. When she got this close, she had to tip her head all the way back to look up at him, but she liked to feel that she was worshiping him. "Come and show me. I might get lost and I'm all naked."

"Opal would've told me if there was anyone else in the building. There are thermal sensors, which set off a silent alarm if anyone enters, and I'm sure you know not to go outside." Pulling his hand out of hers, he went around to the other side of the chest to pick up the lid. Reaching inside, he tossed her a towel and a tee-shirt. "There's soap down there."

So, no fun in the morning, she could accept that. He'd shown her a lot of attention last night, and probably needed his time alone to catch up with whatever he and Opal usually did during the nights. But that gave her the perfect opening.

Holding the fabric to her chest, she hesitated, but narrowed an eye. "Look, I… I know last night I said that I wasn't temporary."

"You're not," he said, folding his arms and hardening his glare. "You're not the only one who can cause trouble to get attention. Walking away isn't an option for you. You had your chance."

"I'm not walking away," she said, smiling and pressing her toe into the end of the mattress they'd made love on. "I just need a few days."

"To do what?"

"Just… personal stuff," she said. His chin lowered, he didn't believe her, or rather he wasn't going to give her a pass. "It's just personal."

"You're standing naked in front of me beside our spunk-stained sheets," he said.

Yeah, ok, so they weren't exactly strangers, and there was no doubt that she trusted him now. Busting up those cars and being arrested on the hope he'd fix her screw up was a pretty good indicator of how deep her faith in him ran.

"Nothing you have to worry about, Flame," she said. "That's what I mean. It's nothing bad. Just… something I have to take care of."

Spinning around, she opened her mouth to breathe in and started for the stairs. Every step brought her closer to escape. She didn't want to look like she was running but wanted to get out of there fast.

"What's the point?"

She stopped and scrunched her face in a wince. So close. "It's not about that… not directly."

But he surprised her with what he said next. "I'm not going to ask you," he said. "Never again. I don't want to know. It isn't that important to me."

Once upon a time, she'd have rejoiced to hear him say that. But now, a rush of defeat hit her, making her sag. "And therein lies a different problem," she murmured.

"What does that mean?"

Surprised to hear his voice so near, she turned around to find him standing just a couple of feet away. "Two people in the world knew the answer to that question," she said, and he searched her eyes, saying nothing. "One of them is dead."

"You think you're in danger?"

If only it was as simple as that. "I don't think it, I know it, but that's not the problem," she said. "No one's coming to kill me. Killing me would be stupid because if I'm dead, I can't answer questions."

Strike didn't seem worried about that eventuality either. "It's a small group who know about it," he said, folding his arms and tilting his head in a nod. "It's a tantalizing notion, but I can deal with that. I can handle anyone who wants to come for you."

Tensing only to release her breath in a rush, she opened her hands, letting the towel and tee-shirt fall. "It doesn't work," she cried, feeling the burden of exasperation and frustration.

"What?" he asked and then shock made his eyes widen. "Whoa, no." Putting his hands up, he shook them and backed off. "Don't talk to me about this. I don't want to know."

He tried to turn and stride away, but she darted around and put herself in front of him. "Who else can I talk to about it?" she asked, planting her hands on his chest when he tried to walk through her. "As long as it's out there, we're both in danger, because you're the only one who can fix it."

"Stop it," he said and actually put his palms to his ears. "I can't hear this."

Clutching his wrists, she used all her strength to pull them down. "I need help, Strike. I need you to have my back on this!"

Stooping to get in her face, his frown was fierce. "I don't want to hear it."

"But why?" she begged. "You were so desperate to—"

"I don't trust myself," he snapped. "I don't trust myself to make the right choice."

Her hands fell from his arms and she stared into the nothingness left in front of her when he strode past her.

"Me," she whispered. "You don't trust yourself to choose me."

He made no attempt at contrition or apology. But, he was who he was, and she'd told him not to change for her.

"Might not be what you want to hear, but it is what it is. No one will hurt you, I can guarantee you that… But don't ask me to resist temptation… I've never been very good at that," he muttered, his voice getting weaker and more grumbly from the first word to the last.

"Ok," she said, the depth of her resolve wavering while she came to terms with the fact that she really was on her own on this one.

Heading for the bed, she grabbed her clothes, ignoring the panties and choosing to pull on only the bra, shirt and pants.

"What the fuck are you doing?" he asked. "Have a shower, take your time and—"

"No," she said, pulling her hair from the back of her shirt and scooping it out of her way when she bent to put on her shoes. "I better get on the road. I'll have to ad hoc myself a vehicle and—"

He grabbed her arm and spun her around, pulling her upright. "Ro…"

Yes, she was hurt, and angry, and wanted to give him a swift kick, but there was an apology in his eyes as he gazed down at her.

"Thank you for being honest," she said. "I'll be back in a few days."

But when she moved, he pulled her back to him. "No specifics," he said. "I'll be the muscle, that's it."

"I don't need muscle for this," she said, twisting to take her arm from his hand. "I need the man I love to give me his shoulder, to offer his arm, to hold me up when I want to pick up that gun and pull the trigger."

His expression hardened to steel. "I told you, that was your one," he growled. "If you think about—"

"I'm not going to kill myself," she said. "But this is a burden I have to carry by myself. And to love me, you have to trust me."

"There's no one else I trust to keep this secret," he said. "Gallagher chose well. Even corrupted, you're purer than the rest of us."

"But for me to love you, I have to be able to trust you," she said. "And you just told me I can't."

"I told you that in Wonderland."

Clarity lifted her chin. "This isn't about me trusting you or you trusting me, both of those things are true... You have to trust yourself."

"I don't."

"Apparently," she said and sidestepped, thinking about how sad it was that he carried that burden. "I have to go."

"Wait," he said, going around her to the chest. Opening it again, he took out three things and then came back to her to hand them over. A roll of money, a set of car keys, and the switchblade he'd given her in the Last Resort parking lot.

"Is that..."

"Found it in the Wonderland debris," he said, touching the edge. "The car's on the corner; press the button and look for the lights."

"Thank you," she said, looking at the items.

He put a fingertip to her chin and pushed it up, forcing her to look at him. "Keep your chin up, Cupcake."

She nodded and accepted his kiss when he bowed to give it. They were never going to be without their issues, but that didn't change her commitment to him. This wouldn't be the last time that they'd come at an issue from opposing sides, and it would take a lot more than that to make her refuse his kiss.

TWENTY-TWO

IT TOOK HER TWO DAYS to get to Benjamin's apartment.

If she'd have been able to fly, it would've been quicker, but without ID, she couldn't get a ticket. And it wouldn't be a good idea for her to go traipsing through an airport full of cameras either.

Rora got over her tension a hundred miles from the room she'd left Strike in, and that's when she began to enjoy the trip. Getting away from everything gave her a chance to reflect on what she'd been through.

Losing Benjamin was difficult to adjust to. He'd been missing for six months, and in many ways, it felt like he was still missing. Seeing him put a bullet in his own head was so surreal that even when she replayed events as she remembered them, it felt like she was watching a nightmare, not recalling reality.

She spent one night in a hotel and drove the whole second day. It was night when she pulled into the parking lot behind Benjamin's apartment. Putting the car in park, she leaned forward and looked up at the building.

Great idea, Rora, she thought to herself. Coming here seemed simple in theory, but in practice, it was a different ballgame.

Closing her eyes, she steeled herself, telling herself that she was strong enough to do this. Climbing out of the car, full of determination, she checked her jacket pocket for the switchblade. Squeezing it tight as she went into the building and started to ascend the stairs, she knew she was strong enough to face whatever she had to.

Benjamin's apartment key was hidden beneath the plant at the end of the corridor, she retrieved it and unlocked the door ready to storm in and do whatever was necessary to get in and out fast. Turned out that wouldn't be a problem.

Rora didn't expect to see the sight that faced her. The apartment was completely empty. There wasn't a speck of dust, let alone an item of furniture or a picture on the wall.

Turning on the spot, she couldn't take it in.

Benjamin owned the apartment. It belonged to him. It wasn't a rental. There was no landlord to come in and clear the place. His mortgage was paid to the bank and there was plenty of money in his account to cover his bills, she'd kept on top of that for him, expecting he'd be returning to his life as soon as she found him.

Shaking herself to her senses, she ran through the apartment, but found only blank white walls and hardwood floors. Someone had gone to great lengths to get what they wanted. Someone ransacking the place she might understand, taking paperwork and trinkets maybe. But did they need to take his clothes and his pictures? This was awful, it was like he'd been erased from existence.

Getting out of the apartment when she felt like her lungs were getting smaller, she fell against the hallway wall and breathed out.

Strike's assertion that the group who knew the secret was small might still be true. But that group was more determined than she'd given them credit for.

But all wasn't lost.

Shoving off the wall, she went back to the stairwell. Instead of going down, she went up. Ascending all the way to the roof level, she checked the light fitting on the internal wall, but it was above her head, out of her reach. Turning left and right, she couldn't find anything to stand on. There was no way for her to get up there on her own.

Balling her fists, she cursed the air. This could be crucial and she hadn't realized that she was on a clock. These people, whoever they were, they were ahead of her.

Taking strength from Strike, she told herself to calm down and not to be discouraged. What had happened was in the past, she had to focus on the future and that meant she needed a plan.

Running down the stairs as fast as she could, she flew out of the building and ran across the parking lot. Fumbling with her car keys, she got the car unlocked and dropped into the driving seat to take a breath and rub her face with both hands.

Ok, she regrouped and tried to stay calm because freaking out would get her nowhere. She needed height; a ladder or a box, anything that would get her to that light fitting. Blowing out her adrenaline, she put the car into gear and looked straight ahead with her hand on the key. There on the dash on the other side of the steering wheel was... a cupcake.

Her mouth fell open.

Thrusting the car out of gear, she leaped out of the vehicle, twisting left and right to look around the parking lot.

"Flame!" she called out and stopped when she saw a figure step out of the shadow next to the back door she'd just come through. Triumph made her rush across the asphalt to get to him.

"Baby, I—"

Grabbing his hand, she didn't slow down and rushed back into the building. "I need you."

"Babe, the apartment is empty," he said, following her up the stairs as she ran up them, pulling him along. "Didn't you go in?"

"I should be surprised that you got here before me," she said, passing Benjamin's floor. "But I'm not."

"Where are we going?"

Taking him all the way to the top, she yanked him over to the light fitting and pointed up. "Can you reach up there? At the top, there's a box behind it."

He frowned, but stepped forward to feel behind the light. All the air rushed from her body when he took the palm-sized black box down. "Oh, thank god," she said, grabbing it from him to clutch it to her chest.

"What is that?"

She put in the combination and peeked inside. "You don't want to know."

"It's not…"

Glancing up at him, she snapped it shut and grinned. "No, not that. This is mine."

"Naked pictures?" he said and tried to take it from her, but she stuck it in her pocket.

Taking his hand again, she spun him around to pull him back down the stairs. "You better have assumed it was naked pictures of me," she said over her shoulder.

"Well I wouldn't want them of Gallagher. I've got a dick of my own if I want to look at one."

"I've got an ass, but I still prefer looking at yours," she said and he yanked her back, jolting her to a stop.

His glower made her smile. "Did you just flirt with me?"

So, she could sleep with him and love him, but she couldn't flirt with him? Maybe he didn't like it on principle, it did involve implication.

But Rora loved teasing him too much to just let it go. "What? You have a nice ass, baby. It's a compliment."

"We're not safe here, anyone could be watching. A bullet could come from anywhere."

Putting a foot on the stair he was on, she pushed to her tiptoe to whisper. "Then I guess now's the last chance I might have to tell you. I'm in love with your ass, your abs, your dick. I love your body, Flame… I love every inch of you, even that frustrating mind and stubborn glare."

Swooping his arms around her, he grabbed her ass in both hands and spun to pin her against the wall. "I stalked you here. You didn't have a fucking clue," he said, opening his mouth to tempt hers, but when her lips parted, he kept his mouth a whisper away, tempting, teasing, only to disappoint and hold back. "I spent the night in your motel room watching you sleep."

"I'm flattered," she said.

"I could've slit your throat."

"I don't care if you don't trust yourself, baby. I trust you." Stealing her mouth, he forced his kiss hard onto hers causing her to moan and grab for his neck, digging her nails into him beneath the collar of his jacket. "You'll always choose me, Strike... I know you will."

"Motel room's on me tonight."

The guy who never slept wanted to get a motel room? "You got one already?"

He nodded. "Bed's right there."

Her smart smile told him that she knew exactly why he'd planned ahead. "Cocky for a stalker," she said, stroking his face with the length of her fingers. "What if I'd called the cops?"

His mouth slanted. "You've got a kinky idea of foreplay, baby. But it works for me."

"We have to get across town first," she said. "Do you think you can take care of the research department's security? My codes will work, but I don't know if they should know we're there... and there are cameras—"

He kissed her. "What would you do without me, Cupcake?"

Putting her back on her feet, he took her hand to take her down the final flight of stairs. "Oh, I don't know, live an honest, danger-free life."

"You're welcome," Strike said, kissing the back of her hand before nudging her toward the passenger side of the car.

The key was still in the ignition, so he got them underway and she nabbed her cupcake from the dash to tear pieces off for both her and Strike to share the sweet treat.

"Don't you have a car?" she asked. "No, wait, let me guess. You ad hoc'd one." He didn't respond, but that was enough of an answer for her. "Will we need to swing by the motel for Opal? It's not like you to leave her alone anywhere."

Tipping his head back, he nodded to the rear of the car. Twisting to look into the backseat, she was surprised to see Opal there. "You put Opal in the car with my cupcake?" she asked. "How did you know I'd… why didn't you just leave yourself in the car?"

"You know I like to position myself to make a quick exit."

Putting the laptop in the car was a sign he trusted her, and she wasn't going to let that slip by without pointing it out to her love. "But you left Opal with me?"

"You like the ladies," he said.

While she smirked, he kept a straight face. The streets weren't too busy, but there were people in the more built-up part of town, going to dinner and out to bars and clubs. People were going about their lives oblivious to the kind of danger that was around them.

Rora tried to remember the last time she'd been on a date or the last time she'd been oblivious to life without tragedy or drama. Neither coincided, she'd lived with both tragedy and drama since Kyan's crime. But it had been potent in her life again over the last six months, since Benjamin was taken.

"Do you think I should tell anyone that he's gone?" she asked, watching the world go by.

"Gallagher? He didn't have family, did he?"

"He and his ex-wife, Leandra, had a daughter," she said. "But the little one died when she was six. He said she was the best and worst thing that ever happened to him, a blessing and a curse. It was just a sad accident—"

"She drowned in the pool, I know."

Course he did. Sucking it up, Rora made herself smile though she didn't really feel like it, and slid toward him. "I'm sorry. I know you don't like backstory."

"What I wanna know is why you never told me you were with him."

Surprised by the thread of either anger or accusation in his voice, Rora didn't like that he believed she'd lied to him. "I wasn't," she said. "When he went missing—"

"Before that."

Turned out the Black Jewel liked to cause drama, though that wasn't the worst of her crimes. There could be no other reason Bella would bring up Rora's previous relationship except to torment Strike.

"Bella told you that—"

"I saw you together, Ro," he said, his hands sliding further around the steering wheel. "I saw the way he looked at you. I know what it's like to feel that way about you; I'm just better at hiding it than he was." Her gaze drifted back to the side window. "You dumped him, didn't you?"

And her guilt about that had been difficult to live with before he'd taken his life for such a noble cause, now that Benjamin was gone, she'd never be able to convey how sorry she was for hurting him like she had.

Rora sighed. "It was too complicated. He was my boss and—"

"Yeah, 'cause what we've got going is way less complicated than that," he said. "You don't give up on a guy if you've decided to be with him. You make excuses for him, and accept everything there is about him, even if good sense should tell you to run."

Squinting at his profile, she licked her lips. "Are we talking about Benjamin now or you?"

He raised his brows at her and then looked back at the road. "We're talking about Gallagher. Our whatever is still on. But you dumped him. I want to know why."

"Don't worry," she said. "You won't make the same mistake he did."

"You know I don't give a damn about making mistakes. You said you didn't want me to change, I take you at your word... But you being cagey like this intrigues me. Now you've gotta tell me."

Rora could feel him stealing glances at her. In this enclosed car, she couldn't run away or make excuses.

Instead, she beamed at him and slapped a hand onto his leg. "Want head?" But he wasn't going to fall for that and she'd known he wouldn't. She groaned. "If I tell you the truth, you'll think I'm a horrible person."

"You've seen me break bones for kicks," he said. "My right to judge anyone else's choices went out the window years ago, decades ago."

She hadn't expected that he would be so disgusted or offended that he'd throw her out onto the sidewalk, but she didn't like to admit that the reason wasn't dramatic or due to anything Benjamin had done.

"It makes me sound like a horrible person to say it out loud."

"He was shit in bed?"

"No!" she exclaimed. "God, no! You're the second person to say that to me and it's not true. He was perfectly sweet… maybe a bit too gentle sometimes, but that's ok, every guy is different."

"Then what was it?" he asked. "You know I won't stop until—"

"He was too normal," she said. He took a second to think about it, his scowl growing more intense as the seconds passed. "It sounds horrible because he was an incredible guy. He was so passionate, especially about his work, he would just light up when he talked about it… But the truth was, I was most in love with him when we weren't talking."

"So when you were fucking?"

"No," she said. "Sometimes he did talk to me in bed, and…"

A private smile warmed her lips; she didn't acknowledge Strike's double-take.

"Ok, get that look off your face. I can't kill the guy twice… but I can piss on his memory if you don't stop thinking whatever you're thinking right now… Dirty talk?"

"It wasn't dirty," she said, twisting to face him, though she didn't really look at him, she was looking past him, out his side window. "He would be romantic… Not about me, but he'd talk about the sky and the stars and—"

"I'm falling asleep already. You're telling me you came with that guy? I don't believe it. Who else said he was shit in bed?"

"Bella," she said, and curled her legs under her. "I guess she didn't really say that he was shit, she used the word peculiar."

Deadpan, it was obvious Strike wasn't enjoying this conversation, but he'd been the one to start it. "To Bella, that means shit," he said. "But if he talked about the stars with her, she'd probably have laughed in his face."

"It wasn't funny, he was being sweet and I'd never been with a sweet guy before, not like him. But he could be passionate too… When he worked, I could sit across the room and watch him for hours, the way his expression changed, the speed of his fingers, the way he'd stop to ponder… I was… mesmerized. He'd get so excited about his work, it would be infectious. He'd talk at a thousand miles a minute and I would just sit there, taking it all in."

"He was obsessive," he said. "It's a trait of those with superior intellect."

Which would include Strike too, the two men were the same in that way. She exhaled. "But the… other stuff… Setting the alarm, going to the same deli every day for lunch, planning to go to the fair at the weekend… He wanted normal. He talked about houses and cars and kids and I… I started to have panic attacks. I didn't want suburban; he did. Our relationship became routine, brushing our teeth, talking about the latest budget report, then ten minutes in missionary twice a week, and… We had this fight one morning…"

"About what?"

"Him leaving his damp towel on the bed," she said and exhaled a laugh, rubbing her face because it was such a ludicrous memory to stick in her head as significant. "It wouldn't have registered, I guess, if he'd just moved it, but he apologized… He apologized. It was so… normal… and he was so sissy about it. He didn't move it or tell me to go to hell, he groveled. He wouldn't let it go. I was this nagging wife and he was the kowtowed husband and I just froze, I knew I couldn't do it anymore."

They rode in silence for a minute and she was replaying those times, numb to what had ultimately happened to Benjamin. It was difficult for her to connect the two events; such normality to such tragedy.

"Twice a week?" Strike asked.

Snapping from her daze, they made eye contact for a second when he took his focus from the road, probably trying to stop her from dropping into the darkness of grief.

"It's funny," she said. "Bella had you and I had him, and then we switched… Guess she wasn't wrong about us being an intimate foursome…" Benjamin was her past, and she had her future beside her. "If we'd had sex before going to Wonderland, you and me I mean… Would you have joined us in bed when Bella drugged me, or that last day?"

"Drugs, maybe," he said. "But not on the last day."

Trying to figure that out, she rested an elbow on the back of the chair. "Why not on the last day?"

"But you'd be ok with me doing you while you were drugged?" he said, glancing at her like it was ridiculous, which it kind of was.

Maybe she hadn't conveyed her reaction in the right way. "I guess if we'd done it before, like now, we're actually together, there's implied consent. I don't think I'd want you to drug me on a regular basis, but if we were in peril, in a life or death situation and you had to, then I wouldn't judge you for it."

He smirked and dropped a hand from the wheel to touch her knee for a second. "I can't wait to see what that situation will look like. What the hell's gonna happen to us that it will be life or death for me to screw you while you're unconscious?"

Punching his shoulder, she laughed. "You know what I mean… If Bella had held a gun to your head and told you to do it or she'd shoot, I don't know."

He might not be a smiler, but he was definitely amused by her. "Love the imagination, Cupcake."

"Tell me," she said, curving a hand over his bicep. "Why not the last day?"

"I could see it in your face that you didn't want to be there," he said. "I don't know how Bella didn't know it."

"Because she doesn't know me like you do," she said. "You're against rape, aren't you? Because of your mom."

His shoulders rose and fell. "I don't have a lot of morals, you've seen that for yourself. But it's the one thing I won't do under any circumstances."

He'd picked on her for elevating one scenario over another, yet his answer made just as little sense. "Wouldn't someone say that a drugged person didn't want to have sex? Why is one different to the other?"

"I'd have kicked Bella out when you were drugged, I wouldn't have shared you with her."

Rora would've appreciated that. Waking up in bed alone with Bella was a horror until she knew Strike was there keeping an eye on things. So, if he'd kicked Bella out and Rora had woken up with him... well, it wasn't like she'd never woken up with him before. That would have definitely been less of a violation, even if he had been naked like Bella was.

"So, it would've been just you and me, which makes a difference because..." she asked, opening her mouth and bobbing her head to goad him into explaining.

"You were hot for me," he said. "You didn't want to be in bed, in your underwear, under Bella... But if I'd been the one on top of you, kissing you... touching you..."

Boosting herself over the console, she kissed his cheek and rubbed the back of his neck. "I love you, Flame," she whispered.

He stopped at a light and turned to kiss her. "You're the one who wanted to go across town and skip the motel. Don't get frisky."

"Not skip it, delay it," she said, opening her mouth on his cheekbone. "And if we do this now, we don't have to get up in the morning. We can stay in bed all day if you want."

"I've got to get on the road back to town tomorrow," he said.

Though she didn't mean to whine, she was disappointed. "Why?"

"Business."

She waited for him to elaborate but got nothing. So Rora tried to prompt him with a poke in the ribs. "Strike?"

He glanced to her. "What? We don't have to tell each other everything." But there was enough of a smirk on his face that she took his statement as a joke. Catching his earlobe in her teeth, she bit hard, though not hard enough to draw blood, and sat back on her feet. "You've got a thing for biting, baby. We're gonna explore that later."

Later. In the motel room, when they were alone and in bed, safe and warm together, open to enjoying each other. She still didn't understand why he hadn't wanted to have sex before they did or why Bella had flipped out so dramatically when she learned that she and Strike hadn't slept together.

But they were nearly at the research building, so those questions would have to wait until another time.

TWENTY-THREE

THROWING THE MOTEL room door out of her way, Rora tipped her head back and screamed as she strode in. "How can they do it?" she shouted to the heavens, holding up her hands. "How can they get away with erasing a man's life like that?"

Spinning around, she watched Strike come in and close the motel room door behind himself. He put Opal on a side table and took off his jacket. "You're angry."

"You're damn right I'm angry!"

Turned out that going to her and Benjamin's old workplace was a useless exercise. The building had been torched. Literally. They'd driven around the corner onto the block and seen a dozen firetrucks sprawled across the complex tackling the fire that engulfed the ten-story building.

"Might have been an accident," he said, cool as always.

Glaring at him, she tore her own jacket from her body and pulled her top up over her head to throw it away too. Everything was annoying her and making her feel itchy and claustrophobic; she hadn't known it was possible to be so riled with frustration.

"There's no way it's a coincidence," she said.

He shrugged. "There were other things in that building."

He came to her and laid his hands on her hips. Rora didn't know if he was trying to comfort her with his touch or enflame her with his nonchalance.

Snatching the hem of his tee-shirt, she tugged it up. "Take this off," she said, and he helped her pull it over his head.

Closing her wide mouth on his chest, she sucked and licked, digging her teeth into his pec and her nails into his shoulders.

Strike growled. "Like that, is it?"

Planting his hands on either side of her face, he thrust her head back, pushing it so far so fast that pain shot through her neck. He bowed, kissed her hard and then bit her lip. Pulling her bra from her body, he didn't worry about clasps or decency; just kept kissing her while he tore it off.

Turning in circles as they fought for dominance on the way to the bed, they shed their clothes and were naked when he snatched her hips and threw her down onto the mattress.

Seizing her knees, he forced her legs open and mounted the bed between them. His grasp on her breast was so harsh that it bruised, firing her heart into overdrive. Yes, this was what she needed, pleasure, pain, him, here, now.

She scratched her nails down his back in response to his bite on her nipple. Inflicting that pain caused him to rear up to drive his tongue into her mouth. He needed her, but she needed him more. Rora fed off the desire burning from his being and coiled her legs around his thighs.

But when she tensed to pull him forward, he stole her ankles, pulling them away from him and flipping her over onto her front. Landing on top of her, the weight of his body made it difficult for her to breathe.

Gathering her hair away from her cheek, he pulled it hard, forcing her profile down into the bed. Laying his cheek on hers, he rubbed his scathing stubble into her softer skin. It stung, making her pant and fumble for him, but he captured her wrists and slammed them to the bed on either side of her head.

"You angry, baby?" he mumbled into her ear. "Are you?"

Bringing his mouth to hers, she did her best to turn and meet the fervor of his tongue kiss, but in her position, it was difficult to seal their mouths.

"Yes," she panted when he licked his way around to her ear. "I'm angry."

"Good," he purred.

Wriggling beneath him, she needed to take a deep breath, but enjoyed being at his mercy, pinned beneath his weight. He drove a knee between her thighs and rose, grabbing a handful of her hair to yank her up.

Instinct made her hands go to his, the knot of his fist embedded in her hair made her scalp scream. But her grip couldn't loosen his. He pulled her up high on her knees and knelt behind her, one leg between hers and the other on the outside.

She yelped when he tugged hard, forcing her head around so he could growl in her ear. "You think you're angry now? I'm gonna fuck you, and you're not gonna come, and you're gonna be pissed as hell when I'm done using you."

Trying to pull forward, she cried when he yanked her back, forcing her spine to collide with his chest. "Strike," she said, but the word was lost when he thrust her forward, pushing her face into the mattress as he pushed her legs further apart to get between them.

His fist stayed in her hair, holding her down, and then he slammed into her from behind, his dick pushing all the way into her pussy in one hard thrust. Calling out with an open mouth, Rora was held immobile under his hold on her hair.

With his other hand on her hip, he pulled her back to meet every advance. Her belly felt each push, the deep impact of his dick hitting her so far inside. "Strike," she panted his name, clenching her thighs to keep her hips up and her core tight to give all the resistance she could to his hard thrusts.

He let go of her hip and spanked her, maybe for saying his name, maybe to piss her off, didn't matter. The harsh force of his hand on her ass tossed her into the oblivion of an orgasm so powerful that her body spasmed around him and slowed his pace.

After spanking her again, he pushed into her. "I told you not to do that," he growled and fired into her faster again.

Forcing her pussy to take every inch of him, he leaned back, angling her head from the mattress so her chin rested on it.

His growl started low and got louder until he cried out and emptied himself into her before shoving her forward onto her face.

Boneless and panting, she stayed still for a score of seconds. She was sweating and exhausted and sore everywhere. Slowly rolling onto her back, she saw Strike standing next to the bed looking down at her.

For a full minute, they just looked at each other, the burning intensity of their eyes exchanging defiance.

Opening his hands, he let his arms rise a foot from his body and took two steps back. "I'm yours," he said. "Use me. Punish me. Hate me."

But she didn't hate him. She couldn't hate him. He didn't deserve to be punished. Rora hadn't said no. She hadn't fought to get away. She hadn't told him to stop. She didn't want him to.

What he'd done… taking control of her, holding her down, filling her with all of him… It was exactly what she'd needed to expel her frustration. He'd given her what she needed.

She wasn't angry anymore. With him in control, she was… free.

Taking time to balance her weight on her shaking arms, Rora trembled as she sat up. Twisted her legs to one side, she let her arms hold her up at the other. Adrenaline and endorphins were still pulsing through her enlivened body. Curving each leg off the bed, she managed to get herself onto her feet.

Then with her eyes on his, one careful step followed another until her upright body was parallel to his. Again, they just looked into each other. Rora wished she could see into his mind. What did he expect her to do? Hurt him? Hit him? Cut him?

His anticipation was probably as intense as her love and that was all she had now, standing in front of the man who gave her what she needed. Love. When she lifted her hands, he inhaled, just a tiny sign that he might be bracing to absorb whatever came next.

But instead of lashing out, she laid both hands on his cheeks and rose to her tiptoes, pulling him down to let their lips just brush each other.

"I love you, Strike," she said, sliding her hands from his face around to the back of his neck. "I love you." Grabbing her ribs beneath her arms, he pushed her back an inch and peered into her like he didn't understand. "You give me everything I need. You are all I need… I'm not angry anymore."

"Why?"

He must have been sure that she was going to unleash fury on him, and he just didn't get why she hadn't or maybe he didn't understand why she loved him.

"I don't have to be angry when I'm with you. I don't have to be angry or afraid. Whatever this is, we'll figure it out. You make me strong, Strike. You make me invincible because you'll always be there to scare the demons into their holes, to clear my path home… to you. You're my home, Strike."

"Death's no obstacle to the devil," he murmured, pushing her hair away from her arm, sending it tickling down her spine.

Rora pulled him down for another kiss. "There isn't anywhere you can go that I won't follow."

TWENTY-FOUR

"WHAT YOU GOT there?" Strike asked, coming toward her across the convenience store parking lot.

Given that he didn't need to sleep, he'd refused to stay in another motel the previous night and instead, had driven while she slept. Not even the promise of sex could dissuade him from getting back to town for his business.

Rora was leaning against the hood of their car, her ankles crossed, her switchblade open. She held the end of the handle between two fingertips, dangling it in front of her to let it swing left to right. She nodded past him and he turned to see the group of gangbangers on the corner.

"They bothering you?" he asked and tossed her a bag of chips. "Get in the car."

He turned around to start toward the gang. She threw the chips and knife onto the front seat of the car through the open window and had to run fast to get hold of his arm to stop him from going over to confront the group.

Rora laughed. "You don't have to break the arm of every guy who makes me uncomfortable," she said, boosting up to kiss his jaw.

"Says who?"

"Let's go," she said. Strike gave her a water bottle and took her hand to start back toward the car. "I've got this weird creepy feeling… don't you feel it? Like we're being watched."

"You're paranoid, Cupcake," he said.

"Where is my cupcake?"

The reminder of the request she'd made before he went into the store made them both stop. But before he could respond, sounds shattered the air; a pop preceded an ominous whizz.

Grabbing her head, Strike shoved her down into a crouch and pushed her toward the car. Keeping his grip around the back of her skull, he used his body to shield hers while hurrying her forward. Another pop. Another one. Strike got them around the vehicle and pushed her to the ground beside the wheel.

"Not so paranoid now, huh?" she panted. "The gangbangers?"

Rora hoped that maybe this was just an unfortunate coincidence.

Strike shook his head. "One's on the sidewalk, the others are gone."

She grabbed for him when he began to crawl toward the car door. "Where are you going?" she hissed. "There's a sniper out there."

"That's not a sniper," he said. "Not a professional. If it was, we'd both be dead already."

"You don't know that," she said, pulling on his tee-shirt.

"I do," he said, peeking up through the window above him. "There's a guy I know who could line that up to take both of us out with one shot… and he's the only one anyone would send after me."

This was like nothing to him, his awareness was definitely switched on, but he wasn't even really fazed that someone was shooting at them. Someone was shooting at them! "What?" she asked, exasperated by the casual insight. "Why?"

"He's the best," Strike said and pulled her hand from his shirt.

But Rora didn't share his confidence. "Maybe he's out there," she said, falling onto her hands and knees. "Maybe he just missed."

He shook his head. "Raven doesn't miss," he said. "I've crossed paths with his best friend enough that he'd give me a heads up if there was a hit out on me… probably. We're in a similar line of work… kind of."

Opening the door, he leaned inside. She heard the glovebox open and then he closed the door over. With a gun in his hands, he checked the clip and then put a hand on her shoulder.

"Strike."

"Stay low, back up a bit," he said and she shuffled backward to let him move forward. As soon as he could, he peeked up over the hood and almost immediately a gunshot echoed.

To her horror, he didn't immediately duck down, he stayed up there in his crouch until there was a second shot.

"Strike," she said, grabbing for him to try pulling him down. "Stay down would you, please? I like your head on your shoulders."

"Two shooters," he said, coming back to her level. When he moved to rise again, she grabbed him, begging him with her gaze to stay down. He took her hand from his shirt again. "This will be over in three seconds."

"What?"

But he was already up on his feet with the gun extended in front of him. He fired off two shots without blinking and then let his arms relax.

He scanned the area, then offered her a hand. "What are you doing down there?" he said. Rora gave him her hand and he pulled her onto her feet. "Get in the car."

He tried to hand her the gun, but she pushed it back to him. "You might need it."

"They're dead, baby."

Panic was making her pulse erratic; she couldn't believe he was so calm. "You said there were two of them."

"Yeah, and I fired two shots."

Giving her the gun, he urged her toward the side door and went past her to skirt the hood. Rora was still blinking in shock when he came marching back a minute later. His expression was set in a tight scowl, his jaw working like he was full of fury.

"Get in the car," he barked.

"But, I—"

"Get in the goddamn, motherfucking car, Aurora," he snapped and tore open his own door to get inside.

Her ass had barely touched the leather before he was skidding out of the parking lot. The thump of her heart in her chest was nothing to the heat of anger radiating from the man at her side.

"Strike," she said, reaching over to touch his forearm.

He snatched it away. "Don't," he growled. "Say nothing."

"But… where are we going?"

"To visit an old friend."

***

HIS MOOD DIDN'T improve on their journey back to the city. It took another three hours for them to get there, though it probably should've taken five, but Strike didn't care much about speed limits at the best of times. When he was this mad, she doubted that he cared about anything.

They drove to a decent part of town, pulled up at the curb at a steep angle without caring about finesse, and slammed out of the car.

Rora had to run to catch up with him after he went inside what appeared to be a fairly up-scale apartment building. He took the stairs two at a time and went all the way to the top then marched straight along to the door at the end.

Planting a hand on the door frame, he used the side of his other fist to bang on the door. A second later, the door opened, but Strike didn't let it get more than an inch before he flung it out of his way and stormed inside.

"Strike!" Rora called and hurried along the corridor to catch him.

He was inside a beautiful apartment that had walnut floors and an internal balcony, but that wasn't the focus of her view. Rora was horrified to see that Strike was holding a tiny woman, even smaller than Rora was, by the upper arms, shaking her with his fury.

"Where is he?" Strike growled.

"I—"

"Shula, I'll rip your fucking throat out. I swear to God I will."

Rora rushed up beside him and tried to pull him off, but Strike thrust an arm out, pushing her away. She was going to run back into the fray with her nails out until she caught sight of the woman's face. The stranger wasn't afraid. Not one bit. She was surprised, that much was clear. But afraid? No, not so much.

"Try it," Shula said. "It's been a long time since we trained together, Strike."

Strike pulled her higher. "Don't fuck with me, Silk. Where is he?"

"Not here, obviously," Shula said. "You know he saw you walk in here."

"Good. I can't fucking wait to take him apart," Strike said, letting go of the woman to take off his jacket. "Tell me he's on his way."

Marching into the corner, he opened a long wooden box that stood on a cabinet. "I doubt it," Shula called out. Rora could only see Strike's back and wondered what he was doing. She almost missed the way Shula was eyeing her. "He doesn't miss you like I do, and he'll stupidly think I might be safe with you."

"You are fucking safe," Strike said, turning around to face them. "Until he gets here."

Rora gasped when she saw him adjusting knuckledusters on his hands. "What the hell do you think you're going to do?" she asked, rushing over to stand in front of Shula.

The woman exhaled a sound of amusement and strode around her and over to Strike. "I should charge you storage for those," Shula said and folded her arms. "You know you can't fight him. He'll kill you."

Strike sneered. "He's already tried that once today, didn't work out."

Some of Shula's ease disappeared when she frowned. After a second, she shook her head. "No," she said. "He wouldn't."

Taking one set of the brass knuckles off, Strike put them in his pocket and took out his phone. "I executed two of his slaves today, they'd say different."

Shula's hand went to her mouth. "Oh my God, Strike, you didn't! It wasn't—"

"None of his precious high council," he said and turned the phone to Shula who looked at it. "Recognize them? Tell me they're not X."

She breathed out and put a hand over the screen to push it down. "I don't know what happened. It's a mistake. Thane would never come for you."

"No, it's not a mistake," Strike said. "It's the price of doing business."

Although she tried to appear calm, there was a new kind of urgency in Shula's tone. "Listen to me, he would never come for you. I know you've had your differences, but he would never—"

"I wasn't the target," he said. "Your boyfriend's an idiot, but he's not a fool."

"He's none of those things," Shula said, moving her hands onto her hips. "He's not a fool, or an idiot… or my boyfriend."

Taken aback, Strike actually took a reverse step. Rora was just watching the pair from the other side of the room, but even she was shocked, but only because Strike's whole expression opened. She'd never seen him look so stunned.

"Shu—"

"Don't, ok?" Shula said, holding up a hand. "It just happened and I'm still… adjusting."

"And you didn't call me to come rip off his limbs because…"

"He's one of your oldest friends," Shula said. "Because Emeritus would hang us all by the neck… because he did nothing wrong… and because you're never in the country."

Shula turned to walk away from him. Dropping onto the couch in a slouch, she let her head fall into her hands. Rora didn't really know what to do; this woman was obviously tired, and probably heartbroken if she'd just broken up with her boyfriend. She looked to Strike for direction, but his focus stayed on Shula.

"This is about Lawrence," Strike said.

Shula let out a burst of laughter and lifted her head, letting her hands flop down between her knees. "How the hell do you do that? Not even Thane can get into my brain and pick it apart like that and I've been sleeping with him for more than a decade."

"He's too close to you," Strike muttered. Rora felt a bit better when she saw the familiar frown settle over his features. "What did Lawrence do? You might as well tell me because you know I'll find out."

Resigned, Shula sighed. "He has this legal thing… hack all you want, but don't dare tell Thane a thing," she said.

"You know I love keeping secrets from your First," he said and winked at her.

Shula groaned like she was out of patience. "Don't fuck with his head. I'm already afraid he'll go on a rampage."

He tipped his head. "City better watch out. Good weekend for looting I guess."

"If you're up for a challenge, go to Xylo tonight. He's opening the sanctum, all bets, all in." Strike shook his head. "Chicken?"

He sneered at her. "You're assuming that your ex is going to live long enough to toss in his token."

Something warm crossed Shula's features. "When you and Thane fight, it goes on for hours," she said. "Anyone else would yield in a fight like that, but not you two. You're both as bull-headed as each other."

"Oh, I'm not gonna beat him, I'm gonna call Raven."

Shula leaped off the couch with a renewed kind of panic. "You can't call Raven!" she said, storming over to him. "Look, I don't know what happened today. But it was obviously a mistake. There will be an investigation and—"

"I'm not a member of your little cult."

"It's not a cult," she said. "And you don't have to remind me that you don't follow our rules."

"I don't follow anyone's rules," he muttered. "And I will take Thane down if he doesn't call off his dogs. I don't care who he is or how far back we go."

"You're nuts, you kill two of our guys and *you're* threatening *him*?" Shula said, finding her anger.

"He needs to learn to stick to his business, which is this city, nowhere else," Strike said.

Shula scoffed and drew an invisible circle in the air with her finger. "The whole world is your playground. Rich of you to tell anyone else to stick to their own sandbox, isn't it? If those guys were operating out of the city limits, it was for an important reason. You know Thane only lets our cause leave the city in exceptional circumstances. And you said you weren't the target. So please accept X's apologies that you were caught in the crossfire," she said and then muttered, "though I've never known you to shy away from a fight whether it was yours or not."

Strike grabbed her arm again. "This is my fight," he said and glanced past Shula to look at Rora, who was still there near the door.

He didn't look for long, but it was long enough to make Shula twist to check her out. "Who is she? A little vanilla for you, isn't she?"

Strike didn't do a great job of hiding his smirk, but Rora huffed. "What the hell does that even mean?"

"I'll tell you later," he said.

Recognizing the distant promise of heat in his eyes, Rora smiled, proud that whatever it meant, it wasn't something he disliked about her.

"Wow, ok," Shula said. "Well now that I've clearly slipped into a parallel dimension, I should probably go shoot myself." Strike broke his stare on Rora to look down at Shula.

"I will talk to Thane for you. But, please, don't do anything stupid, he's got a lot on his plate right now… We heard a rumor."

"What kind of rumor?" Strike asked.

He and Shula eyed each other for a few seconds before the woman exhaled and gave in. "A potential global threat. We don't know much. Thane's dedicating all of X's resources to it, but we're not getting far. Word is the Black Jewel's involved."

"Possible she's on the deceased list."

"You killed her?" Shula asked like she couldn't quite believe it. Strike just lifted a shoulder. "I can't tell you much, not until we find out—"

"What's the point?" he said.

Shula blinked. "Yes," she gasped. "How did you know that? Shit, look at who I'm asking. But, seriously, Strike, this is dangerous, even for you. We're trying to track Gallagher and—"

"He's dead."

"What? How do you know that?"

" 'Cause I watched him put a bullet in his brain," he said.

Shula folded her arms again and crooked an unimpressed brow. "You have been busy, haven't you?"

"I didn't kill him," Strike said and held up his hands, but he couldn't look innocent if his life depended on it.

Shula exhaled. "I have to call Thane, I have to tell him. We need to know everything we can about this threat. If Gallagher's dead, there's only one last hope." She started forward. "There's a girl—" Strike caught Shula's arm and held it while he looked across the room. Rora was put in the spotlight when Shula looked once, then twice. "Shit, Strike, trust you. The entire world is scrambling, looking for Gallagher's assistant and you're sleeping with her! How the hell do you do that?"

Bowing down, Strike whispered in Shula's ear. The woman's frown deepened, then loosened. Her head tipped a fraction and then she exhaled.

Strike leaned back to look into her eyes. "Shu?"

"Fine. We'll let it go. But no Raven."

In another shocking move, Strike kissed Shula's cheekbone before turning to head for the door, his façade of indifference back in place. Picking up his pace, he snagged Rora's arm on the way past to pull her out of the apartment with him.

He took her back to the car and drove off, leaving Rora confused. "Strike?" she asked. "Is Shula your ex too?"

"If I'd thought about touching Shula, you wouldn't have the pleasure of my company now," he said. "Her man is so in love with her he isn't rational. He lost his mind over her when they were kids, he never got it back."

And now they'd broken up. "That's heartbreaking," she said, gazing straight-ahead. "He must be devastated if they've separated."

"He'll get her back," he said, checking his mirror.

There wasn't an ounce of doubt in those words. "How do you know?"

" 'Cause if he doesn't, I'll kill him," he said. "I'm gonna drop you off with Buddy."

Tensing, she forgot about Shula and grew suspicious. "Why? Where are you going?"

"Business."

TWENTY-FIVE

BUDDY WAS SNOOZING when they got back to his place, so Strike gave him a kick and told him to watch her. Rora wasn't really sure if that was meant to be for her protection, or if he meant lock all the doors and windows so she couldn't get herself arrested again.

Rora didn't mind the dig because any reminder that he shouldn't fuck with her was ok in her book. That didn't stop her from asking Strike half a dozen times if he was definitely going to come home to her. He assured her that he would, that he'd only be gone for an hour… or two.

Buddy went back to sleep and she didn't begrudge him his nap. As long as Strike upheld his vow to come back to her, she had no desire to be arrested again.

Rora had been flicking through a newspaper for a few minutes when she noticed Buddy's phone on the table. She couldn't remember the last time she'd seen her phone, but Buddy didn't mind her using his phone to play games and read news, so she guessed he wouldn't mind her checking messages either.

Her email was mostly spam. She responded to one message and then dialed into her voicemail. There was nothing on her personal system, so she dialed into the one for the office. The building might be a pile of rubble now, but that shouldn't affect their phone accounts. The first couple of messages, she tried to memorize the details, but when she started to lose track, she grabbed a pen and started to take notes around the edge of the newspaper. Names, numbers, call back, ignore, cancel. It wasn't her job anymore, but organizing Benjamin's career had been her rock for so long, there was something numbing about pretending for a few minutes that this was just any other day.

A cop had left a message saying they were still investigating the disappearance but that leads were starting to dry up. They wanted to interview her again. They wanted to interview everyone again.

Everyone was a brief list.

Rora felt a surge of guilt. This guy was doing his job without any idea it was a futile one. Benjamin was dead, his body either destroyed or lost in the waste of Wonderland. She was sitting on the floor between the armchair and coffee table, drawing hearts on the corner of the newspaper, waiting for the next message to start, thinking about Strike and how long she'd wait before popping some tires.

Hanging up the phone, Rora ran out of patience with the past. Taking a breath, she acknowledged to herself that she shouldn't be sitting here pining and waiting. There was a major piece of business she'd neglected so far, and it wasn't going to deal with itself.

Before letting Strike dash off to deal with his own business, she should've asked him for a favor. She didn't have the time to go out there and get herself arrested because she'd have to wait to be released, which could take hours. So how else could she get her man's attention?

Chewing on her lip for a minute, her attention caught on Buddy's phone again. Snatching it up, she opened some of her online accounts, using the usernames and passwords from her former life. Searching for expensive items, she started to make purchases using the saved card details. The transactions would bounce, but she wouldn't be around for delivery anyway. It wasn't like she needed any of the objects, they meant nothing to her.

But if she knew Strike, and she was beginning to get some insight, he'd have some sort of alert setup to tell him that there was attempted activity on her bank accounts.

When she had tried to charge about twenty thousand to her accounts, she sat in her armchair and fixated on the door. Not so long ago, she'd sat in this chair, staring at that door hoping and praying he'd walk through it. This time she was somewhat more optimistic—he'd promised to come back.

He'd promised her.

Sure enough, twenty minutes went by and the door opened. Strike strode in, his face set in a scowl, his focus on the phone in his hand. A few feet into the room, he stopped typing and took his attention from the screen to lift it to her. They made eye contact for a few seconds and said nothing.

Rora was trying to judge if he was mad because that might impact his willingness to help her out.

His brows rose in time with his shoulders. "What?" he asked. "I'm here, what do you need?"

Ok, good, he knew what she'd done and why, he didn't seem mad just suitably impatient, but he was always impatient.

Leaping out of her chair, she dashed across the room, past the sleeping Buddy. Coming up on Strike so quickly that her body bounced on his, Rora descended from her tiptoes while wiggling a fingernail into his torso between the edges of his open jacket.

"Will you ad hoc me a car?" Rising to her tiptoes again, she tipped her head all the way back and let her fingernail trail south until she could open her palm over his fly. She began to massage him through the denim of his jeans. "I'll make it worth your while."

Picking up his phone, he read something on the screen before looking at her again. "I'll get you a car. You don't have to do that."

Falling onto her heels, she grabbed his hand. "Good, 'cause I don't really have time."

Pulling him along, she led him out of the apartment and down to the street. They walked a few blocks over and around to a parking lot in an alley. Strike didn't seem to ponder, he walked straight to a car like it was his, typing on his phone as he did.

Rora liked to tell herself that she was playing look out, even though Strike hadn't asked her to. But he didn't pause for more than a heartbeat before opening the passenger door for her. As she descended into the seat, she noticed him looking around for the first time.

"This is a nice car," she said when he got into the driver's seat. "Can you hot wire cars like this?" But he wasn't bent over or crouched looking to open any panels like she expected him to be. His frown was set on his phone. "The owner could come back any second. Is this really the time to be texting?"

But the car burst to life and her jaw fell. "Perfect time," he said and put it into reverse to pull out of the lot.

"I can't believe you did that," she said a block later. "You can really start a car without actually touching it?"

He shrugged. "Modern cars are basically just computers. Trick is to disable the trackers and security systems first. Starting it's an afterthought… The start button will work without the key now."

Nodding, she sought out the start button next to the steering wheel. That was good because it meant she would be able to stop to sleep if she had to without worrying about getting the thing going again.

"Ok," she said, moving onto her knees. She put a hand on the dash and the other on his shoulder to lean over the console and kiss his cheek. "Thanks. You can, you know, pull over and get out whenever. I just have a couple of things to take care of."

"Sure," he said.

But he didn't stop. Rora stayed suspended over the console, her eye going from him to the steering wheel. Deflated, she sagged back into her seat. "You're not going to stop and get out, are you?"

"Yeah, no, that's not going to happen." Her face fell into her hands and she cursed herself for thinking he'd walk away without a fight. "North or south?" Turning to the windshield, she saw they were coming up to two different routes and she'd have to make a decision… Would he pass the test? "Babe, I need to pick a lane."

Opening her mouth slowly, she inhaled carefully. "North."

He slid into the lane. She wilted back against her door and glimpsed at his profile. Did he have any idea what she'd just done? There was no hint on his face that he knew she was about to test him, to confront him with a decision he'd said he wouldn't make in her favor.

She hadn't expected him to join her on this journey. She'd wanted to dispense with a problem that hung over them without letting it continue to be an issue. For her, it was about living up to her responsibility to Benjamin. But Strike coming along wasn't part of the plan.

Rora told herself that she was proving a point to her love, but that wasn't completely true. There would be an answer at the end of this; she just hoped she hadn't set herself, or Strike, up for failure.

***

DIRECTING STRIKE to the secluded resort she'd stayed at with Benjamin, Rora could feel her anxiety rising. Instead of going into reception like a normal couple and requesting a reservation, she asked Strike to go into the resort's mainframe and make sure they got exactly the right room.

"You like the view?" he asked when they entered the suite on the top floor.

"Something like that," she said, but it wasn't the grand windows filled with the view of the lake that she fixated on.

It was the bed that caught her eye.

The huge four-poster number was all ruffles and silk lace. She smiled remembering when she'd first seen this bed. Benjamin had been so in love with the resort, he thought it was romantic, and it was. They'd taken walks around the lake under the midnight stars and eaten outside on a terrace lit by twinkly lights.

"Benjamin and I had sex in that bed," she whispered, but snapped out of her daze a second later to see that Strike was more unimpressed than usual. "I don't know why I said that, I… I just meant that we came here together."

His eye twitched. "Literally," he grumbled and stormed on past her to toss his jacket on the end of the bed. "You bring every guy you're screwing here?"

She shook her head. "I'm sorry, I didn't… expect it to feel so… fresh."

Bending, Strike caught her wrist to yank her over to him. Angling her to face the bed, he stood behind her and pushed her head forward until her chin met her chest. Shoving her hair away from the back of her neck, he licked her spine and then dragged his teeth over it.

"Strike," she breathed out, opening her fingers against the front of his thigh.

"What?" he asked. Keeping her head forward with one strong hand, he used the other to push her hand from his thigh to press it against the erection behind his fly. "This is why we're here, right? But you say his fucking name and I won't be responsible for what happens next."

She managed a smile. "I don't think I could ever confuse you for him." Stepping from the caress of his mouth on the back of her neck, she curled her fingers into his and turned to face him. "That's not why we're here. I just pray you'll forgive me."

His demeanor grew tight and he pulled his hand away from hers. "Who is it? FBI? Interpol? J-CAT? What did they promise you?"

"No," she said and gave his chest a shove. "And you're forgiven for thinking I'd ever do that to you. If I didn't have you around, who would ad hoc me vehicles, buy me cupcakes, and make love to me at night?"

Leaving him at the end of the bed, she went down a passageway at the back of the room and peeked up at the vent above the closet. Inhaling, she then blew out the breath and steeled herself. This was it. The moment of truth. Retrieving a chair, she opened the closet and from the outside, she had to reach up inside to the lip beneath the vent.

His voice came from the direction of the bedroom. "What are you doing?"

"Just give me a second," she said, her tongue meeting the corner of her lip as she found the bump she was looking for. Smiling, she began to pick the tape and worked it side to side to pull it from the adhesive. Pulling out the metal USB stick, she held it up, triumphant. "I got it!"

When she looked down, she found Strike right there in front of her. With a hand on his shoulder, she leaped onto the floor and grabbed him to drag him back to the bedroom.

"What is that?" he asked.

Shoving him onto the bed, she climbed on beside him and crossed her legs to lay the metal rectangle on the middle of the bed. Looking at it for a second, she exhaled and then looked up at him and gestured at it.

"Strike," she said. "This is the Point." He leaped up and staggered back a step, his hand rising to his mouth. "Don't be afraid of it."

She reached for him, but he didn't take her hand; he took a good minute to breathe before pointing at the small object. "That... that's..."

His next inhale was ragged and she laughed. "Strike—"

"Why the fuck didn't you tell me that's why you were coming here!" he said, lunging forward to grab his jacket. "I'm out of here."

"No," she said and scrambled off the bed to catch up with him. Rora squeezed herself between him and the door. "Please, just... hear me out, ok?"

Dubious though he obviously was, he let her turn him around to push him back into the room. Except when they got near the bed, he turned out of her advance, leaving her to stumble forward.

"I don't want to get too close to it."

Seeing him like this was funny until she saw how tense his expression was. "Baby, why?" Rora asked. "What could possibly happen to—"

"You remember what happened to your driver's license, right?" he asked. Yeah, he stole it from her. Oh. "Shit."

Grabbing something from a secret pocket in his jacket—a piece of tech, small and flat—he gritted his teeth and snapped it in half.

"What the…"

He tossed the broken pieces to the floor. "I'm stealing from you and every other person every minute."

"That absorbs data?" she asked.

"Designed to do a lot of things. Does nothing now."

Going to him, she took his hands, one at a time, letting them hang loose in hers. "Ok, let's just take a breath," she said and shook his hands. "I'm sorry I didn't tell you, but… I needed to come here and get this, and you didn't want to get out of the car and—"

"If you'd given me a hint, I might have pulled over," he said and to her surprise, he lifted his curled fingers to let the back of them brush the underside of her jaw. "Cupcake, I can't be in the same room as that thing."

Now to make him understand. "You won't be," she said. "I had to come and get it because I want us to destroy it."

His mouth opened a fraction, but she wasn't sure he actually breathed in. Sealing his lips again, he swallowed hard. "You want me to destroy cutting-edge technology? You want me to destroy it without… playing with it?"

She smiled and nodded. "Yes, and I know you will."

"How do you know that?"

Moving in closer, she let her head fall back to gaze up at him. Sure in her resolve that she could have faith in him, even if he didn't have it in himself. "Because I'm asking you to and you love me."

"I…" Taking his hands out of hers, he walked away, gripping and squeezing the fingers of one hand with the other. "Babe, I told you this wouldn't end well if you gave me the chance… I warned you."

"I'm not worried," she said, and followed on to take his hand again. "Please, I think if you let me explain the implications, you'll see that I'm right. There's just no way this can be released into the world."

Rora tried to take him over to the bed, but he resisted, so she diverted to seat him on the couch by the window. "Ok," he said, drawing in a long breath through his nose. "Tell me, Rora… What's the Point?"

"An algorithm," she said and felt a sense of relief. "An algorithm that basically quantifies the human soul." His mouth opened, but she put a hand to it. "It can see inside a person. It learns everything a person cares about, every weak spot, every vulnerability, every crime, every humiliation… every secret. It figures out 'the point' of each person's existence. For some, it's their kids, some their career, some their secret fetish, or a clandestine affair. It doesn't matter, the point is it can access every piece of data that ever existed on any person ever, and it runs them through this formula and figures out where a person can be squeezed, and it doesn't just come up with the obvious answer.

"It actually does a psychological profile and monitors communications as well as measures the frequency of visits to websites, physical locations, etc. It's extremely complex. It analyzes thousands of bits of data and finds out the truth. It doesn't just answer with kids because a person has them, it figures out what really drives that person, something that sometimes even they don't know about themselves… It finds out their price without ever asking them a question or having any contact with them."

Her hand fell from his mouth to his thigh. "That's—"

"And it does it in a fraction of a second. It's… spectacular."

His eyes widened. "You've seen it?"

She nodded and her lips rose. "It had a one hundred percent accuracy rate. A hundred percent, Strike. Isn't that incredible?"

"But you said it didn't work."

"Well," she said, her hand sliding from his when she sat back. "It needs to be refined. Benjamin designed it to give people an opportunity to protect themselves, you know, to help us learn about our own vulnerabilities and how easy it would be for our weaknesses to be exploited."

"Oh yeah," he said, a purr of anticipation in his voice as his eyes drifted toward the window.

Slapping a hand to his cheek, she brought his attention around to her frown. "You don't understand the implications," she said, unhappy that he seemed excited by this idea.

"I do, baby. Hypothetically, someone could program it to blackmail and manipulate thousands of people simultaneously. Once the user sets it loose, they wouldn't have to lift a finger, just sit back and wait for the capital to pour in."

Getting frustrated, she hoped he would see past the potential personal reward. "And that's the terrifying part. If this gets into the wrong hands someone could run it and extort people. Part of the reason it doesn't work is limited capacity, and that's why it needs to be refined. The code is unwieldy. At the moment, it can only work on a handful of people at a time, but hypothetically, anyone who wanted to use it for their own sinister reasons could, if they had the ability—"

"With the right tech, they could run it on every person on the planet simultaneously," he said, his eyes flicking back and forth between hers. "I understand exactly what the implications are. With that kind of information, someone could control the world. It goes beyond ransom and extortion. Keeping secrets like that, personal, private secrets, that gives the user the ability to control everyone on a permanent basis. Sure, you can start with, 'give me all your money' but easily move onto, 'I want your wife on weekends' and then it's just a quick hop to insider trading and directing governmental affairs… on a global scale…"

Rising from the couch, his hands went through his hair and he moved to the window. Examining him, Rora hoped that giving him a minute to think about it would make him see how it was wrong to let one person or group have that much power.

"It's scary how it takes every piece of digital information about a person, everything from their deleted internet history to the frequency they use phone apps. It can track the GPS of every phone you've ever had to map every place you've ever been and cross reference that with every other phone to see who you've been near… it gets into all the minutia," she said, a frown slowly forming on her face. "No one would be immune… including you."

Whipping around he searched her for a second. "And you."

"There are those of us who have nothing to exploit," she said. "You have my money. I have no family anyone could threaten, even Benjamin's dead… The only way anyone could get to me is through…"

"Through?" he asked.

Resigned to the truth that she knew and he couldn't see, she confessed. "You. You're the only thing I care enough about to fight for."

Rushing to her, he sat at her side and grabbed both her hands onto his knees. "But we control it, baby. We have it. Right there. No one can hurt us with it as long as we have control of it… We could control the world, baby. Everything."

When his hand moved toward her face, she ducked back. "No," she said, shaking her head. "No, Strike. We're not going to control it; we're going to destroy it."

"Aren't you curious?" he asked, peering into her. "Think of what you could learn. Information, Cupcake… it really is power."

Frustration made her exhale. "I don't want to learn," she said. "I don't want to know anything." Balling her hands on her knees, she hit them and stood up. "Goddamnit, what is it with men?"

Rising in front of her, he explored her features. "Gallagher wanted to use it."

She lifted a finger of warning because Benjamin never wanted power like Strike was talking about taking. Benjamin had a professional curiosity, not a vendetta.

"He wanted to try it, he wanted to let it loose, to let it learn and refine itself."

"But you wouldn't let him," he muttered.

Guilt chilled her, forcing her to wrap her arms around herself. She'd tested Benjamin once and he'd passed. The jury was still out on Strike, but she'd get her answer when he decided where his priorities lay, with her or with this opportunity.

"I asked him to destroy it, but I knew he hadn't," she said. "There was one copy left…" Her eyes drifted to the bed. "When I confronted him about it, we fought… He came up with a compromise, he told me we should hide it, that no one would ever know."

"So, you hid it here?" he asked.

Making eye contact with him, her guilt tightened her throat. "I came back and hid it here alone… The storage device that he and I hid together… that he thought the Point was on… it was worthless. It was full of landscape images."

As far as she knew, Benjamin had never learned of her deception. Hiding the Point might have been a compromise, but she hadn't wanted him to ever be tempted to go back on his word.

He'd passed his test by agreeing not to pursue his plan and then sticking to that agreement. But all that meant was that he'd never learned about her switching one powerful storage device for a useless one.

"You tricked him?" Strike asked and his mouth slanted. "You're a grifter."

Strike's satisfaction came closer when he leaned in to try to kiss her. Rora leaned away, pressing a hand onto his chest. "I wanted to help him," she said. "I wasn't thinking about myself. I was thinking about him and about taking away the temptation. I had no interest in it. I knew how dangerous it could be. I could trust myself not to use it; I don't have the skills to refine the code anyway…"

"I do," he said, looming over her and bowing to rub his face in her hair. "You are a clever girl."

"Strike," she said, easing him back. "You do understand, don't you? I love you so much, so much more than I ever loved Benjamin… I need you to get rid of it for me, wipe it, incinerate it, do whatever you have to, just… free the world from the threat… please."

"Cupcake…"

It was difficult to hear him in pain and he obviously was. "I'm trusting you. You love me, Strike. I know you love me… Prove to yourself that you can resist this temptation, pass this test for both our sakes…"

He growled. "Fine," he said. Her head fell onto his chest between her flat hands. "But I can't do it here, I have a piece of tech at the loft, it will destroy every trace."

"Thank you, Flame," she whispered. "Oh, thank you, baby."

Looping her arms around his neck, she leaped up to wrap her legs around his hips. He dropped forward, catching his hand on the back of the couch to lower her into the seat. Their kiss grew in heat and she helped to strip both of them.

Just when she was braced for him to slide into her, Strike took her into his arms and picked her up. "I want to screw on it," he said and carried her over to the bed.

"The bed or the Point?" she asked, happy to accept him on top of her when he laid her down.

"Both," he said and pushed into her. Sliding her fingertips over his shoulders, Rora felt him shiver and the surprise of that reaction made her blink at him, but he growled at her. "All this frilly bullshit."

She couldn't imagine a setup that was less Strike. Rearing up, he snagged the silk trim from one of the bedposts and ripped it down.

"Strike!"

"Better," he said and seized her wrist.

"What are you doing?" Wrapping the fabric around her wrist, he looped it around the headboard and then captured the other wrist to tie her hands together. "Strike," she said, laughing. Rising to his knees between her legs, he looked down at her naked form and she tugged at her hands. "I can't move."

Bowing over her, he slid his tongue between her lips and began to caress her body. His rough hands were heavy; he'd never been delicate with her and she loved it when his need was this potent. Tugging her nipple to a point, he lowered to breathe it into his mouth and then traced his lips down the middle of her stomach.

"Strike," she whispered his name when he tasted her center. "Oh, God."

"Mm," he moaned and circled her clit with his tongue. "Delicious."

Pulling at her hands, she wanted to be free so she could touch him. "Oh, Strike," she said his name and he rose again, pulling the silk from the other bedpost and this time he wrapped it around her head, gagging her.

Resting his mouth over hers with the silk between their lips, he breathed into her whimpering mouth. "What have I told you about using my name?"

Bound to the headboard and gagged, all Rora could do was move her hips when he pushed her thighs apart and slid into her again. With their eyes searching each other, she sank into the rhythm of advance and retreat.

He was choosing her, making love to her on the promise that they were going to do what was necessary together. Tricking Benjamin had been one of the hardest things she'd ever done. Instinct had made her do it, she'd made a split-second decision, and he'd died never knowing that the Point wasn't even in the place he thought it was.

Rising on the crest of her climax, Rora was on the descent when Strike's hit him hard. For a second, he stayed there, suspended above her, and she tried to smile behind the gag. Rora wanted to touch him, wanted to ask him what was in his mind. But she couldn't because he'd trussed her up.

Strike eased back, returning to his position on his knees between her thighs. She was still admiring him, filled with her love for him, when his hand rose and she noticed what was between his first two fingers. The Point.

"You know, I never thought… I never thought this day would come," he said. "And the funny thing is, I actually meant what I said in the loft. I would never have asked you about it again."

Bending over her, he kissed her forehead and then slid off the bed. Trying her best to call out behind the gag,

Rora pulled and kicked, but he went over to the couch and got dressed.

He got her jacket and took something from the pocket. Bringing it over, he kept his distance from her flailing legs when he slipped the cool metal handle between her bound hands.

"Be careful, it's open," he said like he was handing her hot coffee on any random day of the week.

Screaming, Rora clung to the switchblade handle he'd just put into her hands, though she had no idea how she'd cut herself out of her bindings from the position she was in.

Picking up his jacket and the broken tech from the floor, he took a second to examine the mangled pieces. "This doesn't have the capacity to hold something like the Point." So that was why he'd destroyed it rather than being more covert about his betrayal. "I'm sorry, baby. I am. But I've said it from the start…" He went to the door and opened it an inch. Rora was screaming as loud as she could, but the sound was so muffled, it didn't matter. Even though the fabric was cutting into her wrists, she didn't stop fighting. "You're so naïve… Chin up, Cupcake."

Turning around, he went out and closed the door. Kicking, screaming, desperate, and tired, Rora wasn't sure what was worse, the physical pain of the fabric cutting her wrists or the weight in her chest.

He'd betrayed her. Dumped her. Failed the test. But he was right, he had warned her, she should've listened, should've known better.

The devil was not immune from temptation.

TWENTY-SIX

AT LEAST THE CAR was still there when Rora went down the stairs.

Cutting herself free from the fabric wasn't difficult when she stopped blubbering and concentrated. She'd ripped the gag from her mouth, put her clothes on and run down to the parking lot.

But did it matter? Even if he'd been here, she wouldn't have been able to stop him. He was bigger than her. Stronger. More ruthless. Willing to go to any length to get what he wanted.

Rora was on her way to get into the car and then slowed. Did she trust a car he'd stolen? There was still money in the inside pocket of her jacket. Hesitating, she thought about what had happened upstairs.

It would be easy for Strike to make sure she was caught by cops and this time, he'd want her to stay in jail, there would be no Torres and no rescue.

Turning her back on the car, she walked away, heading down the private access road that led away from the resort. It was about two miles, maybe more to the highway, she could thumb a ride at least to the next town, and she could get a bus. Yeah, no more ad hoc vehicles, she was back on the straight and narrow.

With her family history, it was ridiculous of her to think she could even dip her toe into the world of criminality. While she might not have coveted it at first, she hadn't resisted it. Benjamin's work started her on this path, but she hadn't needed to so fully embrace being bad after she met Strike.

Even the smell of pine and fresh air couldn't make her feel any sense of peace. In fact, she was pleased to get away from it when the first driver stopped and gave her a ride to the closest town.

Rora went to the bus station.

She stood looking at the departures board for the longest time, except she had nowhere to go. No one needed her. There was nowhere she needed to be. It wouldn't be possible for her to track down Strike on her own. Not that it mattered; he'd probably seek her out on his own when he realized what she'd done to him.

Having given up the rental on her apartment and put her possessions into storage while she was looking for Benjamin, she didn't have a home. She still had some clothes at Buddy's, but she might not be welcome there anymore.

Rora couldn't decide. Did she risk going back to Buddy's where she could get her throat slit, or did she crash at Benjamin's cleared-out apartment?

"Waiting for someone?"

Glancing over her right shoulder she saw a tall man at her side, as interested in the board above them as she had been. "Trying to decide."

"Death in the family or break up with the boyfriend?" he asked.

"Excuse me?"

"That's usually when people decide to do spontaneous things like pick random destinations to travel to," he said, turning to look down at her. "We feel our own mortality and want to cross things from the bucket list, or we're looking for a fresh start to mend a broken heart. So, death in the family or break up with the boyfriend?"

Breathing out, Rora turned her attention back to the board. "Both," she said and decided that since the bus that would take her back to Buddy's was first and Benjamin's apartment would always be sitting there empty, she'd try her luck at Buddy's first.

Walking forward, she intended to go to the ticket desk, but the guy who'd been talking to her grabbed her arm and turned her around. She was going to call out, maybe scream in his face; messing with her today would be a big mistake, she'd taken all the bullshit she could.

But he didn't say anything or try to move her. There was a curiosity and a knowing in the way he looked at her. Like maybe there was something he wanted to say, or that he expected her to say.

The depth of his interest felt profound. She shivered, getting that creepy feeling like she'd had in the convenience store parking lot, and she had been right then. Rora got her wits back and pulled her arm away from him.

"Excuse me," she said and walked away.

Trying to keep her head down, she scanned the vast space and suddenly everyone felt like a potential threat. Strike knew snipers, he knew thugs, he'd introduced her to a cult member. Rora was known and now that Strike had given into temptation, he might consider her expendable.

With a new respect for the danger that she might be in, Rora bought her ticket and kept herself in corners until the bus door opened to let passengers on. Strike had once accused her of being paranoid, she could never have known he'd become the greatest threat to her life.

***

IF BUDDY WASN'T HOME, she'd go inside, pack her shit and bolt. Rora was deciding that she liked the idea of going back to Benjamin's less and less. She couldn't go anywhere that she'd easily be found. She had to lay low for a while. But without money, or real skills, that might be difficult.

She couldn't go to her storage unit with ID because that would put her on too many people's radars and, yeah, she didn't have her ID anymore. But she could always buy bolt cutters and break-in the old-fashioned way.

The bus journey had given her the chance to face a lot of truths; one being that ending up in jail might be her destiny. Kyan was locked up, and he was the only family member she had left. Maybe they weren't meant to have a home in a quiet suburban street. Maybe home for the Maguires was the cemetery or maximum security.

Buddy's was the closest thing she'd had to a home since Benjamin was taken, so it was bittersweet when she vaulted up the stairs to start along the corridor to the apartment door knowing that this would be the last time she'd ever be there.

The door was never locked. Buddy was scary enough that people knew not to mess with him, and he didn't have much worth stealing anyway, so she didn't hesitate to go inside.

But as soon as she crossed the threshold, she stopped dead, coming up short when she saw someone was in her armchair on the other side of the room.

Strike.

Shit. She may just have walked into her tomb.

He wasn't glaring and angry, he was focused on Opal, who he had upside down on the coffee table in front of him. His fingertips were resting on a rectangle in a corner, but he quickly lifted them to snap the back of Opal's case into place.

As he began to secure the screws, he glanced up and noticed her, that was the moment she spotted the open silver box on the table beside Opal, the one the NSA had given her. Next to that was the Point USB he'd taken from her at the resort.

Picking up the USB, he held it between his palms and sat back. "You going to swear at me?"

"What are you doing here?" she asked. "I thought you'd be long gone."

His arrogance was on rare form, he was proud to the point of smug. "Well, I thought… hoped… that maybe you'd have had a change of heart," he said. "This is happening, whether you support it or not."

Her chin rose, and she eyed the long metal box she'd gotten from Torres all those weeks ago. "What is that? You never told me."

"Newest hardware install for Opal," he said, turning the laptop over. "Gotta love DARPA's paranoia, the box is fireproof, thank fuck. I had it in Wonderland, thought I'd need it up there since I planned to work there for a while, but I had to check out the tech for bugs before I could install it. You can't trust the NSA, you know? So I hadn't added the hardware to Opal before the fire."

"That's why you went back to Wonderland?" she asked. "You were getting your toy."

"Yep," he said and stood up.

She took a step back, coming up hard against the door.

Strike dropped the Point onto the table and came toward her. "I'm not gonna hurt you, Rora. There's nothing in it for me… Keeping you alive on the other hand…"

"What does that mean?" she asked. "You have what you want. You knew it would come down to a choice between me and it… You chose it. Congratulations. I hope you'll be very happy together."

Breathing in and holding her mouth closed, she braced when he came up in front of her and picked up her hand. Her throat was shaking, her lips dry, and the terror that consumed her was like nothing she'd ever felt with him before, or with anyone.

She didn't just fear death or physical pain with him, this man had made her fall in love with him. He had her in every way a person could have another, and he knew her vulnerabilities.

"It doesn't have to be that way," he said, holding her hand, palm up, between them. Easing back the cuff of her jacket, he touched a fingertip to the bruising left by the fabric he'd tied around her wrists. Lifting her hand higher, he touched his lips to one of the abrasions. She tried to pull away, but he was stronger and held her hand under his mouth. "Stay with me… We'll do it together."

"No."

"Come on," he said. Touching his fingertip under her chin, he pushed it higher. "You love being bad with me, Cupcake."

Strike bent lower, touching his lips to hers. Rora didn't hesitate to lunge forward and sink her teeth into his lip, satisfied only when she tasted blood. He hissed and pulled back.

"Now I know how Bella felt about you," she spat.

Growling at her, he pounced, snatching her wrists and planting them on the door behind her. "You love to sink your teeth in," he snarled. "Be vicious, baby. No rules. No fear, my queen, we'll build our own world."

"No," she said. He tried to kiss her again, but she brought up her knee to smash it against his groin, making him buckle. Rora shoved at him before stamping on his foot. "No means no! No to this! No to your sick, evil little plan! No to being your queen! No to kissing! And definitely no to sex!"

"Fine," he hissed and spun around to march back to his seat.

Fury and adrenaline pumped through her chest, killing little pieces of her heart with every beat. "You don't have to do this," she said when he dropped into the seat and opened Opal. "Please, Flame, just... just toss it and we'll forget this. You can still have me. I'll be yours. We'll belong to each other." He sneered up at her and grabbed the Point from the table to open it; he angled it against the port. "No! Please! Baby, just let it go! You can still choose me!"

He didn't know it, but this was the final exam. The test she'd set in motion when she chose north over south. Every atom of her being wanted him to pass but putting the USB into Opal proved his intention to choose the Point over their relationship. But there was still time, he could still choose her, he could still pass.

"You were temporary," he grumbled, his fingers curling tighter around the device. "Always knew it."

"No," she said, hoping the angel on his shoulder might find her voice. "There's still time, I want to be permanent. Forever, for all eternity permanent, just please, please..." She begged and actually dropped onto her knees with tears streaming from her eyes. "Please, Strike, I'm pleading with you. Don't do this. I'm yours until you put that into the port. Connect it, and I'm gone forever, Strike." His cold eyes rose to hers. Desperation flavored her throat when she sobbed. "Please, baby… My Flame, my love… put it down… don't force me to leave you… I don't want to walk away. Let me stay with you, please."

"You can," he said, his fingers clenching around the device. "We'll do it together."

But that wasn't the deal, he couldn't have both.

"No," she whispered. "This is the moment of temptation you talked about. If you connect that to Opal, I'll walk out of here and you'll never see me again."

For half a minute, they looked at each other across the room, him with his hand poised to push the device into the computer, her on her knees, her hands clasped beneath her chin, her face stained with tears.

"Please," she whispered one more time.

"Satan's son is beyond redemption," he said and pushed the device into the computer.

He might as well have been driving a knife into her heart. In that instant, he took her soul. Her hope. Her faith. All of it was gone.

Rising from her knees, she swallowed her grief. Rora was consumed by numbness; there was nothing to fear because she had nothing.

Turning around, she said nothing else, she walked out of Buddy's apartment and left her love to his triumph.

Autopilot took her down the stairs. Her head was bowed; she didn't even see anyone enter the building until she was just a couple of meters from the door.

"Isn't this convenient," a female voice exclaimed. "Victims are just delivering themselves right to the front door."

Rora gasped, her attention flew up and she was stunned to see Bella there in front of her. The dark silhouette of the black-souled woman was haloed by the light from outside. It didn't make her look angelic, in fact it managed to make her look downright demonic.

"Bella," Rora said and tried to take a backward step, but there were men closing in around her from every direction.

Something stung her neck, making her grab for the source of the pain.

"We'll take this one to go."

Bella's laugh was the last thing Rora heard before she blacked out.

TWENTY-SEVEN

THE SHOCK OF ICY WATER hitting her face woke Rora up with a sputtering gasp.

She struggled to breathe against the impact of the cold. Coughing and choking, she tried to lift her head to see where she was, but darkness surrounded her, and she… she couldn't move her hands.

Pulling on them, she felt something wide and metal around her wrists, holding her in place. And when she tried to move her heavy feet, the jangling sound of a chain came from the floor. The wall at her back was cold, it scratched on her, tormenting her skin, creating a cascade of prickling pain over her exposed back.

Blinking down at herself, Rora let her eyes adjust to the lack of light and managed to get a rhythm to her breathing. She was naked, cold, in the dark. Her feet were locked in lengths of chain that were attached to the floor and her hands were connected to metal stocks on the wall.

Someone touched the curtains of her hair that hung over her face and she recoiled, but there was nowhere for her to go against this exposed-brick wall. Whoever it was, they got closer and pushed her hair away from her face with a… feminine touch.

"Bella," she croaked.

The Black Jewel was there in front of her, smiling, perfect, gorgeous, and glittering with anticipation. "Hello, Arousing Aurora… We have unfinished business, duckie."

The woman was alive. Strike had said he didn't know if she was alive or not. But Rora wasn't too surprised. If anyone would have the ability to bounce back no matter what, Bella seemed like the type.

"He's not coming," Rora said. "Or did you take him too?" Though the truth was, Rora was so dazed right now, she couldn't make sense of much. "Or were you in on this together from the start?"

"My prince will come," Bella said. "But not for you… This isn't about him."

"Then what's it about?" she asked. "The question? Because your prince knows the answer. He has it. All of it. You took the wrong person if that's what you're looking for."

Except that was a lie.

After Rora walked away from Strike in Buddy's apartment, her former love would have accessed the USB device they'd taken from the resort only to discover it contained nothing more than the landscape images she'd hidden with Benjamin.

Benjamin had thought the Point was there in that hotel room, just as Strike had, both men were wrong.

If Strike had chosen her, he'd never have needed to know about her deception, just like Benjamin never had. But he'd picked the device thinking it did contain the Point.

In that moment of choosing between the north and south routes, she'd decided to test her love, but she'd been smart enough to have a failsafe and chosen not to take him to the real device.

Rora had put temptation in front of the man she loved believing that he would never give in to it. But he had.

The real Point was safe where she'd hidden it alone.

Strike would be on the warpath.

"Well," Bella said, creeping even closer and tracing the back of her finger down Rora's shoulder and over her breast to circle her nipple with a knuckle. "That is, of course, part of it… I expect my prince to do whatever he has to, that's who he is and… he's a man. Men are pathetic in their weakness. But you… you should've known better. You corrupted him. You hurt him."

Now that was so incredible that Rora regained some of her wits, enough to make eye contact with Bella. "And people call *me* crazy?"

Stepping back, Bella backhanded her hard, making Rora taste blood. "You took him and twisted his mind! You tried to take advantage of me! Tried to use me! I cared about you!"

"You knew me for ten minutes," Rora said. "You didn't care. You just wanted to play with me and I'd have let you if he hadn't interrupted us."

"Don't," Bella spat, lunging forward to dig a sharp fingernail into Rora's upper chest. "Don't you blame him! This was your weakness! Not his! He's a bastard, a weak, sniveling male. I hold you to a higher standard!"

"Because I have a vagina?" she asked, her head dropping. Her arms were burning, her shoulders aching, and the shivering was becoming more than numbing. "If it's him you want, have at him, he's on the market… You thought he loved me; you accused him of it like it was a dirty crime… Turned out, he agreed with you. He used me… He wanted one thing, and it wasn't me. He doesn't love me, Bella… He still belongs to you."

Grabbing her hair, Bella hauled her head up just to slap her again. "He always belonged to me! They all belong to me! Everything I want is mine and you will learn that… no matter how long it takes."

The sinister statement felt like a promise and a threat at the same time. Curling her lips in a smile, Bella leaned in and kissed her, pushing her tongue into Rora's mouth before purring on her retreat.

"Mmm, you taste so sweet…"

Taking one step back, and then another, Bella admired Rora's figure for a second then spun around to march across the room.

Two men who'd flanked the entrance, turned to loosen the lock and opened the heavy door for Bella.

"Wait," Rora called out. "What do you want with me? Let me go! Bella! Bella!"

The door closed behind the threesome and darkness closed in around Rora again. She was trapped. Imprisoned. There was no way out and no one coming to save her.

TO BE CONTINUED...

Thank you for reading this tale!
If you can, please take the time to review.

~

Ask your local library for more Scarlett Finn novels!

~

For all things Scarlett Finn
check out:

www.scarlettfinn.com

BOOK TWO

kiss CHASE

SCARLETT FINN

OUT NOW!

www.ingramcontent.com/pod-product-compliance
Lightning Source LLC
Chambersburg PA
CBHW060813190726
48285CB00002B/654